PLAYING PASSION'S GAME

By the Author

Truth Behind the Mask

Playing Passion's Game

PLAYING PASSION'S GAME

by
Lesley Davis

2011

PLAYING PASSION'S GAME

ISBN 13:978-1-60282-223-8

This Trade Paperback Original Is Published By
Bold Strokes Books, Inc.
P.O. Box 249
Valley Falls, NY 12185

First Edition: May 2011

CREDITS
Editor: Cindy Cresap
Production Design: Stacia Seaman
Cover Design by Sheri (graphicartist2020@hotmail.com)

Acknowledgments

My sincerest of thank-yous to Radclyffe for your endless encouragement and support of my writing.

For all at Bold Strokes who work hard behind the scenes to get these books out there.

For Cindy Cresap: Words cannot express my deepest admiration or gratitude for your marvellous editing skills. You make my words read so much better. Thank you always.

To Stacia Seaman, for taking "one last look around the house before turning out the light" on the whole editing process. Thank you for your discerning eye.

Thank you, Sheri, for another wonderful cover.

For Wayne Beckett, my precious and much loved friend.

To my Number One Stalkers, most dedicated readers and truly marvellous friends—Jacky Hart and Jane Morrison.

And to all my readers: I really appreciate all your support and wonderful e-mails spurring me on to write more. Thank you. And I'll try to put aside the controllers a little more to get back on the keyboard for you!

To my Cindy

For understanding the necessity of my playing
"just one more level!"
Thank God you're a gamer too! My love is yours always.

And to all the gamers out there, be they casual or hardcore:
Game on!

CHAPTER ONE

The increasingly loud shouting coming from outside finally drew Trent out from under the table where she was working.

"What the hell is going on out there?" she asked her friend Elton, who was running a length of cable behind her. When he ignored her she grabbed at his pants leg and yanked hard. He looked down blankly at her, then swept back his long hair and removed his earbud.

"Say again?"

Trent scowled up at him. "Some use you are. It sounds like World War Three is starting up outside and you're plugged into your MP3 oblivious to it." She connected her last lead, then scrambled out from where she'd been linking together computer cords. She headed to the front of the hall they were in and opened the large metal door to peer out. She slammed the door behind her and was more than pleased with the startled reactions from the group of boys who were causing part of the noise.

"Is there any particular reason why you're disturbing the peace out here, boys?"

The group took a step back at her presence. Dressed all in black, towering over the boys at a solid six foot, and wearing a scowl she had perfected for just that moment, Trent was certain she was putting the fear of God into them.

As they all stepped back, the boys revealed what they had been huddled around. A little blond girl stood holding her ground, fists balled before her, ready to start swinging.

Trent growled low in her throat. "Tell me you guys weren't bullying this girl?" She scanned the faces and found more than one she knew. One especially she was disappointed to see. "Wade? I thought you were a better man than for this kind of childish behavior."

The boy cringed at being singled out of the group. "We were just seeing who she was."

"By backing her into a corner and crowding round her like a pack of wolves? Some welcome committee." Trent stepped forward and gently lowered the girl's fists. She stood before the girl, effectively blocking her from their view. "Wade, don't make me mention this to your brother." She had the satisfaction of watching his face turn ashen. "Imagine how he'd feel to find out his brother consorts with *big* boys who terrorize *little* girls." She looked around to stare down each boy. "I ought to let her pound each and every one of you." Trent began to roll up her sleeves as if preparing her own hands for battle. "Get the hell away from this property and leave this kid alone or you'll have me to deal with." She took one step forward. "Understand?"

The boys tripped and tumbled in their backpedaling haste to escape Trent's wrath.

"Kids," Trent muttered. She looked behind her. "You okay?"

The girl puffed out a breath that blew her hair out of her eyes. "They were just being stupid." She straightened her shoulders and tried to look composed. "Boys are like that."

Trent looked her over. "They didn't hurt you?"

"No, they were just crowding me even though I asked them to let me pass." The girl watched as the boys disappeared from view. "I don't think they'll do it again. You scared them off." She held out a small hand. "Thank you…?"

Trent took the offered hand and shook it solemnly. "I'm Trent Williams and you are very welcome…?" She waited and got a sweet smile in return.

"I'm Kayleigh Sullivan." A frown creased her forehead. "You're a girl, aren't you?"

Trent bit back the sigh. Her masculine features, though perfect for her butch persona, often led to awkward questions. "Yes, I am."

"I thought so. Where did you come from?"

Trent flipped a thumb over her shoulder at the Rowley Civic Center. "I was working in there when the commotion started."

"That was me. I was kind of yelling at them. I figured if I was loud enough I would frighten them off. Boys don't like screeching girls."

"Good work. It was you squealing like a stuck pig that got me out here to see what all the fuss was about." Trent turned back to the Center. Kayleigh followed after her, obviously not wanting to be left behind.

"What are you working on in there?"

"We have a big games meeting tomorrow. Me and a few guys are setting up the room for the event."

"I play games. I have a DS Lite."

Trent relaxed. Now this was something she could relate to. "Good gaming choice. I have one too."

Kayleigh's face lit up at finding someone who understood. "It's my birthday soon. I'd like my parents to buy me a Nintendo Wii, but they have no clue what I mean when it comes to stuff like that. They'll probably buy me something girly they hope I'll be more interested in." She made a face. "I won't be, though."

"That sucks," Trent said. She looked up at the darkening sky. It was getting late. "What were you doing around here anyway?"

Kayleigh looked abashed. "I had to get out of the house. My folks were too busy and I was just getting in the way. I thought I'd go for a walk, but I lost my direction a few times and got all turned around."

"How old are you?"

"Ten."

"Then I think it's time you went home. It's going to get dark soon."

Kayleigh nodded, then added sheepishly, "I'm still a little lost."

Trent shook her head at Kayleigh's pitiful tone. "How about I just finish up in here and then I'll walk you home. You do know your street name, right?"

"Of course. I'm just miles away from my house, that's all."

"Miles, eh?" Trent hid her amusement at Kayleigh's serious tone.

"Well, at least one. I was walking for quite a while, though."

Trent coughed to cover her laughter. "Okay, follow me. I'll go get my coat and we'll start your long trek home."

"If I had a cell phone I could call my sister. She'd come get me. She's cool like that."

Trent pulled her own cell phone from her pocket. "Here, use this."

Kayleigh made a face. "I don't know what her number is."

Trent sighed and put the cell phone back. She opened the Center's large door and yelled inside. "Elton? Can I leave you to clear up here?"

Kayleigh's eyes widened as she took in Elton as he walked toward them. "Wow, he's even taller than you are!" Kayleigh viewed Elton's six feet five inches of lanky length, taking in his long dark hair, mustache, the long wispy beard that today was plaited in two like a Viking's, and the wild tattoos that decorated his arms and neck. She fixed on his ornate eyebrow ring.

"Did that hurt?" she asked, running a finger over her own eyebrow in sympathy.

"Not as much as I thought it would."

"Is your name really Elton?" Kayleigh was obviously intrigued by Elton and his Gothic clothes.

He nodded. "My mom named me after her favorite singer."

Kayleigh considered this. It amused Trent that Kayleigh was obviously a child who questioned everything and anything.

"It's different, like you are. It suits you."

Elton bowed courteously. "Thank you." He cast a curious eye at Trent. "She with you?"

"This is Kayleigh. She was outside fending off Chris's kid brother and his friends."

"Actually," Kayleigh said, "the red-haired boy that you made turn really white was the only one who wasn't being cruel. He kept telling the others to leave me alone."

"Maybe Wade isn't such a little bast—" Elton hastily curbed his tongue at Trent's warning glare toward Kayleigh. "Sorry."

"I'm going to walk her home to make sure she's safe."

"No probs. We're all done here anyway. You've got the servers all set and the monitors are plugged in. We're good to go."

Trent scanned the room and nodded. Rows of monitors were lined up ready for tomorrow's gaming. "You'll wait for the security guard to come?"

"I'll make sure Todd is here to watch over the consoles and computers, and then I'll head off home myself." Elton flexed his hands and popped his knuckles. "Ready to wipe out the competition tomorrow?"

"Always," Trent said and snatched up her leather jacket. "You, me, frag fest at nine a.m."

Kayleigh waved good-bye to Elton as she was steered out of the Center.

"What's a frag fest?"

"It means my team is going to beat the Harley Hurricanes for the third year running at a game they keep thinking they can win."

"What's your team called?"

Trent struck a fierce pose and growled out her reply. "We are the Baydale Reapers and we rule the consoles." Trent looked down at the giggling Kayleigh. "We are very good; I promise you. We have the trophies to prove it." She cast her eye down the road. The evening traffic sped by. It wasn't safe for a young girl to be out on her own. "What's your street name, Kayleigh?"

"Castleview Street."

"You *did* wander a little far from home. Good thing I know where that is. Come on. Let's get you going."

"Juliet should be there by now." Kayleigh looked at her watch. "I hope she brought pizza. Mom and Dad don't like it, but I love it. Juliet brings it for me as a treat sometimes."

"Juliet?"

"My big sister. She's twenty-seven years old so she's my really *old* big sister. How old are you?"

"Thirty-two." Trent suddenly felt even older by Kayleigh's standards.

"Are you a lesbian?"

Trent stumbled off the curb and had to quickly get back on the pavement before she was run over. "Excuse me?"

"You look like a lesbian. You're like some of the ladies I've seen at Juliet's parties. But they weren't as nice as you are. You talk to me. They couldn't be bothered to."

Trent was a little lost for words so she just stared at Kayleigh chatting away at her side.

"Juliet's a lesbian. That means she goes out with other girls on dates."

Trent began to seriously wonder what she had gotten herself into rescuing this kid.

"Do you go out with girls?" Kayleigh asked.

Trent nodded dumbly.

"I thought so. And you beat boys at games. You are so cool!" Kayleigh took a breath. "Maybe you could tell my parents I want a Wii. They'd probably listen to you."

Trent listened to Kayleigh's endless chatter all the way back to her street. Once past the minefield of the lesbian queries, Trent and Kayleigh discussed favorite games, what kind they liked to play best, and what they were good at.

"Yes! Juliet's here! That's her car." Kayleigh pointed to a small red Honda parked against the curb. From the line of houses a front door opened and Trent looked up as Kayleigh's name was called.

The woman standing at the door was tall and slender. Her long blond hair was held back by a loose tie, but tendrils escaped to frame a face that instantly captured Trent's attention. She couldn't help but stare at this woman whose beauty was undeniably unique. With a self-conscious act, Juliet pushed her hair back behind her ear when she caught sight of someone with Kayleigh. It was only Kayleigh's shouting that brought Trent back to her senses.

"Jules, come meet Trent." Kayleigh raced ahead, and her sudden departure broke the spell that Trent had woven around her. She shook herself slightly as Kayleigh hugged her sister. Hanging back at the gate, Trent was entranced by the way the much older sister gave her full attention to the younger. Kayleigh led Juliet down the steps to where Trent stood waiting. Her breath stuck in her chest as bright blue eyes singled her out and seemed to pierce through to Trent's very soul.

"I understand you have been Kayleigh's knight in shining armor, and not only have you rescued her from a gang of boys but walked her all the way home too."

Trent looked at Kayleigh. "You tell her all that in one breath, kid?" She shrugged at Juliet. "It sounds more exciting than it was, believe me."

Juliet ruffled Kayleigh's hair affectionately. "I've got pizza warming in the oven. Go wash up and then you and I will talk about you not just leaving the house as and when you want to."

Kayleigh nodded quietly at the censure in Juliet's voice. "Thank you, Trent, for walking me home."

"You're welcome." Trent waved as Kayleigh ran inside the house.

"See you tomorrow for the frag fest!" With that tossed over her shoulder, Kayleigh disappeared inside.

Juliet faced Trent. "*Frag fest?*"

"I help run a gaming club at the Rowley Civic Center, and tomorrow we are in competition against other local teams."

"And you invited my sister?"

"Actually, no. She's too young to watch the competitions I'll be taking part in, but she's more than welcome to come and try out in the kids' competitions we run." Trent withdrew a flyer from her inside pocket and handed it over. "She seems very interested in her games. I think she'd enjoy playing with the other kids."

Juliet looked at the flyer. "She hasn't made any friends here yet. This might be good for her. I'll see if I'm free tomorrow to bring her."

Trent couldn't hide the delighted grin that escaped at the thought of seeing Juliet again. She stifled the feeling down just as quickly. *Look at her, Trent, you stand no chance there.* "I'll look forward to seeing you both tomorrow, then."

"Thank you for bringing her home safe." Juliet reached out and touched Trent's hand. The slight pressure sent tingles of pleasure through Trent's body.

"It was no problem. She's a great kid." Trent hastily pulled herself away from the gate. Part of her could have stayed there all night, just staring at the shifting shades of blond that streaked through Juliet's hair. She didn't usually react so strongly to a woman she'd only just met, but there was something about Juliet that seemed to call to the place that had lain long dormant inside her. Feeling unusually edgy, she decided to beat a hasty retreat before she embarrassed herself. "You'd better go inside before she eats all your pizza."

"Good night, Trent."

"Be seeing you, Juliet." Trent took a step then stopped. "Do me a favor?" She liked the way Juliet's eyebrow rose as she waited for Trent to continue. "Talk to your sister about Stranger Danger. I promise she'll always be safe with me, but not everyone on the street is as understanding when they find a kid alone. Please stress that to her."

"Don't worry. I'll make damned sure she never wanders off again," Juliet said with a steely edge to her tone.

❖

Juliet remained at the gate, watching the retreating figure of the woman who had brought her sister back home. She tore her gaze away from the edge of the woman's jacket where the tight fit of jeans accentuated a trim rear end. *Goodness, but she's handsome.* Juliet knew she shouldn't be hanging outside admiring the lean form of Trent as she walked away, but she didn't really want to have to go inside and have *that* talk with Kayleigh. Knowing she couldn't put it off any longer, Juliet closed the front door and went to find Kayleigh in the kitchen.

"I thought you knew better than to leave the house without telling anyone where you were going." Juliet busied herself at the table laying out the plates. She sat on a stool by the counter and waited for an explanation. When Kayleigh was quiet for too long Juliet asked softly, "Would you like to explain to me why you were out walking alone and had to be brought back home by a total stranger?"

"Everywhere I went in this house to escape I was in the way, Jules, so I thought I'd just get out before I got yelled at again." Kayleigh diligently washed her hands at the sink. "I was safe. I promise."

"But you weren't. You had to be rescued from a gang of boys. They could have hurt you." Juliet's blood ran cold at the mere thought of what could have happened to her sister.

"But they didn't and Trent saved me so it's all okay."

Juliet was annoyed at her happy logic. "Trent is a total stranger."

Kayleigh shook her head. "No, Trent is the next step up from a stranger and one step down from being a friend."

"She could have been worse than the boys were. Not all adults are safe to be around either."

"I know that. I'm not a baby," Kayleigh said. "But Trent isn't a bad guy. She's a bad *ass*."

"*What?*"

"That's what one of the boys called her," Kayleigh said matter-of-factly.

"Kayleigh, that isn't a compliment about someone."

Kayleigh dragged herself up onto a stool beside the kitchen counter. She leaned on her elbow, unconsciously mirroring Juliet's pose. "She was nice to me. She listened to me and talked to me. And not like I was a dumb kid either. She was setting up the equipment at the Center for the competition tomorrow," Kayleigh said as if this explained everything.

"Sweetie, you didn't even know that center existed until today."

Kayleigh shrugged. "She's a good guy. She's gay like you."

Juliet let out a sigh. "That doesn't make her any safer." She reached out to brush the hair out of Kayleigh's eyes. "And how exactly do you know she's gay?"

"I asked her. I told her you were too."

"I wish you'd stop outing me to anyone and everyone you meet," Juliet muttered.

"You said you didn't care who knew. It's just who you are," Kayleigh said.

"Yes, it is, but you can't tell just anyone. It may be who I am, but it's still private. Do you understand?"

Kayleigh nodded reluctantly. "I guess, but Trent goes on dates with girls too so I don't see what the problem is."

Juliet closed her eyes and counted to ten very slowly before she opened them again. "Enough about Trent. You know it was wrong to leave the house without a word, don't you?"

"I guess," Kayleigh mumbled.

"Mom and Dad are trying so hard to get this new house all set for you all, sometimes I think they forget that you could help too. You're a big girl now. You shouldn't have to be excluded."

"Did they go out tonight as usual?"

Juliet nodded. "I lied and told them I knew where you were. Otherwise we'd have had the police on our doorstep."

"So you got to tell me off instead of them?" Kayleigh asked hopefully.

Juliet graced her with an all too knowing look. "No, I'm sure you'll get all this replayed tomorrow over breakfast."

Kayleigh's face fell. "Lucky me."

Juliet ran her hand gently through Kayleigh's blond hair. "How about you and I see if there are any after-school classes that you could attend to keep you occupied?"

"I'd like to go to Trent's competition tomorrow."

"You and your games. You need to get out more, be with people."

"Jules, we've just moved here. I'm still the odd kid out at school. And besides, I've just been 'out' and you're mad at me!"

"I'm not mad. I just don't want you getting hurt. Those boys could have been worse than they were."

"Trent chased them away."

"She won't always be there. You were lucky this time."

Kayleigh nodded. "I won't do it again."

Juliet reached for the oven mitt. "Are you ready to eat?"

"I'm always ready for pizza."

Juliet placed the pizza on the table and began cutting it into manageable slices. She caught sight of the brightly colored flyer that Trent had left with her. "So this competition tomorrow? What time am I picking you up?" Kayleigh cheered around a mouthful of cheese and pepperoni. "Try not to choke yourself. We'll go see what these gamers have that draws you to them, eh?"

"Trent is gonna win," Kayleigh said. "She always wins."

"Does she now?" Juliet couldn't help but wonder at the power this mysterious woman had to draw her usually quiet sister out and bring a light to her eyes. She figured she'd get another chance tomorrow to see for herself.

CHAPTER TWO

Trent was in a reasonably quiet corner of the hall getting into her black robe. She made sure the long draped sleeves were hanging just right and lifted up the cowl to cover her head. She pushed past Elton, who was picking invisible lint from his pristine robe.

"Looking good," Trent said. "Not every Reaper can boast such sharp creases in their sleeves."

"At least mine is clean. Have you walked by Eddie yet?" Elton made a disgusted face in the general direction of their fellow teammate.

"Hey! Our washing machine isn't big enough to cram this thing in." Eddie pulled the seriously crumpled material over his face.

"You are sitting downwind from me, Eddie Gray," Trent said, her nose wrinkling at the stale smell of unclean wool and goodness knew what else. "You could stand to have that dry cleaned once in a while, you know."

"He'll give us a bad name," Elton said, fixing his cowl just right to hide his features from the audience they were about to face. What part of his face that was free of beard and mustache was painted a deathly pale color to emphasize his death skull visage. Black under his eyes hollowed out his lean cheeks and made him appear decidedly ghoulish.

"I'll have another word with him later," Trent said. She leaned in closer to Elton's face to get a closer look at his handiwork. "You are a living work of art, my friend. I've never seen a man more skilled with makeup to create the desired effect."

"Except perhaps for the Divine Danny?"

"She…or actually, *he* was truly an artist. A drag artist, but a beauty nevertheless."

"I miss him in the shop. He made the day seem so much brighter."

Trent agreed. The flamboyant drag queen had been with them for a year at Gamerz Paradise before the bright lights of the stage had called him away to better things. "I don't think management ever quite got over him turning up at the Christmas party as Daniella and not Daniel."

"Daniella was a hottie."

"And she just adored you." Trent nudged him. "Pity he wasn't your type."

Elton sighed. "Alas, it was not to be. He was not enough girl for either you or me."

Trent agreed. Her nose wrinkled as an offending smell wafted under her nostrils. She growled as that something came to stand next to her. "And he would have kept his robe clean. Eddie, move your skanky ass away from me. You're supposed to embody the swift kill of a Reaper, not smell like his rotting corpse!"

❖

"So tell me again why we're here consorting with the geeks and freaks of the gaming world."

Juliet cast an eye at Monica, who was sitting with her chin rested on perfectly posed hands as she leaned forward watching the endless procession of people streaming into the hall. Juliet was a little underdressed sitting next to her friend; her blue jeans and sky blue sweatshirt paled in comparison to Monica's long black dress. Each layer was ornately trimmed with an intricate lace that also edged the high-necked collar. Monica wore knee-high black boots with lethal heels as opposed to Juliet's white Nikes, and where Juliet's hair was swept back and held by a small tie, Monica's jet black hair hung straight down her back. Juliet had long since realized they were as different as night and day, in both attitudes and coloring, but looking at Monica now, her dramatic makeup was undeniably the finishing touch to a beautiful Gothic lady.

"We're here to bring Kayleigh to get to play with some other kids," Juliet explained again. She twisted around in her seat to catch Kayleigh's attention. Kayleigh was all but leaning over the barrier, her eyes racing over the activity below.

"Have you seen Trent yet?"

"Not yet, but she'll be here."

Monica leaned back and regarded Juliet. "Such certainty over one whom she only met yesterday."

Juliet hitched her shoulder. "There's something about her. Even I can't begin to explain it."

"I can't wait to see her. From how you've described her she sounds quite delicious."

The atmosphere in the hall grew charged as the lighting changed. Juliet was amused by how excited Kayleigh was getting. She enjoyed seeing her enthusiastic about something.

"What do you think is going to happen now?" Juliet whispered in Kayleigh's ear as the lights began to pulse out a rhythm that echoed the piped music's beat.

"The Reapers are coming!" Kayleigh said assuredly.

A loud voice over a microphone welcomed everyone to the hall and started to announce the teams one by one. Troops of teenage boys, twenty-something men, and the occasional girl came out to great applause. Juliet craned her neck to try to see where Trent's team was.

"Patience, Juliet. Your geek will be out shortly, I'm sure," Monica said sweetly.

❖

Behind the curtains Trent waved forward each team on their mark and looked over at her own team. She could see Elton still steering well clear of Eddie.

"Eddie, you clean that robe by next week or you are off the team, understood?"

"I'll get my mom to wash it tomorrow. I promise."

Trent rolled her eyes at Elton. "He is why gamers get a bad reputation." She ushered out the last group, their main rivals, the Henley Hurricanes. Elton good-naturedly booed them as they stepped through the curtains and got a one-fingered retort from their captain.

"That's very un-sportsman like conduct," Elton said, blowing a large raspberry at the rest of the team and earning a gentle slap from their lone female player. "See?" He turned to Trent. "I told you she liked me."

"And here I was thinking you were waiting for your vampiress to come to you out of a dream."

Elton shrugged inside his robe. "I keep waiting. I just keep meeting the ones who want a pound of flesh more than a bite of eternity with me."

"That was very poetic. I like that."

"See? I'm the answer to a maiden's prayer." Elton listened to the cheering going on for their rivals. "I don't know why you don't just use a fart machine to announce them," he muttered.

"Because they deserve all the respect we can give them back here because the minute we hit the consoles, we wipe the floor with their sorry asses." She waved to the guy manning the equipment to load up their music. The sound of piped organ music creepily echoed around the hall. A wolf howled, and an evil chuckling began to sound out menacingly. With a solemn air, the team members all flipped up their cowls and prepared to make their entrance. Trent got into position in front of Elton who, as their team leader, always brought up the rear. Trent listened to the crowd getting ready for the home team to make their appearance, and one by one her team filed out. They all kept their faces hidden, their hands tucked away in the long sleeves of the robes. Trent walked out to the sound of the audience cheering for their recognized talent and their showmanship. Elton stepped out from behind the curtain, a lethal-looking scythe in hand and his ghoulish face just visible beneath his hood. The cheers grew louder as he played to the audience, swinging his weapon above his head.

"Ladies and gentleman, give it up for the reigning champions, the Baydale Reapers!"

The team removed their cowls and the audience cheered for their home team. Trent scanned the audience and unerringly found Juliet among the crowd. A smile broke out unbidden at the sight of her. She flashed a thumbs-up sign to Kayleigh, who was waving to her excitedly. But her eyes were captivated by the beauty of Juliet. She got a soft nudge in the middle of her back from Elton.

"Basking in adoration done now. Let the gaming begin."

Trent reluctantly followed him as they left the stage and the emcee took over to welcome everyone to the games.

❖

Juliet sat back down with a thump.

"Wow, talk about a production." Monica fanned herself comically. "Please tell me that next to the last Reaper is this Trent because, girlfriend, she was all but eating you alive with her eyes."

"That was her."

"She's handsome, in a leaner, meaner incarnation of Mariska Hargitay kind of way."

Juliet had to laugh at Monica's description of Trent. "It's only a slight resemblance, I'll give you that. But Trent is so much more…"

"Butch? Studly? Damn sexy as hell for a woman?" Monica sighed. "I can see it all written as clear as the lust on your face." Monica leaned in closer. "Wouldn't you just love to run your fingers through that short hair of hers?"

"I hadn't really gotten to the part about mussing up her hair." She did, however, appreciate how Trent's dark brown hair was cut to accent her lean face.

Monica nodded sagely. "I see. You mentally skipped the foreplay and went straight for the down and dirty parts. I like your way of thinking!"

Juliet was scandalized. She checked that Kayleigh's attention was still elsewhere and hushed Monica. "I just mean I hadn't really thought about her in that way."

"Much."

"Much. Okay. I admit it, I thought about her."

Monica leaned back in her chair. "Well, she couldn't keep her eyes off you, so I'd say the feeling is mutual."

"She could have just been checking to make sure Kayleigh was here."

"Oh, honey, I don't think it was your sister she was looking at with *those* eyes. And think about it, she plays these games. She's going to have dynamite fingers. I bet she could push all your buttons *very* nicely."

"I can't believe I'm sitting here cruising her with you helping me along."

"She's just looked up here at you again. Who is cruising who?"

Juliet couldn't resist any longer and looked over to where Trent was helping to set up the first tournament. Their eyes met, and for a long moment the dull noise filling the hall disappeared and all Juliet knew was the pull from those dark brown eyes. She had to blink to physically break the spell.

"Juliet, she's coming!"

Juliet was shaken from her introspection by Kayleigh grabbing her arm. True enough, Trent was heading toward them.

Monica leaned in to whisper in Juliet's ear. "She's on her way. Be on your best behavior." She paused for a second, then added, "Stick your tits out!"

Red faced, Juliet hissed at her. "Will you stop that!" She looked up to find Trent bounding up the steps to lean over the barrier and greet Kayleigh.

"Hi, kid." Trent looked over at Juliet. "Juliet, glad you could make it today too."

"Kayleigh would never have forgiven me if we'd have missed this."

"Can I steal Kayleigh away from you? We have some competitions starting in the next rooms that are for kids her age." She gave Kayleigh an apologetic look. "The games we're playing first aren't meant for your age, but you can come back in later to see me drive."

"Why can't I see you play everything?" Kayleigh was obviously disappointed.

"We don't allow anyone to see games unsuitable for their age. But I promise you, you won't miss out." She turned her attention to Juliet. "Would you like to see where I'm taking her?"

Juliet stood, leaving her denim jacket on the chair. Monica stood too. "This is Monica Hughes," Juliet said. Trent reached over to shake Monica's gloved hand.

"A pleasure."

"Monica is Juliet's roommate," Kayleigh said.

Juliet caught the polite smile on Trent's face slip a little and her eyes clouded. Was she imagining the look of disappointment on Trent's face?

"We just share an apartment," Juliet said and was surprised by the visible relief that sparked through Trent's eyes before she hid it swiftly.

Monica looked down at Trent from her higher position on the steps. "I have a question for you, Trent."

Juliet held her breath for whatever Monica was about to utter.

"Mr. Tall, Dark, and Ghoulish on your team, the ever-so-gorgeous Grim Reaper, is he taken?"

Trent looked over her shoulder to where Elton was towering over a console watching the action unfold. "No, he's surprisingly unattached."

"Excellent. You must introduce me when you've all finished playing whatever it is you people play," she said. "Now, where are you taking the child?"

Trent held out her hand to help Kayleigh down the steps. "Let me introduce you to some games you are going to love."

❖

The back of the hall was separated from the main area by a series of room dividers. The sound of children's high and excited voices came from behind the screens. Trent led her group inside. She waved over a young man who was supervising the children with a parental eye.

"Conrad, we have another convert to add to your fold." Trent introduced Kayleigh to him and then Juliet and Monica. She bit back a grin at his obvious double take of Monica's stylish appearance. Trent guided Kayleigh along with Conrad to get her settled in. "I have two sets this morning that I have to compete in, but I'll be sure to come back here to see how you're doing, okay?" She pointed to all the consoles lined up. "This is where you get to test your skill at sports. Trust me, the bowling is brilliant." She drew Kayleigh's attention to another area. "Here's where the DSs take the lead, and you can go head-to-head with people here in the room, or we have Wi-fi set up and you can challenge people online anywhere." She cast Juliet a look. "All safe, all monitored. And the people here are great. They'll keep Kayleigh occupied."

"Do we stay with her?"

"You could or you can trust Conrad and his merry band to keep an eye on her should you decide you want to watch the main matches on today."

"Is the Grim Reaper playing?" Monica's question was innocent enough, but the accompanying look in her eyes was not.

"Yes, ma'am, he is. He and I have a match against another team in about fifteen minutes should you care to watch."

"What are you playing?"

"We're in combat teams against zombie hordes for our first game of the morning." Trent looked over at Juliet and rubbed her hands together gleefully. "There's nothing like an early start on killing the undead."

Juliet addressed Monica. "You go take your seat in the main hall and I'll come join you once I know Kayleigh's settled in." She turned to look for Kayleigh. "I guess that answers that, then." Kayleigh was already standing in line with some other children, strapping on her Wii remote, ready to play baseball.

Trent noticed that Wade, who had been with the boys terrorizing Kayleigh just the day before, had snuck in line behind her. Kayleigh acknowledged him and Trent was pleased to see him flush a brilliant magenta as he was obviously apologizing to her.

"Does Kayleigh know him?" Juliet asked.

"He's a good boy. He was just with the wrong crowd yesterday." Wade's shoulders relaxed as he started chatting more freely to Kayleigh, who obviously didn't hold a grudge. "I think she's just made a friend."

"Thank you for letting her come here."

"No, thank you for bringing her. Every kid needs someplace to go to explore who they are and what they like."

Juliet looked around her, taking in the sounds of many games all going at once and the children's delighted chatter. "As long as she's happy, I'm happy."

Trent drew Juliet's attention to Kayleigh taking her stance before the screen. With a look of intense concentration she swung her remote, and on the screen the ball flew out of the stadium to cheers and a "Home Run!" announcement. Kayleigh's team all cheered and high-fived her as she stood aside for the next player to take his turn. Kayleigh's face glowed as she caught Trent's eye and struck a winner's pose.

"I'd say she's happy." Trent discreetly winked at Kayleigh and turned to leave the children's area. Juliet's hand on her arm stopped her.

"I'm looking forward to seeing your match."

"I'll be sure to do my best to impress you."

"You think I need to be impressed?"

Trent straightened her shoulders. "Your sister has just scored a home run on her first go; I'm not having a little girl outplay me. How would it look if I got myself killed in the first minute of my game? How could I possibly hold my head up high before you? I have a reputation to uphold after all." Trent's tone was serious but she failed to hold her smile in check.

"You take this all very seriously, don't you?"

"Gaming *is* serious, even though it's just a bunch of people getting together to press a series of buttons to move pixilated characters around a screen."

"It sounds silly when you put it like that."

"But then would we still dance if it was described as just sticking your bodies together and moving your feet across the floor in time to a beat?" Trent was almost pushed into Juliet as a young child barreled past in their haste to reach a new game. "It takes the romance out of what can be a very intimate act." Trent could see the pulse in Juliet's neck beat out its rhythm. She was mesmerized by it.

"Do you dance, Trent?" Juliet's voice was low.

"I haven't for a long time, but I think I could still follow the beat." She was all too aware that the tone of the conversation had switched track just a little. She cringed as the siren went off to announce the next tournament but was thankful for it. "I have to go play."

"Good luck."

"Will you cheer for me?" Trent hoped she didn't sound as desperate as the words appeared.

"If I can be heard over Monica screaming for your partner the Grim Reaper, then yes, I will."

Trent laced her fingers together and cracked her knuckles. "Then let the contest commence." She gestured for Juliet to go before her. "But first, let me walk you back to your seat."

"What is it with you escorting the Sullivan sisters wherever they need to go?"

Trent kept her gaze fixed on Juliet. "Seems like the best thing I can do."

CHAPTER THREE

The game between two of the Henley Hurricanes' top players and Elton and Trent had been running for a set time of twenty minutes. Trent had very quickly gotten her concentration back into why she was there and away from the distraction of Juliet Sullivan. She grunted with satisfaction as she managed to kill off another set of moaning undead and set their score higher than their opponents'. When the final score was tallied, she and Elton had taken a very healthy lead, and she was proud as their scores were the first to be added to the board and the Baydale Reapers were far ahead of the competition. She walked over to congratulate her opponents on a good game played. However, Elton was not as gracious, and instead he played to the audience, building up their cheers.

"He's such a pain in the ass," Dave said as he shook Trent's hand.

"He knows that this is what the audience likes. We're not supposed to all get along and be friends outside the arena." Trent shook her head at his antics. "I told you to come work at our shop and not go to the other branch; that way you'd have been on our team and wouldn't have to put up with his showman antics."

"Your game was excellent today," Dave said.

"I had extra stimulus," Trent muttered and tried not to look out into the crowd of people to see if Juliet was still watching. She'd never worried before what anyone thought of her playing except for her own team members. She was a little disconcerted to find she was interested to hear what Juliet thought of her win.

"You're in the racing later?" Dave eyed her curiously.

"I'll be dogging your tail all around the track, yes." She caught Elton's attention. "Will you stop working the crowd into a frenzy?"

Elton sauntered over to clasp an arm about Dave's shoulders. "How about I buy you a drink, loser?"

"You really think a can of pop is going to stop me from breaking your fingers if you keep goading me?"

Elton looked over at Trent. "Did you hear that? He threatened actual bodily harm."

"Leave Dave alone. You've had your fun; now play nice with the other boys."

Elton ruffled Dave's hair into a mess. "I'll buy you a beer tonight and you can drown your sorrows in that, okay?"

Dave began trying to get his hair back into some semblance of neatness. "Two beers."

Elton nodded. "Two beers *and* a bag of chips." He waved him off the stage. "No offense, but he's such a girl."

"You'd think you'd be nicer to him, him being your cousin and all."

Elton wrapped his arm around Trent's shoulder and led her backstage. "In gaming there is no family except for your buddy beside you in the field of play." He pulled her back behind the curtain and pushed her against the wall playfully. "So spill, sister. Who got you pulling some fancy tricks while we were playing, because you were either touched by divinity or you were shooting to impress."

Trent knew she couldn't keep anything from him so yanked him back with her to peek through the curtain. "Second tier, fourth row."

Elton's jaw dropped with comical speed. "Oh my God. She's beautiful." His words whispered out like a prayer. "And damn you for seeing her first!" he said, not moving from between the curtains. "God can't be that cruel could he? To make such a gorgeous woman, one so obviously meant for me and have her fall for you instead?"

Trent stuck her head beside his out the curtain and realized what and who he was salivating over. "The Goth chick is all yours, Elton. She's already asked me to introduce you to her. I'm talking about the blonde next to her."

Elton shifted his gaze and looked where Trent was indicating. "Wow, she's pretty damn hot too. If you like blondes with big—"

"Elton! Eyes up!" Trent growled.

"I didn't think your tastes ran to the darker femmes of the Gothic bent. But I swear, that woman beside your ray of light is a vision of dark beauty."

"That's Monica."

Elton rolled the name around on his tongue. "Mon…i…ca, even her name is a benediction."

"Try not to drool on your robes there, Reaper."

Elton closed the curtain swiftly. "You'll introduce me, right?"

Trent nodded.

"No, I mean now, right this second." He began straightening his robe.

"Elton, we have another match in a few minutes. We don't have time for you to go meet and greet."

Elton pouted, which given his face paint, was not a good look for the angel of death. "But you've showed her to me now," he whined.

"And you can get up close and personal with her after the matches, but for now we need to have your concentration on the games and not on Morticia Addams out there."

Elton sighed dreamily. "She does have a little Carolyn Jones going on around the cheekbones, doesn't she? Then there's all that black hair, the pale face, those black lined eyes…"

Trent snorted. "She's actually wearing less makeup than you at the moment."

Elton put a hand to his cheek. "I need to go make sure nothing has run. I can't meet her with my Reaper guise anything less than perfect." He disappeared into the men's room.

"Great, now neither of us is thinking about the games."

❖

Juliet handed Monica a can and waited while Monica tried to pull the ring tab without damaging her false nails. Juliet rolled her eyes at her and retrieved the can to pop the tab.

"You're a high-maintenance date," she grumbled good-naturedly.

"But you love me anyway." Monica's attention was drawn to the stage where the next game was being set up. Juliet followed her line of vision. Trent, minus her flowing robe, was standing with her arms folded talking to an official. Juliet enjoyed the fact she could study Trent without censure. Dressed in blue jeans and a T-shirt bearing the face of a gaming character even Juliet recognized, Trent was stunning. She towered over the man she was talking to, her body solid and powerful, yet now that she was out of the shapeless robe Juliet could see the subtle curve of her breasts. Juliet's palms itched and she absently wiped them on her thighs. Trent's face was unashamedly masculine, but her smile broke up what could have been a moody countenance. Trent suddenly laughed at something the official had said, head thrown back and her face wreathed in delight. Juliet's heart clenched at the sight.

"If you continue to look at her like that she's liable to burst into flames," Monica said softly. She took a sip from her can and added, "Either that or you will."

Juliet reached for her own drink and took a long swallow from it.

"I know you normally like the more butch lesbian, but this one is not your average butch, me thinks."

"Why do you say that?"

"You usually go out with tomboys, girls who would cream themselves to be as big and bad as that one looks. She's not playing. She's the real deal."

Trent walked off the stage and headed to the back of the hall. "This one is so different, she doesn't seem to pretend to be something she isn't. And she cares. She walked Kayleigh all the way home yesterday. She didn't need to do that."

"She's a geek. She plays with boys on games where they shoot aliens and zombies. None of your previous dates would have been seen dead doing such things."

Juliet acknowledged that and tried not to crane her neck to see where Trent had disappeared to. The hall seemed strangely empty with her off the stage.

Monica leaned closer to Juliet when Trent reappeared to take her seat at a console beside Elton. "Other than her looks and how she eats you alive with her eyes, what makes you think she's a lesbian?"

"My sister told me."

Monica snorted at her. "Is there nothing that kid can't find out?" She leaned back in her chair and regarded Juliet. "So are you going to see if this woman can put down her toys long enough to play with you?"

Juliet drained the remaining pop from her can to delay her reply. She was saved from answering by Kayleigh's exuberant return.

"Jules! Trent's going to play next and I can watch this one. She came and got me especially." Kayleigh flung herself into her seat and then leaned forward over the railing.

Juliet reached over to run her hand through Kayleigh's hair. "You having fun, kid?"

Kayleigh's eyes were sparkling. "This is the best day ever!"

"And how about you?" she asked Monica.

Monica shrugged. "Ask me after I've met Reaper Boy." She then cast a sly eye at Juliet. "But I'm really glad I came, if only to watch you fall under the same spell your sister obviously is where that woman is concerned."

❖

Trent tuned out Elton's repetitive grunting as he guided his car around the track ahead of their competitors. His lead was virtually untouchable. Trent was driving to secure second place and bring the race home for the Baydale Reapers. Her concentration was totally fixed on the screen before her to the exclusion of the crowd behind her, the two men seated at the screens opposite, and her best friend beside her. Focused on the road before her, she felt the rumble from the control pad as she took a corner wide and the gravel crunched beneath her wheels. Her eyes were fixed on the car ahead of her, a rival who was confident the game was his. His erratic driving across the track was to keep Trent from overtaking him. Trent bided her time. She had driven this track so many times that she knew every curve and line like a lover. She ignored the man's taunting voice that she could just hear over the partition, having long since turned off the headset so she wouldn't have to listen to his blow-by-blow account of his superior driving skills in her ear. When his car hit the blind curve too fast because of his showboating, Trent pulled past his fiercely spinning vehicle and sped forward to a comfortable victory. Elton cheered and the audience erupted as her second place behind her teammate was broadcast around the room. The slap of a hand on her shoulder brought her back to her seat and she looked up to see Elton's victorious face. She looked over at the losing team. Only Dave put his hand out over the tables to congratulate them. The other player had thrown down his headset and stormed off the stage.

"Your new teammate plays dirty," Elton said to his cousin.

"And that is why he fails," Trent said in her best Jedi Master voice. She shook Dave's hand. "Nice driving, Dave. Pity you got pushed off the track by your own man so early in the game."

Dave's disappointment was obvious. "He won't try that trick again. You two are amazing, though."

"I've had a lot of practice chasing after this guy." She patted

Elton's shoulder as she eased herself out of her chair and looked over to where she could hear a small voice shouting her name above the row. Trent nudged Elton who was also looking in that direction. "If we win the tournament today, what say we take the ladies out with us to celebrate?" She surprised herself with the wager. She usually kept gaming and girls entirely separate. *I'm doing this for Elton, so he can meet Monica*, she told herself.

Elton's eyes were transfixed on Monica, who easily stood out from the rest of the crowd. "No pressure, then."

"You want the girl to be impressed, we had better frag the ass off Mick's team for the finale."

"Bring him and his team on."

Trent stepped down off the stage. Elton's voice made her turn around.

"Hey, where are you going? We have our last match soon. We should talk strategy and game play and—"

"We kick their asses. Enough said." Trent walked away. "I just have someone to see first."

❖

"You two totally beat him!" Kayleigh said, her excitement lighting up her face.

Trent enjoyed her infectious glee. "He was a careless driver. He deserved to wipe out and lose."

"He was a bad loser too. He stomped off the stage like a five-year-old."

"I think he'll have to get used to that if that's how he wants to play. I think his teammates might have a few words with him about his conduct. We don't like bad sports." Trent tried to be nonchalant about looking over at Juliet. She couldn't control the shock of pleasure that ran through her body when she met the bold eyes staring back at her. "I'm going to see how badly your sister can beat me at Wii bowling before I have to finish the last game of the day. Is that okay with you?" She glanced over at Monica, curious to know her connection to Juliet. "Elton, Chris, Eddie, and I are going up against the first placed team, which should be decided at the end of this game now starting."

"The Baydale Reapers have ruled the scoreboard all day," Kayleigh said seriously.

Trent was proud of that fact. "That we have, but our last game is against the top players of the second place team. I have half an hour before that game starts. The other teams are still playing, but I thought you and I could go get some time in together before I have to leave you in there because the next match is seriously for adults only."

Kayleigh sighed. "Shooting again."

Trent nodded. "I know it sucks, but age restrictions are in place for a reason. For now, though, I'm in the mood for some fun before I have to shoot aliens. You up for it?"

Kayleigh was out of her seat in a flash.

Trent addressed Juliet. "After the last competition the Baydale Reapers will all go out to celebrate or commiserate with pizza. We were wondering if you three would care to join us?"

Kayleigh looked imploringly at Juliet. "Can we?"

"I promise we won't keep anyone out late. We just eat, then go home. And it's a family restaurant so we'll be on our best behavior. I promise."

Juliet looked at Kayleigh's expectant face. "You're well in the lead already. I'd say your victory was pretty complete."

"We've played well, but this final match is the signature of the whole competition. If we lose this, we lose status points. But either way, win or lose, we have a pizza party after." Trent eyed Juliet. "So you'll come with me?" Juliet's eyes widened and she hastily added, "And the rest of the team?"

"Please, Jules, I want to see Elton and meet the rest of the Reapers. There's another girl on the team I want to meet," Kayleigh said.

Juliet looked over her shoulder at Monica, who nodded her assent. "Count us in and thank you for the invitation."

Trent helped Kayleigh down the step and then looked back at Juliet. "Are you going to join us now?"

Juliet once again turned to Monica, who shooed her away. "Go be with your sister. I want to see what this flag thing is these guys are chasing after. I know the Reapers are in the lead, but I'm sure the extra points the members of your team bring in will all help to elevate you to the dizzy heights of unequalled victory."

The large screen displayed a "Capture the Flag" game going on with two of Trent's teammates against another team. "You're watching two of our youngest members, but both Rick and Zoe are excellent players."

Kayleigh tugged at Trent's sleeve until she bent to hear what Kayleigh wanted to whisper to her. "This is yet another shooting match I shouldn't be seeing, isn't it?"

Trent nodded and whispered back. "Don't worry. When you're old enough you can learn how to play these games too."

"But you're going to play with me now?"

"Well, I'm told you're a dedicated gamer. I only play with that kind of person."

"I'm very dedicated," Kayleigh said. She shyly shifted her hand into Trent's and squeezed. "Let's go play."

Trent tried not to jump at the feel of someone's hand in hers. She was even more surprised when Juliet put her own hand on Trent's arm.

"So come on, then. Show me this world you both are so keen to inhabit."

"Have you never played a game, Juliet?" Trent asked, letting Kayleigh lead them back into the children's area.

"Not properly," Juliet said. "I don't ever seem to have time these days."

Trent shook Kayleigh's hand in her own. "I think you need to show your sister how we do things, squirt."

Kayleigh pulled away from Trent's grasp to go gather up controllers for a game that was free from players. "I think she'd rather you show her, Trent."

Trent was intrigued by the rosy hue that suddenly heated Juliet's cheeks.

"Out of the mouths of babes," Juliet said. She reached for the controller that Kayleigh held out to her. "Come on then, either one of you, show me how to play." She flipped the controller over in her hand, testing its weight. "And don't come crying to me if I manage to beat you."

Trent liked the determined set of Juliet's face. "Oh, I do so love a challenge."

CHAPTER FOUR

T he crowd was cheering as the teams took their places at their screens for the final match of the day. The Baydale Reapers were already way ahead on points, but the final game was more a grudge match than anything else. Two teams of four players, one team an elite squad of soldiers going up against members of an alien race, all hell-bent on killing the other. Elton took his seat beside Trent and glowered at Eddie, who sat as far away from him as he could. Trent put on her headset and they all checked that the microphones were working and they could hear each other's commands as they took up their controllers and prepared for war.

"Nobody gets a bullet, or I will personally make sure you are stocking the 'pre-owned' shelf for weeks to come." Elton's dire threat hung in the air.

"Good luck, team." Trent rallied her people as the game began. She instantly made her character dive for cover as the other team began firing rockets. "Bastards, they learned that from us," she said. "Chris, shoot their launcher and let's get to higher ground."

The battle raged and they raced across the harsh terrain, ducking behind shattered buildings and shooting the enemy with everything they had.

"I swear, Eddie, if you don't drag your guy's ass back and take cover I will shoot you myself," Trent said as Eddie's soldier got shot at from all angles. She edged forward, scanning the area carefully, then popped up from behind her wall and took aim at one of the enemy. The target dropped and the crowd cheered behind her.

"First kill to us," Elton said, "Great shot, Trent. Now let's get the others. I can smell the scent of victory pizza from here."

❖

The game was hard fought but the Baydale Reapers had earned
their reputation through dedicated playing, and that shone through with
their defeat of the other team. The last alien fell and Trent punched the
air as the crowd erupted. Elton flung down his headset and faced the
audience to roar at them. Trent got up to congratulate her team and
mentioned for the last time that Eddie wash his robe or else. Then she
leaned over to shake hands with the losing team, acknowledging each
of them for what role they had played in the game.

"Nice trick with the flamethrower, Evan," she said, then narrowed
her eyes at him. "And don't think we won't be ready to counter that
next time."

Evan basked in her praise. He was an assistant from another shop
in the same mall where Trent worked. "You still in for next week's
online game?" he asked.

"Got it written on my calendar. And this time, you have to show
me how you pulled off that move, the one where you all but fried
Eddie. Thankfully, Elton pulled his dumb ass out of the fire just in
time."

"You want me to show you my best move?"

"In exchange, I'll show you how you could have got Elton in that
last play if you hadn't left yourself wide open for me to sniper you,"
Trent said.

"You're on!" They shook hands on it.

"Well done, everyone. That was a brilliant match. But I need to
go rescue Elton before he has the room whipped up so much they start
a riot."

"He's frightening with that face makeup on," Evan said.

"He's just as scary without it," Eddie muttered.

❖

Trent loved it when everyone got their trophies for playing. She
knew the sponsors got a great deal of publicity for their wares. Her own
company got a huge chunk of the recognition every time the Baydale
Reapers won, and the teams got the satisfaction of playing with others
just as dedicated as they were. She dutifully took her place at her team's
side as team leader Elton accepted the first place trophy.

"Next stop, Chicago!" Elton said.

Trent knew they were edging ever closer to being able to take on the professional teams that competed all around the world. She knew Elton hungered for that, and there was a part of her too that enjoyed the competition. Trent enjoyed the games, win or lose. It was more about taking part and the experience. Jubilation was written all over Elton's face as he lifted the trophy high. Trent had to admit that winning was a whole lot better than losing. She looked out through the crowd of faces and spotted Juliet on her feet applauding with the rest of the audience. But Juliet's eyes weren't on the team. They were fixed on her. Trent couldn't help the fire that burned in her as she acknowledged Juliet's stare. She barely remembered taking her place for the group photo that would be displayed in the shop to announce their victory to all budding gamers. All Trent could see was the bright blue of Juliet's eyes seeking her out among the many.

❖

Trent pulled on her leather jacket after carefully folding up her robe and packing it away in her sports bag. Elton was beside her, making sure his hair was just the right amount of messy. Trent tried not to let him see her amusement at his preening, but sometimes he was way too fastidious in getting his appearance just so. She called to the rest of her team.

"Everyone ready for pizza?"

She was greeted by a chorus of "Hell, yes!" as they all filed out from behind the stage. There were still a lot of people in the hall. Some were playing in the children's area, some chatting with the other teams.

"I'll come back later to help you all clear up," Trent said to one of the men who had helped her and Elton set the place up the previous day.

"I thought once the games were done the folks would leave," he said.

"This is a huge gathering of geeks, my friend. They don't go until you physically pick them up and show them the door. The organizers are used to it. They'll let it run for a little longer and then they'll start flashing the lights to signal it's time to go. I'll go have my celebratory meal and then I'll come back and help you all clear up." She reached into her pocket and flipped open a small notebook. "There were ten of you yesterday, right? Same number today?" She scribbled something down as the man nodded. "Any preference to your pizza topping?" He rattled off a few pizzas and thanked her. "It's no problem. You helped get this all set up. I'm just sorry you can't join us, still being on duty and all, so we'll have them bring the pizza to you." She put away her pad. "I'll get Elton to have them sneak in some beers for you all too."

"You're a star, Trent."

"You contributed to our win. We can't play if we don't have the equipment." She checked her watch. "I'll see you guys later to help pack everything away."

"No one else buys the techie guys pizza," Eddie said.

"No, they don't, which is why they don't get the most comfortable seats or the cleanest controllers. We do," Elton said, holding out his hand. "Everyone cough up ten bucks to pay for them." He gathered the money and put it in his pocket. "That is how you earn a reputation, my team. We play fair, we look after our techies because they look after us, and we win with honor. And if you're lucky, you get the girl at the end of it," he added sotto voce for Trent's ears only.

With the team all gathered together, Juliet found herself intrigued by the unusual group they made. Elton and Trent literally towered above everyone else. There was a handsome red-haired man who bore a striking resemblance to the young boy Kayleigh had been friendly with all day. Then there was a younger girl who looked way more fashionable in her carefully torn jeans than the man beside her, who looked in desperate need of an ironing board. Both were chatting with another young man who was so blond his hair was almost white.

"Strange little group, aren't they? Led by giants," Monica said.

Monica's comment registered but Juliet couldn't tear her eyes away from Trent, who was bounding up the steps toward them.

Kayleigh spoke to her first, her excitement bursting from her. "You guys won the biggest trophy!"

Trent took the trophy from Elton's hands. She held it out for Kayleigh to hold. "Careful, it's heavy."

"This is so cool," she said.

"Get used to holding it. I'm betting in years to come you'll be here holding a winner's trophy all of your own."

Kayleigh's eyes sparkled up at Trent. "Really?"

"If you're serious about playing, then I'd have to say yes."

"I would like that a lot." She handed the trophy back to Trent. "I didn't get to see everything you did today, but I know your team did excellent. Can I meet everyone now?"

Trent introduced everyone to Kayleigh who was quickly taken in by the group as they chatted with her.

"You've made her day," Juliet told Trent.

"She needs to make new friends. Nearly everyone on the team has younger siblings around them, so they are used to kids. Except for Rick, but he hangs round with Zoe, so he has her little sister Sam by proxy." She stepped back to introduce Elton to Monica. "Monica Hughes, may I introduce Team Captain Elton Simons."

Monica held her hand out to shake Elton's, but he gently turned it over and kissed the knuckles hidden in her glove. "The pleasure is all mine," he said gallantly.

"You've removed your face paint," Monica said with disappointment.

Elton scowled at Trent. "She said I would scare the patrons of the pizza restaurant so I had to wash it off."

"It was very fetching."

"Thank you." His eyes were drawn to a small tattoo visible on her neck. "You're a fan of Within Temptation?"

Monica fingered the band's symbol on her skin and faked a swoon. "I want 'Ice Queen' played at my funeral."

Elton clenched his fist and punched the air. "Finally! A *real* woman! I want 'Deceiver of Fools' played at mine. Please, let me escort you to dinner." He guided Monica past Juliet, tucking her arm in his, and they began chatting together as if they were old friends.

Juliet blinked as they passed by. "So much for that awkward first meeting."

"Fate obviously meant for them to meet. You and I were merely their conduit," Trent said.

Folding her arms loosely across her chest, Juliet regarded Trent steadily. "And what about us?" she asked softly.

Trent froze, caught off guard by Juliet's obvious teasing. She hesitated, then offered her own arm to Juliet. "I too have a healthy respect for fate and destiny and little sisters lost in the wild streets of Baydale." She gave Juliet a shrug. "But forgive me if I haven't picked my funeral music out just yet."

"I'm very glad to hear it."

❖

The meal was a lively affair, full of loud talking and laughter. The gamers were seated at a large table that ran along the back of the restaurant in front of the windows. Kayleigh wasn't the only child to join them at their table; Chris had gathered up his brother Wade, and Zoe had brought along her sister. The children were interspersed among the adults and kept highly entertained by their stories and jokes. Trent reached for a piece of pizza while speaking to Monica.

"I wondered if you'd remove your gloves."

Monica lifted her own piece of pizza and sighed. "Had I known that today's festivities would culminate in this food free-for-all, I would have dressed more accordingly."

"I think you look beautiful," Elton said, his eyes never leaving Monica's.

She glowed at his obvious sincerity. "I can do jeans. I just prefer to express myself a little more differently on the weekend."

Trent stuffed a piece of pizza in her mouth and chewed, savoring the tangy cheese taste. "You look amazing. I'm used to seeing Elton all gothed up, but there's something very striking about a woman in her regalia. You're handsome and all, Elton, but you just wouldn't look the same in that dress."

"Sad, but true," he said.

"Monica, I couldn't help but notice your ornate earrings. They really are unusual."

Monica touched her ear and twisted the black bejeweled design so it caught the light. "Thank you. I found them in a little antique shop."

"Elton, show her your ring. I think she'll love it." Trent leaned back as the two dark heads bent together as Monica excitedly exclaimed over Elton's devil's head ring.

"Are you quite finished matchmaking?" Juliet spoke softly into Trent's ear. Trent's whole body tingled at the soft breath that had whispered against her skin.

"They make a perfect couple," Trent said quietly back, looking directly into Juliet's eyes and marveling at how blue they were. Juliet blinked and Trent hastily drew back, conscious of how close she had been leaning into Juliet's personal space. *Step away, Trent, this lady is not for playing and you're certainly not the sort she'd play with.*

Juliet moved back also and regarded Trent a moment before addressing the table. "So, you all work in the same shop?"

"Elton is the manager and the rest of us are his underlings," Zoe said. "He commands and we all bow before him."

Elton snorted. "I wish."

"So you started the team at work?"

"Elton and I started working together at Gamerz Paradise at the same time and we'd been playing for years before that," Trent said. "Then when Chris came and was interested too, we started to go online as a trio, which grew into a larger group. We turned professional two years ago when the gaming business really began to take off. Since then we've gained Eddie, Zoe, and Rick and become a formidable team."

"Why the robes? I noticed no one else dressed up today," Juliet said.

"It was Elton's idea. He said we should bring a bit of showmanship to the proceedings. Everyone else had their name printed on a T-shirt, but we storm in wearing our Reaper robes. It makes us stand out."

"Whether we win or lose, the crowd remembers the Reapers when the gaming is all done with," Rick added.

"And the skull face?" Juliet looked over at Elton, who was in deep conversation with Monica.

"That's Elton's own special trademark. He's the team captain, and he's very aware that the face makeup unnerves some of the younger crowd we play against. He's as purposely ghoulish as possible. He's our version of those Maori rugby players who do the haka to frighten the opposition." Trent signaled the passing waitress for another round of drinks and got a saucy wink in return. Trent caught Juliet looking from the waitress to her and back again.

"She seems to know you."

"She should. We come here nearly every other week."

"Didn't you go out with her once?" Eddie asked around a mouth stuffed with pizza crust.

"Once," Trent said stonily. She couldn't remember how long it had been, but the encounter had been brief and characteristically one-sided. The waitress had thought it was a turn-on when Trent had purposely kept her hands pinned to stop her from touching her back. For Trent it had been necessary, but the sex had left her as unfulfilled and empty as always. One-sided sex was Trent's way. It was quick and lacking in true intimacy, but it was the only way she would allow herself to be. She couldn't afford to be vulnerable; she'd learned that lesson. Trent studied the pattern on her plate for a moment before turning the conversation away from herself. "So what line of work are you in, Juliet?"

"I work for a bank."

Trent grimaced. "In this current climate? Not a safe bet for a long career."

"True, but I've been with this company ever since I left college."

"Several years in one job is a long time," Trent said. "You must love your work."

Juliet shrugged. "I used to love the challenges it created, but I can't help wondering if I'm truly destined to stay there forever."

"I love my job," Trent said. "I work with a great group of people, get to talk games all day, and meet new folk to talk games with."

"It's perfect for you. You're lucky to be so settled."

"You're not so settled?"

Juliet ran a hand through her hair which almost distracted Trent from her reply. "I'm bored. I can't help but wonder if there's something more."

"There's always something more. You just have to decide if you want to take it up on its offer when it presents itself to you."

"Do you want more, Trent?"

Trent was stopped from answering by the waitress deliberately leaning over her to set her drink down on the table before her. By the time she had removed herself, Kayleigh had engaged Juliet in conversation and the moment was lost.

❖

Once the meal was over, everyone started to ready themselves to leave. Trent worked her way around her friends saying good night and answering the kids' questions while she slipped on her jacket and prepared to go back to clear up the hall. She was amused to find Elton with Kayleigh fast asleep in his arms, her head on his shoulder.

"Guess we wore her out," she said as they walked back to Juliet's car.

"She hardly slept all night, she was so excited about today." Juliet opened the car door and Elton carefully lowered Kayleigh into the front seat and fastened her seat belt. She never made a murmur.

"When that kid sleeps, she's dead to the world," he said.

"The sleep of the innocent," Monica said, hooking her arm back through Elton's once his charge was settled.

Elton gave Trent a look she knew all too well. "I need to ask you a huge favor. Will you be able to finish up at the hall without me? I would really like to take Monica out for a drink."

Trent nodded. "Sure, go ahead."

"We'll help you finish up, Trent," Rick and Zoe said.

"Haven't you got somewhere else to be?"

"No, not really. And Sam here can help wrap the controllers. We'll see you in there."

The threesome headed over toward the hall. Trent gave Elton the thumbs up. "There you go, all sorted. Those three will pick up your slack."

"I owe you one," Elton said.

Monica kissed Juliet's cheek and promised not to wake her when she came home. She held out a gloved hand to Trent, who shook it dutifully.

"It was wonderful to meet you, Trent."

"Likewise, Monica. Something tells me I'm going to be seeing you a whole lot more." She smirked at Elton's uncharacteristic blush. "Elton, just make sure that trophy makes its way into work tomorrow unscathed. We'll want it on display before the doors open."

"I'll remember." They waved good-bye and began to walk away, already in deep conversation.

"It's really a shame those two didn't hit it off," Trent mused at their departure. "I'm sure they would have made a lovely couple."

"I've never seen Monica so instantly smitten. It's nice to see her happy. She's a good friend and deserves to find a nice guy."

"Elton's the best," Trent said. "And he's a gentleman, so Monica is in good hands."

Juliet leaned back against her car. "So what are you going to do now after such an exciting day?"

Trent tucked her hands into her coat pockets and rocked back on her heels a little. "I've got to help pack everything away again. I'm usually chief cable layer. Now I get to roll everything back up."

"And then?"

"Then I go home and prepare for a busy day at work tomorrow."

"You have to work on a Sunday?"

"This week, yes. I'm covering for one of the guys there. He has a wedding to go to so I'm taking his shift."

"That's very nice of you."

Trent shrugged. "I don't have the same commitments as some of the others. I can usually swap or change at a moment's notice." Trent peered into the car window to make sure Kayleigh was still sleeping. "You sure she's asleep?"

Juliet nodded. "She's out for the count. Why?"

"Is it her birthday soon?"

"Next weekend," Juliet said. "Is there nothing she didn't tell you on that walk back home?"

She didn't tell me just how beautiful you are, Trent thought as Juliet's eyes danced with amusement. "Have you gotten her a present yet?"

"No. My parents and I are stumped as to what to buy her."

Trent chewed her bottom lip and debated her next words. "I can tell you exactly what she wants, but she's worried you won't get it for her because of the whole moving thing and the fact you usually stick her with girly presents."

Juliet rolled her eyes at Trent's statement. "My parents can't quite get used to having a more 'energetic' daughter this time around. I'm told I was much easier to look after." Juliet closed her eyes a moment. "But then, they didn't have me so late in life."

"There does appear to be quite a gap between your ages."

"Kayleigh was an 'oops' baby but very much wanted by my parents. They had her when I was seventeen, late in the day for both of them, and I regret that I was already way beyond wanting a little sister to tag along with me. But I love her to pieces and try to spend as much time as possible with her when I can."

"She wants a game console for her birthday. I know exactly which one and what else you'll need for her. I hasten to add this isn't so I can make a sale here. It's what she told me she wanted."

"If I come into your shop could you set me up with her dream present?"

"I could do exactly that and make you the best big sister ever in her eyes."

"I could live with that. You say you're in tomorrow? I could pop in then. Sunday shopping is a perfect time for me."

"Do you know the Baydale Shopping Center?"

"I'm getting to. Monica does all her shopping there and delights in dragging me around every square inch of the place when I go with her."

"We're on the ground floor, opposite the food court. We open at eleven a.m. Come see me and I'll hook you up with everything you need."

"This is very sweet of you," Juliet said softly. "After all, she's just a kid you met by chance yesterday."

"Everyone should have what they want if they want it hard enough." Juliet's undivided attention made Trent's chest ache, and warmth began to radiate between her thighs.

"Is there anything that you want hard enough?" Juliet asked, her voice suddenly husky and low.

"At this precise moment I find myself quite content with my life."

"You're very lucky."

"I had a really great time today. I'm so glad you came." The smile Juliet gave her took Trent's breath away and she was glad she'd given voice to her thoughts.

"I don't think Kayleigh would have let me *not* bring her." Juliet walked around her car to get in.

"Then I owe your sister. Until tomorrow, then?"

Juliet nodded. She unlocked her door and started to get in but at the last minute stopped. "Trent? I had a wonderful day too. Thank you."

It was my pleasure, Trent thought as Juliet got in her car and started the engine. Trent stayed to wave her off and didn't move until the car turned at the end of the road and disappeared from her sight. She shifted uncomfortably at the steady thrum of arousal radiating over her body. "Oh, she is way out of my league," she mumbled to herself and kicked at the pavement petulantly. She forced herself to take a deep breath. "Okay, she's gone now, time to get your brain in gear and go clear up the gaming hall." Trent wandered back to the civic hall. "So maybe I'll see her again tomorrow. Maybe I won't. Maybe I'll just get one of the other guys to just deal with her and I won't have to see her again." She swallowed against the excitement the mere thought of seeing Juliet caused and the unwelcome rush of unease that followed it.

"This had better not put me off my game."

CHAPTER FIVE

Trent tried not to be obvious about the fact that every four seconds she was checking out the customers entering the store. She busied herself by neatly arranging the empty game boxes on their shelves. She made a concerted effort to keep her hands busy and her focus away from the front of the shop. Elton finally caught her.

"Are you waiting for someone in particular or just looking to make your escape from the hordes of Sunday shoppers?"

Trent leaned her hip against the counter and straightened her tie, unconsciously fidgeting to make herself presentable. Elton stilled her hand as she fiddled with her name tag.

"Okay, now you're making me nervous. Have we got a visit from the head office that I haven't been warned about?"

Trent ignored him as a flash of blond hair distracted her at the door. One of the guys behind her made a comment about the new arrival. It was sexist and derogatory and Trent was grateful he was just a temp because she wanted to kick his ass out the shop that very second. Any thoughts she had about hiding in the storeroom until Juliet had left were shattered; there was no way she was leaving her to the mercies of a Neanderthal.

"Back off, Greg. This one is all mine," she said.

Elton peered over to where Juliet was making her way through the shop.

"God, no wonder you've been antsy all morning." He leaned his chin on Trent's shoulder as they both stared in her direction. "She really is a pretty lady."

"Yes, she is." Trent stepped forward to make her presence noticed. Her heart raced at the smile she received when Juliet caught sight of her. She couldn't stop her answering one.

"Good morning, how may I help you?" Trent fell into her customer service training deliberately, trying not to be distracted by the simple lilac sun dress Juliet wore that showed off her creamy skin to perfection. She purposely kept her eyes way above the cleavage that Juliet was modestly displaying. She hoped by being professional she wouldn't have time to wonder what scent Juliet wore that was teasing her nostrils and making her slightly giddy.

"You can cut the salesperson's spiel and show me what it is my sister wants."

Trent led the way to the middle of the shop and set about explaining what Kayleigh had mentioned.

Juliet nodded as Trent pointed out everything that would be a part of the bundle she recommended. "And how about the games themselves?"

Trent recommended which games she thought Kayleigh would get the most enjoyment from. "Of course, the machine comes with a free game in it. It has the bowling that you proved to be very talented at yesterday."

"I never came close to Kayleigh's score."

"True, but it was your first time and practice makes perfect. Which is why I am recommending that you get an extra set of controllers." Trent took a step back, aware that she had been leaning ever closer to Juliet, so close she could smell the faint perfume of her hair. Trent forced herself to take a deep breath and try to be impartial, but she couldn't seem to help but be drawn to Juliet. *She's so beautiful and I really should know better. This woman isn't a one-time only kind of lover; she's an all or nothing. I cannot afford to get involved with that kind of woman.* She tried desperately to focus on the job at hand.

"So if I buy all this, what is the damage to myself and my parents who have promised to go halves with me."

Trent reeled off the total and was pleased Juliet didn't balk at the cost.

"Sold. I'll also take the two games you said would be perfect too."

"You don't have to get them all today. You could always come back." Trent hoped like crazy that none of her fellow assistants had overheard her say that. Making the sale was the ultimate goal in retail.

Juliet just shook her head. "I think it's a safe bet I'll be in here more often than not with Kayleigh in tow wanting to spend her birthday money, her allowance money, and any other money she can wrangle out of the folks." She made a wry face. "She is way more savvy than I ever was at her age." Juliet's attention shifted as she looked over Trent's shoulder. "Hi, Elton."

"Juliet, it's good to see you again. Did Trent here convert you into becoming a believer?"

Juliet stared at him for a moment, then laughed. "No, this is for the convert already at home. Apparently, this is what Kayleigh wants for her birthday and she told Trent all about it." She turned back to Trent. "I'm glad she did; otherwise we'd have been none the wiser. For a chatty kid she can keep quiet at the strangest of times. She's not your usual little girl."

Elton grunted. "Trent would know all about that." His attention was distracted by another customer. "She wasn't a normal little girl either." He walked away to deal with someone else.

Trent stared at his retreating back. "Elton and I go way back. We grew up as kids together."

"No wonder you are so close."

"He's my big brother and best friend all rolled into one."

"You're lucky to have that."

"Yes, I am." Desperate to change the conversation, Trent quickly rubbed her hands together. "So how about I go get your console and extras and we go run it through the till?" She disappeared to the storeroom to find everything that Juliet had picked out. She picked up a new console box and gathered the extras and the games. Then she stopped, aware that her breathing was patchy and her palms were damp. She leaned back against one of the shelving units and took a moment to just think.

"I can do this. She will buy this stuff, and I probably won't ever see her again. I really like her, but she is not what I can afford to start dealing with in my life right now. My life is settled and I like it that way." Trent knew she was deluding herself, but she'd used the excuses so many times that she was starting to believe them herself. "Besides, she's probably just flirting because I'm the first new lesbian she's seen for a while. She's beautiful and she's smart and she's out of my league." Trent gathered all the items up into her arms. She hastened back toward the shop floor and halted again in the process of opening the door. *But God, she's so damn gorgeous.* She groaned out loud and resisted the urge to bang her head off the door. Trent straightened her posture and prepared to re-enter the shop. "Just make the sale."

Juliet was waiting when Trent came out with all her goods. She reached into her handbag to get out her wallet as Trent guided her to the counter to pay.

Trent busied herself in the routine of scanning all the objects and packing them up. "You're going to need a lot of wrapping paper," she said.

Juliet agreed. "Are you due a break soon?"

Trent nodded. "I could be. I could walk you to your car with this. It's not heavy, but it's bulky."

"I'd like to ask you something out of the din of the shop."

Trent finished up the sale and caught Elton's eye. "Can I have fifteen minutes, please?"

Elton nodded and shooed Zoe in to take Trent's place at the counter. Trent gathered up the bag and escorted Juliet out. "I feel like I'm absconding with half the shop," she said, waiting for Juliet to lead the way.

"Thank you for doing this." Juliet reached out to touch Trent's arm. "I wanted to invite you to Kayleigh's birthday party."

"Birthday party?" Trent repeated dumbly.

"You've got to come. You're Kayleigh's newest and bestest friend."

Trent's chest tightened at the thought of having to be social with strangers. She looked into Juliet's face, argued with herself, and then caved in. *So much for keeping your distance, Trent.* "Will there be cake?"

"Cake, ice cream, sandwiches, and it's just a few of us. Mainly my parents and me, although Monica has said she will pop in, but she doesn't 'do' my parents. They're a little distracted by her look."

"Then I should totally make their day," Trent said dryly. She'd seen how people looked at her, intimidated by both her size and looks.

Juliet pulled her to a halt. "Why? You're smart, witty, can hold a conversation with anyone and everyone. You have the most amazing sense of fair play that I have ever witnessed. Add to that you are amazingly handsome, what's not to like?"

Trent willed her mouth to close. No one had ever complimented her so nicely. "You think I'm all that, eh?"

"And probably more."

"You hardly know me."

"Maybe we can remedy that over cake and ice cream."

Trent warred within herself for a moment then capitulated. "Okay, but I warn you I'm a frosting fiend."

"You and Kayleigh alike."

The parking lot was busy, and Trent dutifully followed as Juliet directed her to where her car was parked. Carefully, Trent placed the bag in the trunk and lowered the lid.

"You know, I don't think I've seen anyone treat a box so reverently." Juliet accepted back her keys from Trent's hand and their fingers touched. Trent shoved her hands in her pants pockets nervously.

"I love my games and treat them accordingly, whether they are mine or for someone else."

"Kayleigh is going to love this. Thank you for helping me."

"It was my pleasure." Trent was at a loss as to what to do next. She needed to get back to work but was loath to leave Juliet's side. The feeling both unnerved and excited her.

"I'll come pick you up on Saturday, unless you'd rather drive yourself?"

"I don't drive."

"You don't have a car?"

"I have no need for one. I live close enough to work that I can walk, or if I'm not in the mood for a trek I can catch a bus here. I have my own house that I'm paying for. The money I'd use on a vehicle I pay into that instead. I don't need wheels as much as I need a roof over my head," Trent said.

"How wonderful. I want my own place desperately. When I moved back to Baydale, I was still in touch with Monica, who just happened to have lost her last roommate to the joys of matrimony. I took the spare room and have been living with her for the last two months. When Mom and Dad moved here for Dad's job, they did ask if I wanted to move back home. I'd been so long out of the family nest that I didn't like the idea of going back under their roof."

"Well, I know exactly where they live, so I could save you a journey and just walk there."

"No, you won't. I'll come get you. You aren't traveling all that way by foot this time." She reached into her bag and pulled out a business card. She gave it to Trent after writing something on the reverse. "This is my cell number in case you need to call me." She reached back in her bag and pulled out a small notepad. "Now, what's your address?"

Trent reeled it off and Juliet wrote it all down.

"Okay, we're set. Next Saturday, four p.m. okay for you?"

Trent nodded. "I'm not on the schedule next weekend so it's perfect."

Juliet put everything away and flashed a satisfied look. Trent was startled when Juliet leaned up and kissed her softly on the cheek.

"Thank you for everything."

Trent resisted the urge to touch the spot on her face tingling from Juliet's kiss. "No problem," she said around the sudden tightness in her throat as desire rose to suffuse her whole being.

"I'd better let you get back to work before Elton comes looking for you." Juliet suddenly seemed shy, her face turning pink. She touched the name tag Trent wore. "Assistant manager or not."

Screw Elton, Trent thought as she stared at Juliet's lips, but she eventually nodded, knowing Juliet was right. "Next Saturday, then?"

"I'll be sure to save you some frosting."

"You know the way to my heart," Trent said without thought. She wasn't sure, but she thought she heard a *we'll see*, but the parking lot noise drowned out whatever words Juliet had uttered.

CHAPTER SIX

Seated in her office, Juliet was thankful she could close the door on all the excitable midweek chatter that seemed to buzz around the building. *The economy is screwed, and I think we're all about to be screwed right along with it.* She studiously ignored the flashing of her e-mail inbox that told her of yet another message that needed her important input right this second. She was more intrigued with the fact she had no message yet on her cell phone from Trent. *I was so sure she'd have sent me a text to cancel this weekend.*

Juliet leaned back in her chair and thought about Kayleigh's unusual protector. *She's such a damn contradiction; one minute she's giving me a look that begs me to rip my clothes off, and then she's backing away as if she's scared to get too close.* Juliet considered Trent for a moment. *But she's so handsome, especially with that piece of hair that threatens to fall in her eyes. It's so sweet, though she probably wouldn't appreciate that sentiment. I can't help but wonder at the shadows in her eyes, though. She doesn't seem aware they're there, but that night at pizza, I saw a whole world of hurt when Eddie brought up the waitress. I can't help but wonder why. And I wouldn't have thought the waitress was exactly Trent's type either.* She snorted softly at her own musings. *Like I would know Trent's type. I barely know her.* She registered another ding from her computer as yet another e-mail came in. *But I would like to.*

Another e-mail followed quickly on the heels of the last, causing Juliet's temper to spill. "I'm beginning to hate this job," she said out loud, startling herself. But she knew it was true. It had been so much fun at the start, learning all the complexities of the banking world. The job had been rewarding, the pay fantastic. The bonuses alone were worth every single hour Juliet had put in above and beyond her work schedule. But somewhere along the line it had become tedious. The constant backbiting and power games that her colleagues played wore at Juliet's soul, and she was disheartened by just how cutthroat a business it had become. Having to constantly move from branch to branch had also proved tiring. It had left her constantly trying to make new friends only to be relocated again once she'd settled. *Maybe I just never saw it before, but my rose-colored glasses are off now; I'm not happy anymore.* She scanned her office, which displayed all the trappings of a successful career. The polished furniture, the framed awards, the fact she could boast a window with a fairly decent view.

She touched a petal on the orange carnations Monica had given her to brighten up her desk. "Maybe Monica is right. Maybe I need to shake up my cozy little world and try something different." She caught sight of the laptop resting on the desk. "But I have my proposal to finish. If I do it right I could be in line for the senior manager's position at the head office. My job would be secure, my future settled." She ran a hand distractedly through her hair. "Then why is it Monica gets up every day looking forward to work and I feel like I should just stay in bed?" She leaned in to smell the flowers. "I should take her up on her offer of working for her, if only to see what it's like." She thought back to when they were in college. Monica had badgered Juliet to join her on her gardening projects. Juliet had been tempted. She loved being outdoors, but her professors had wanted her to use her talent for finance to reap a greater reward for her in the business sector. She regretted not taking the chance and seeing what she could have accomplished with Monica's help. With a plan in mind, Juliet sat back down and reached for her phone. "I'll speak to her now before I change my mind. If nothing else, I can enjoy being out in the warm weather." *And maybe it will take my mind off the captivating Trent Williams.*

❖

Trent's dilemma was in trying to work out what she should wear to a little girl's birthday party. She sat on the end of her bed, staring into her closet waiting for inspiration to strike.

"So you still haven't decided yet?" Elton asked her over the cell phone she had stuck between her shoulder and ear as she perused the rack of clothing.

"I have absolutely no clue what I should wear." Trent flung herself backward on the bed. "Is it formal so I should wear a suit, or is it going to be just casual and I could wear my jeans?"

"Why not just phone Juliet and find out?"

Trent made a face at the ceiling. "Because I don't want to call her over something so lame. When a woman gives you her number it's not for dumb questions." *And I've written the same "Sorry I can't make it" text five times this week and couldn't work up the guts to send it.*

"So wear whatever you want, then." Elton's long-suffering sigh echoed down the receiver.

Trent let out a groan. "Why am I even going to this thing? It's not like I know the kid."

"Maybe it's the fact her sister is an absolute stunner with amazing eyes and a chest that—"

"Elton, you are not helping me here."

"Treeent," Elton deliberately drawled out her name. "You haven't had a proper date in years."

"This isn't a date. This is a kid's birthday party. And I don't date, Elton, because it just gets too complicated."

"I know that too, my friend. But you need to experience a warm body close to yours for a while."

"I do, occasionally," Trent grumbled.

"No, you don't, Trent. I don't think I've ever seen you with a woman more than once, and you never even stay the night. You need to spend more quality time with these women. You might find someone worth keeping."

Sure, but would she be interested in keeping me? I have never met anyone worth keeping, and certainly no one whose interest kept me wanting to stay around longer than the fumble we go through and then I go home alone. I couldn't deal with the fallout once they realized I don't do things like love and happy ever afters. "I do okay. I'm not a nun," Trent said, all too aware that argument was weak.

"I know that, but I want you to have someone special. You deserve that. You do so much for others, I'd like someone to take care of you for a change."

"You're asking for the impossible. None of the women I have ever seen have done that." Trent could hear the bitter tone in her voice and scrubbed at her face. "Just because you've found a kindred spirit doesn't mean that this Juliet is mine."

"But you like her."

"A little too much, I fear," Trent said. *Fear being the operative word.*

"Does she set your heart all aflutter?"

Trent smiled at Elton's affected high voice as he sought to tease her out of her mood. "She makes the whole planet tilt under my feet. Satisfied?" Trent hated to admit it. She just couldn't control the feelings Juliet stirred in her, and that left her even more terrified.

There was a moment of silence over the line while Elton digested that. "So what are you going to wear to knock this woman off her feet?"

Trent put a hand over her eyes. "Why can't you be gay? It would be so much easier. You could help me pick out something in a flash."

"My disappointing sexuality aside for a moment, I would recommend you go with basic black. It always works for me."

Trent lifted up off the bed and squinted into her clothing. She spotted exactly what would work. "You're a good friend."

"I know; I'm a total catch. Monica said she and I would swing by the Sullivan home to drop off her present to the kid, so I will see you there. That way, your choice of clothing will pale into insignificance when we enter the room. Monica got us tickets for a screening of Within Temptation's Black Symphony concert at the local Goth club. Full-sized screens and music from the gods, and Miss Monica by my side. I'm expecting a stellar evening of entertainment."

"Maybe you could rescue me, because you know and I know I don't really *do* parents."

"You'll do fine, and anyway, if they get too weird staring at your dark beauty than you can just go play on the Wii with Kayleigh. There's nothing a bit of gaming can't cure."

"Amen to that," Trent said, finally hanging up the phone. "It's been my substitute for sex for years now." She sighed at her pitiful whining tone. She got up to stand before her closet and drew out a pair of black chinos and a button-down black shirt. "Black it is." She opened up a small box on a table nearby and removed a pair of silver cufflinks shaped like Space Invaders aliens. "But we'll do black *my* way."

❖

Trent stood on her doorstep enjoying the warm August sunshine. Lazily, she watched the occupants of her street go about their weekend duties. She waved to the ladies across the street when they tried to keep their two dogs from tangling everyone up as they crossed leashes in their excitement to be going for a walk. Trent took note at the picture of domestic bliss the two made. She wondered how they did it without losing themselves in the process. They linked arms as they got their animals under control and set off toward the local park.

"You look very handsome, my dear. Are you going somewhere?"

Trent looked over the adjoining fence at her elderly neighbor Mrs. Tweedy.

"I've been invited to a birthday party," Trent said.

Mrs. Tweedy's face lit up. "I was twenty-one at my last birthday, you know."

"You've got to stop adding years to impress the gentlemen. I was told you were barely a day over nineteen."

Mrs. Tweedy chuckled and waved Trent on. "You're a charmer. It's about time you got yourself a lady of your own for you to use those charms on. Like the two across the road there. Lovely ladies." She paused for a moment. "Can never remember their names, though, too many Js that just befuddle this old lady's mind."

"You're no old lady, Mrs. Tweedy, and you know full well I'm just waiting for you to notice me."

Mrs. Tweedy's eyes widened and then she giggled like a little girl. "You'd never keep up with me, my dear!"

Trent tried not to look too shocked and tutted at her instead. "You're a sneaky old lady; that's for certain. I'll wheel your garbage can down when I get back tonight, so don't you dare try to move it yourself, okay?"

"You're too good to me, dear. I appreciate your kindness. My arthritis holds me back so much now."

"It's no problem." A car pulled up. "I think that's my ride."

"Have a nice time, dear."

Juliet got out of her car and flashed Trent a brilliant smile at finding her waiting.

"Hope I haven't kept you long."

"Not at all. I was just passing the time of day with my neighbor and making the most of this fine weather while it lasts. And believe me, seeing you in that dress has just put the day to shame." She let her gaze run from the top of Juliet's free-flowing hair, over her curves swathed in a sky blue dress that fell demurely to her knees. High heels afforded her an extra inch so she reached just above Trent's jawline.

"You look lovely." Trent was unable to tear her eyes away from the vision Juliet made. She caught her breath when Juliet reached out to brush at her shirt just above her collarbone.

"You look incredible too, may I say even formidable in black."

"Is it too much for a birthday party?"

"No, you look just fine, and Kayleigh is going to love your cufflinks, and the fact your tie has the same motif will just make her day. She's more like you than she will ever be me."

Trent held up her own gift-wrapped parcel for Kayleigh. "Can you hide this until Kayleigh has had her gifts from you?"

"You didn't have to buy her anything."

"I'm not going empty-handed to a birthday party. Not when there's the promise of cake." Trent gestured with the gift. "Besides, she had to have this game. It only came out yesterday and it's brilliant."

"You've bought yourself a copy?"

"And played it for most of the night," she said. "Excellent graphics."

Juliet gave her a censorious look. "Games aren't cheap, Trent."

"No, they're not, so it's a good thing it's her birthday only once this year." Trent brushed aside any further arguments Juliet was going to voice. "I get a staff discount, so it wasn't that expensive, okay?" She opened the passenger door to the car. "So are you ready to take me to meet the folks?" She tried desperately not to let her nervousness show.

"I'll warn you now, they'll probably grill you like a suitor. I rarely take a woman home unless it's Monica. And she's already told them that as much as she loves me, I'm just not man enough for her."

"Maybe you should have told them I'm more Kayleigh's date than yours."

Juliet threw back her head and laughed joyously. "That would so mess with their minds!" Juliet's eyes were alight with amusement. Trent though she had never looked lovelier. "There's a part of me tempted to do just that, but I'll spare them. I'm sure Kayleigh will do her own mind blowing with them as she gets older." Juliet got into the car still chuckling. "They're your usual parents. They just want me to settle down with a nice young woman."

"I'm not that nice."

"That's good, because I don't *do* nice either." Juliet winked in Trent's direction and pulled away from the curb.

❖

Kayleigh's excitement was palpable when Trent followed Juliet through the front door of her parents' home.

"Trent! Did you come for my birthday?" Kayleigh skidded to a halt in front of her. "Wow! You have Space Invaders all over your tie!"

Juliet gave Trent an "I told you so" look and directed Trent forward to meet her parents. "Mom, Dad, this is Trent Williams."

Trent shook their hands politely, silently amused as their eyes widened at her height towering over them both. "Thank you for inviting me."

Trent was spared any small talk when Kayleigh piped up. "Can I have the rest of my presents now? I've been patiently waiting all day, you know."

❖

The front room to the Sullivans' new house had been designated Kayleigh's playroom. Trent reached behind the television and threaded a lead back to connect into the designated socket.

"This is the best present I could ever have had," Kayleigh said for the umpteenth time, her arms wrapped around Juliet's waist as she hugged her.

"Kayleigh, turn the TV to the AV channel. Keep clicking through until you find AV3 and you should see the screen appear." Trent disentangled herself from behind the TV and moved back. The screen appeared that signaled a connection. "There you go. Now get your batteries in your remote and you can start playing."

"It's that simple?" Juliet asked.

"It's hooking up a game console; it's not exactly rocket science," Trent said. "Doing just one is easy. It's setting up a hall full of monitors that takes the time and energy."

For the next hour Trent helped Kayleigh design her own personal gaming character and then stylized versions of her family, much to Juliet's horror and Kayleigh's amusement. With a break for some food and for Kayleigh to blow out her candles on a suitably heavily frosted cake, the Sullivan family all traipsed back into the playroom to watch Kayleigh celebrate her day.

"This is the happiest I have ever seen her," Leonard Sullivan said, his eyes on Kayleigh as she explained a game to her mother.

"Encourage her in this. She has a natural talent for it." Trent leaned back in her seat, licking frosting from her fork. She let out a satisfied sigh. "This is some good cake."

"Thank you. I made it myself," Kathy Sullivan replied. "I'll make sure you take some home with you."

"I'll hold you to that," Trent said. She started at the sound of the doorbell chiming. Checking her watch, she stifled a grin and settled back in her chair. If Juliet's parents had been surprised to meet such a "lean and mean-looking butch babe," as Elton regularly described her, Trent was intrigued to see how they would react to Elton's always *understated* presence.

Elton and Monica made for the most striking couple. Monica entered wearing a black corset over a skirt that trailed on the floor, while a fancy shawl covered her shoulders and cleavage to offer a brief sense of decorum. Elton was resplendent in a suit that any 1950s stylized vampire would have killed for. His shirt was a mass of ruffles, as were the cuffs. His shoes were as pointy and lethal as Monica's stilettos. Trent caught Mrs. Sullivan's open-mouthed stare before she hastily hid it and welcomed her guests. Kayleigh was more interested in showing off her present than in what either of the new arrivals was wearing.

"We can't stay long. We have a concert to attend at eight o'clock, but we wanted to swing by and see the birthday girl." Monica, unmindful of her dress, got down on the floor and hugged Kayleigh close. Elton did the same to embrace her tightly.

"Happy birthday," he said, holding out a gift.

Kayleigh unwrapped her gift from them and pulled out a small black robe. Trent recognized the cut of cloth immediately as Kayleigh squealed and quickly put it on.

"You made me a Reaper robe!" Kayleigh cheered and flung her arms around Monica's neck.

"It's a copy of the ones that the Baydale Reapers wear. I made sure there's room for you to grow."

Kayleigh twirled around in it before everyone. Her parents were at a loss to make any kind of comment but could see Kayleigh was thrilled.

"Guess if you're going to be our mascot you have to be dressed properly." Trent was heartened by Kayleigh's happy face. "Elton, that is a seriously cool gift you orchestrated."

"We came up with the idea between us. This gorgeous woman

makes all her own clothes. A Grim Reaper robe was child's play for those talented hands." Elton tossed Monica a proud gaze.

The door bell chimed again. Juliet excused herself and was soon back with Zoe, Sam, Rick, and Chris with his brother Wade.

"How did you guys know?" Kayleigh asked excitedly as the younger guests rushed over to her to exclaim over her gifts and hand her more.

Wade spoke up first. "My brother overheard Trent say you were turning eleven, so we thought we'd come wish you a happy birthday ourselves."

Zoe leaned down to whisper in Trent's ear. "Sam told me Kayleigh had only just moved here and was in need of some friends, so here we are."

Trent patted her on the shoulder, touched by Zoe's thoughtfulness for a young girl they had only just met. "Thank you." She shifted over as Juliet took the seat beside her. "Sorry if we've suddenly taken this out of your control."

"I'm not. Look at her. She's the happiest kid on the planet."

Kayleigh shared her controllers and the children began to play on her new console.

Mrs. Sullivan nudged Juliet. "I should have made a bigger cake. I didn't know she had this many friends of all ages."

Juliet looked at Trent. "Well, she started with one and the rest just followed."

"It's wonderful," Mr. Sullivan said.

Juliet leaned closer into Trent's side. Trent welcomed her warmth and leaned back involuntarily. "Yes, it is," Juliet said quietly.

Caught up in the happiness of the room, Trent silently agreed with her.

❖

"You have marvelous friends," Juliet said when Trent wandered into the kitchen, stretching her legs and rolling her neck. She handed her a glass. "Here, you look like you could use a drink." She surreptitiously eyed Trent and noticed the faint signs of strain on her face.

Trent held the glass up to the light. "It's brown, but I fear it's not the beer I would kill for."

"Sorry, you'll have to make do with Pepsi for now. But I promise you, if you can last just a little while longer, I will take you out after this and you can unwind."

Trent stared into her glass. "Am I so transparent?"

"Only to me." She met Trent's startled eyes without censure. "Something tells me that, for all the people that are drawn to you, you prefer times of solitude more than the babble of friends and their noisy siblings."

"Is that your polite way of saying I'm secretly antisocial?"

"I think you're trying very hard to be a part of a birthday party that is way out of your comfort zone." Juliet picked up a cookie and held it out for Trent to take. "I only have experience of these things through Kayleigh, and I think this has been her most attended one."

"Those folks in there amaze me." Trent chewed her cookie thoughtfully. "I had no idea they were going to crash the party. I would have warned you."

"I'm glad they did. It's made Kayleigh's day, and I think my parents were fascinated by Elton. He charmed them so much I swear I caught my mother flirting with him."

"He has that affect on women."

"It's a pity they had to leave earlier."

"I think Monica was oddly disappointed too."

"I noticed that. It was fun to see her relax and play with the kids. She does love children. Although, the sight of her playing tennis in her Goth corset and those ridiculous heels will be something I'll have to treasure forever!"

Trent laughed with her. "Wish I'd have had a video camera, the hits we'd have gotten on YouTube…"

Trent seemed to relax in the quiet kitchen. Juliet longed to reach over to brush back the hair that fell across her forehead, to feel its softness and reveal more of the face that it hid. "I think Wade has a crush on my sister," she whispered and was delighted at the mischief that sparkled in Trent's answering gaze.

"I'd noticed that too, but then I witnessed it last Saturday when he made sure not to leave her side while they were playing in the kids' gaming area. Wade's a good boy; his brother Chris makes sure of it."

Juliet edged a little closer and bumped Trent's hip with her own. "How are you really holding up?"

"Well, I'm disappointed the cake is all gone, but I'm very glad you asked me to come. It's been an experience. Kids are so much more draining than adults, though."

"Can I still talk you into a drink after everyone has gone?"

"Do you promise strictly adult conversation over a beer?"

"It will be just you and me as your designated driver."

"I don't drink to excess. Just a couple of beers and I'm as mellow as a pussycat."

Juliet's eyebrow rose. "Now that I'd like to see."

Trent drained her drink and set the glass back on the counter. "What time do you want everyone out, because they'll stay until the birds start their dawn chorus."

"Nine o'clock maybe? Given it's a birthday and a Saturday night."

Trent squared her shoulders and prepared to return to the fray. "Consider it done. I'll go have a discreet word with Zoe."

Juliet enjoyed the steady gait that took Trent back into the playroom. She mentally shook herself at the direction her thoughts were all too busy heading in. She placed the glasses on a tray, still mumbling to herself. "You haven't been here long, and you're still getting settled at work. You do not need the complication of falling for the first handsome woman that comes along." Juliet lifted her tray and paused. *She's not the first woman I've seen since moving here, but she is the first I have been immediately drawn to. So maybe there might be something worth pursuing. Just maybe.* With the tray held carefully in front of her, Juliet returned to the room where the laughter was loud and the party still in full swing.

CHAPTER SEVEN

The bar was bustling with the regular Saturday-night crowd, but Trent managed to snag a table for Juliet and herself. She hastened to the bar to get drinks, then maneuvered through the people mindful not to spill a drop. Finally able to hand Juliet her glass of wine, Trent was astonished to see her swallow half of it in one go.

"Guess you needed that," Trent said taking a more leisurely drink from her own bottle, savoring the bitter taste of beer on her tongue.

"Three children, six adults, and my parents all in one room for more hours than I care to remember. I could drink the whole bottle." Juliet put her glass down and shifted it a little out of her immediate reach. "But I will try not to guzzle the whole glass in one just yet."

"Kayleigh went to bed one seriously happy kid tonight." Trent recalled the long hug she had received before Kayleigh had climbed the stairs. She had whispered, "I know you told them what I wanted," and kissed Trent's cheek before tiredly going to bed still dressed in her Reapers robe.

"You helped us make her eleventh birthday something to remember."

"I like to see kids happy. Childhood is fraught enough."

"What about your family, Trent? Do they live locally?"

Trent traced a pattern in the condensation on her bottle before finally answering. "No, they live far away from here. I don't see them."

Juliet reached over to pat the back of Trent's hand. "I'm sorry."

Trent shrugged. "I'm not." She took a gulp of beer and deftly changed the subject. "I didn't know Monica made her own clothes."

Juliet blinked, obviously recognizing a deflection when it was given to her. Trent could almost see her warring inside as to whether she should call Trent on her action. The small smile Trent received was all-knowing, yet she was warmed by it. Juliet was letting it go for now, and Trent appreciated it.

"She's got an amazing talent for it, but would you believe her heart is in landscaping?"

"Excuse me?"

"She's completing her courses at the local college for landscape and design. She's fitting it all in while working at the local garden center just in the town here."

"But she's so…" Trent searched desperately for a word to explain, "*not* the kind of woman I would have imagined digging holes and planting trees."

"No, she's not exactly how you'd picture a typical gardener when you see her in her Goth regalia. But she can nurture a dying plant back to life and design a yard that you would kill to see in full bloom. I've seen some of the projects she's worked on; they're growing works of art." Juliet played with her glass as she paused. "She always wanted me to go into partnership with her."

"Landscaping?"

"I would predominantly do the bookkeeping, work out the costs involved and handle the paperwork behind the scenes, ordering and such."

"And are you still interested?"

"It would beat being behind a desk for eight hours a day." Juliet pushed her hair back from her face and leaned her chin on her palm. "But I think I'd like to get my hands dirty, both figuratively and quite literally. If I'd be a partner with her I'd want to do more than just sit back and write out receipts."

"You'd want to get out and smell the roses."

"Exactly. But I can't just up and leave my job to go be a gardener for a few weeks to see if it's a more suitable career move. Monica has some big projects she's working on, and I just can't justify the time I'd need to take off to join her on them. She wants something smaller I can putter around with after work to get the feel for it."

Leaning back in her chair, Trent thought for a moment. "You need a place to practice to see if this is really what you want to do. A place to get your hands dirty, somewhere to go to experience what Monica wants you to be a part of. Correct?"

Juliet nodded diffidently. "I guess."

Trent took a deep breath, ignored the roaring in her head at what she was about to propose, and spoke before she could let herself think about it any further. "You can come do my yard."

"*Your* yard?"

"I have a yard at the back of my house. I don't use it. I have no use for it. It would be prime testing material for a budding amateur like yourself to walk in and see what needs to be done."

"You'd trust me to work in your yard?"

"Juliet, believe me, you couldn't make it any worse."

❖

Juliet waited as Trent worked the lock on her front door and pushed it open to let Juliet enter first. Trent quickly keyed in a code in the alarm box that was beeping threateningly.

"You'll find the kitchen straight ahead. I just need to go get Mrs. Tweedy's garbage can ready for collection tomorrow, and if I don't do it tonight the stubborn old biddy will try to manhandle the thing herself in the morning." Trent handed Juliet her keys. "Try not to scream too loud when you see the yard; you'll only wake the neighbors."

Juliet wondered at Trent's sense of humor and walked into the house, grateful of a chance to see inside without Trent's presence. The hallway was long with one closed door to her left which she guessed was the front room and a living room at the back that looked strangely empty. Juliet paused long enough to notice there was a small portable television in there and a sofa. The room looked unused and unlived in. The kitchen had just a few amenities, though there was a washing machine with a dryer beside it. The sink held only one of everything set in the rack. One plate, one bowl, a spoon, a fork. Juliet wondered at the solitude on display here. She knew Trent lived alone, but this home seemed very empty given that someone as vibrant as Trent lived there. She took a step toward the kitchen window and stared out into the twilight.

"Oh my God." Juliet stared at what was outside in disbelief. She jumped at Trent's voice behind her.

"Told you it was bad."

"No, you said I couldn't make it any worse. You did not say that nothing, short of a nuclear explosion, could clear whatever it is infesting your backyard."

"It's a tad overgrown, I'll admit."

Juliet looked back and forth between the yard and Trent's amused face. "Trent, that is not overgrown, that is a jungle that has planted itself in the suburbs."

Trent moved to look over Juliet's shoulder. She towered over her and Juliet could feel her warmth sear through the cotton of her dress. She resisted the urge to lean back and feel Trent's body pressed against hers.

"Think you could tackle it, though?" Trent's voice was soft in Juliet's ear and she shivered slightly at the low tone.

"I couldn't do it alone. I'd need Monica's help."

"I recognize that. You are more than welcome to bring her over to see the disaster zone for herself."

Juliet noticed their reflections side by side in the window. Trent was so much taller than Juliet, yet seemed to fit so well beside her.

"I can pay you, so be sure to let Monica know it wouldn't be a labor of love."

"Monica is nothing if not shrewd. She'll give you a price just to clear this tangle back. Then she could begin to see what it would take to bring it back to some semblance of order." Juliet turned and was so close to Trent she could see golden flecks in the brown of her eyes. Eyes so dark they were almost black as they bored into Juliet. "Are you free tomorrow, maybe around midday? I could bring Monica over and she can be equally horrified by this mess, then tell you what she recommends."

"I don't want a yard I have to mess with." Trent's breath whispered across Juliet's brow.

"I can tell that." Trent's eyes grew darker still. For a moment, Juliet was certain Trent was going to kiss her, but she took a step back instead, shaking her head wryly.

"What's wrong?" Juliet asked.

"Me." Trent leaned back against the kitchen table. "You have got me so mixed up I don't know whether I'm coming or going." Trent studied the tiling on the floor as if searching for her answers there. "I'm usually so much more confident around women, but you," she looked up and Juliet got the full force of Trent's stare, "you just scare the hell out of me."

"Why?"

"Because I have just spent a marvelous evening with you torn between enjoying your company and wanting desperately to hold you close and kiss you."

Juliet's grin spread across her face at Trent's obvious agitation. She wondered why Trent seemed so uncomfortable admitting her feelings. Juliet had felt the same attraction all night too. Trent groaned.

"No, don't give me that smile! It makes you look too damn pretty and only makes my resolve crumble more and more."

"What's so wrong in you wanting to kiss me?" Juliet asked, moving closer until Trent was pinned at the table's edge. "Do you have a long line of women that you string along with your charm and good looks?"

"There's no one, hasn't been for a while. I like my life uncomplicated."

"Are you telling me you are too comfortable in your life not to risk one kiss with me to see what it would be like?" Trent groaned, and the sound vibrated through Juliet's chest in an almost erotic symphony. She pressed in closer until their bodies touched.

"I don't need complications either, Trent. I haven't lived here long. I'm still getting settled into my job and my surroundings. I enjoy being with you and I'd like to get to know you better. No strings attached. Plain and simple. Think you can manage that?"

"Plain and simple," Trent repeated, her hand reaching out to caress Juliet's cheek. "Neither word I would use to describe you. Do you know how beautiful you are?"

Juliet pressed her own hand to Trent's lean face. "I see it in your eyes. I hoped you'd find me so because I can't help but be drawn to you too."

"You deserve better than me."

"I happen to like you just the way you are."

"That's because you don't know me well enough to turn away."

Standing on her tiptoes, Juliet kissed Trent gently on the lips. Trent shuddered against her. "Then I need to get to know you better and for you to know me. You'll find I'm not so easily frightened off."

Trent's hands rested on Juliet's shoulders and gently kneaded, a restless movement almost like she was going to push Juliet away, but she drew her close instead, covering her lips with her own. Juliet gasped into Trent's mouth, astonished by the warmth that poured from Trent as she held Juliet tightly to her hard body. Juliet's breasts pressed against Trent's chest, and she marveled at how strong Trent was. Juliet wrapped her arms about Trent's back and clung to her, letting her control the kiss and set the pace, sensing that was what Trent was used to. Juliet was dazed when Trent finally drew back to grant them both air. She reached up to touch her lips to Trent's just to reestablish a connection. She could almost feel Trent's disquiet for all the arousal that surrounded them both.

"Did you kiss me to save money on the plants we're going to recommend for your yard?" Juliet asked and was heartened to see Trent's brooding look lighten.

"Did it work? Do I get free labor on top?" Trent's voice was curiously shaky.

"Depends what else you have in mind, Trent Williams." She was captivated by the blush that rose up Trent's cheeks. "Why, Ms. Williams, for such an expert kisser I do believe you are really quite shy."

Trent ducked her head and just held Juliet close. "You are a dangerous woman. You make me feel things that I haven't felt for so very long." Trent ran her hand through Juliet's hair. "It's unnerving."

Juliet snorted softly. "You play games where the main objective is to shoot zombies and mutant monsters, and *I* unnerve you?"

"You're *real*."

Juliet digested the softly spoken words and held Trent closer for a while, loving the feel of her body so close to her own. Trent's body was all but vibrating.

"You make it very hard for me to leave."

"You deserve more than a quick fuck."

Juliet flinched at Trent's rough words and immediately Trent's arms tightened around her in wordless apology.

"And what do you need, Trent?" Juliet carefully drew back to look into Trent's stormy eyes. She found confusion there warring with desire.

"I don't know. No one has ever asked me what I wanted before."

"I'm not like anyone else. Just thought I should warn you." She placed one last kiss on Trent's curved lips and slipped out of her arms reluctantly. "And on that note, before I have you test out my theory of how strong your kitchen table is, I'll just let myself out. Good night, Trent."

The long groan Trent emitted followed Juliet as she shut the front door behind her.

CHAPTER EIGHT

I can't believe I just did that! Trent ran her fingers over her lips and tried to capture Juliet's taste again. "So much for taking it slow, Trent," she grumbled and rubbed at her face harshly. She was astonished to find her hands were still shaking. *What the hell is it about this woman that just sets me reeling? And I invited her in. I never invite anyone into my home.*

Moving almost through rote, Trent began to lock up her home for the night, hanging up her jacket and removing her shoes at the bottom of the stairs. She quickly went upstairs, her whole body vibrating with the arousal Juliet had left her with. Getting ready for bed, Trent tried to calm her yearnings by going through the motions of brushing her teeth and finding something to sleep in. She tugged on her sleep tee over a pair of shorts and padded into her bedroom, a much more furnished room than the floor below. A large bed took up most of the room. Shelves lined with DVDs and books framed the walls and small keepsakes were scattered in between. Trent turned off the light and lay down on her bed, but her body thrummed with an energy all its own. She turned on the television to distract her. Trent moaned as the last thing put in the DVD player sparked to life once again on the screen. Two women kissed and fondled each other and Trent grew even more uncomfortably damp. Her body was tight, her skin crying out for contact. Trent slipped a hand inside her shorts and tugged on her already hardened clitoris, rolling it between her fingers, exposing the head from its hood and running her wetness over it. With her free hand she ran her palm over her breasts and circled her tight nipples with her hard-skinned thumb. With the accompanying sounds from the TV urging her on, Trent drew herself ever closer to orgasm, assuaging the tension building inside her with her own touch. Knowing exactly how to press to get her clitoris harder, Trent let her fingers run over her flesh. With her eyes closed she pictured Juliet's face above her, that long blond hair teasing her. Those slender fingers were suddenly the fingers squeezing her nipples and making them highly sensitive. Trent could almost feel Juliet's body beside her, and it was her hands that pushed Trent over the edge, her voice that urged Trent on as the spasms rocked through her. Trent bit her lip to stop herself from calling out Juliet's name as she came hard. Body shaking, her breath shuddering from her lungs, Trent finally lay wasted on her sheets, her mind barely registering the sounds of further excitement coming from the TV.

"Shit, I am in so much trouble." Trent carefully removed her hands from her sensitive flesh. "Just one kiss and she's got me with my hand straight down my shorts." She reached for the TV remote and savagely shut it off, unable to hear any more of the women's groans of pleasure. She lay in the darkness and waited for her body to calm, all the time thinking about Juliet and how she had felt in her arms.

It was going to be a long night.

Trent groaned as a soft tongue teased the wetness between her legs and spread kisses over her clitoris. Each brush of lips made Trent buck and moan aloud.

"Stop teasing me," she growled and pressed a hand to the back of Corrine's head.

Bright green eyes looked up from Trent's body. "You know you like it when I tease. It gets you wetter." Her tongue flicked over Trent's opening and Trent's hips rose as the need to be filled consumed her.

"Just fuck me, Corrine, you're driving me crazy." She grabbed more hair and pressed Corrine closer to her point of need.

"Just because you've just had me screaming out your name with half your hand inside me doesn't mean I can't take it soft and slow with you."

Trent whined pitifully. "I'm too far gone for soft and slow. Just stick your fingers in there and get me off."

"God, you're such a guy." Corrine laughed and sucked Trent's clitoris firmly into her mouth.

"Christ, yes, just like that." Trent panted as the warning rush of orgasm tightened her stomach muscles. Her focus was centered on the feel of soft lips and tongue tipping her ever closer to the edge.

"Trent, why are you home from school?"

The sound of her father's voice coming unannounced through her bedroom door caught Trent and Corrine off guard. He pushed open Trent's bedroom door and found them, Trent spread out on the bed, naked from the waist down, school shirt up exposing her breasts, and Corrine with her face pressed firmly between Trent's legs, her lips covered with wetness.

Trent's father's face turned an ugly shade of purple as he screamed, "You dare bring this filth into my house?" He roughly grabbed Corrine by her hair and wrenched her off the bed. He flung her to the floor and directed his ire on Trent, who was trying to scramble for her clothes. The first blow knocked her back against the wall, the second cut open her scalp as his ornate wedding ring cut into her flesh. Trent dimly noticed Corrine snatching up her clothing and running out the room, but the sound of her feet on the stairs was quickly lost in the sound of Trent's father shouting.

"You bring shame to this household. It's bad enough you have to look like a man without possessing the sinful qualities of one too." The next blow cut Trent's lip open, and she cowered under her father's rage.

"Dad, please—"

"I am not your father; you are not my child. No child of mine would reduce herself so low to be disrespectful to God and give in to the temptation of the flesh. You disgust me, queer."

Trent flinched at the words that she heard so often in the house to describe those her father hated. She'd known it would be all too soon before he turned the words on her. She just hadn't expected him to find out so graphically. She cursed herself for being so stupid as to skip school and bring her girlfriend home. She scrambled back into her clothing hastily, fastening buttons with shaking fingers. Her father towered over her, his face contorted in fury.

"You will not leave this house again. When I get back tonight, we will get the elders in and they will counsel you from your deviant ways." He took a step back and looked about her room. "I've been too lenient with you, indulged your wayward leanings." He swept an arm along her desktop and knocked the game console and its games to the floor. Systematically, he smashed the whole lot under his feet, stomping the game cartridges and breaking them to pieces, crushing the console and ripping apart Trent's books.

"Dad, please no…" Trent's words went unheeded as his anger fuelled the destruction he wrought.

When he had finished, her room was destroyed and everything was ruined. "You need to think on your actions, Trent Williams, because tonight you will be judged. Be thankful I have to go back to work now because I would deal with you myself. I would beat the devil out of you. Wait until your mother and sisters find out what has been going on under our roof. They will be as disgusted as I am by your filthy perversion." He took a step forward, but the sound of his pager going off distracted him. "Don't you dare leave this house. I'll deal with you later, child."

Trent stayed on the bed as her father swept out of the room slamming her door. The door lock slid into place, trapping her inside. She strained to hear his footsteps leave and peeked from the window as his car pulled out of the drive. She rushed to gather up clothing and anything else she could salvage. She grabbed a duffel bag from under the bed, opening drawers and shoving clothes into it. She wiped at the blood trickling down her face and cast a quick look at herself in the mirror. "Christ, I look terrible," she gasped, assessing the damage. She began to cry at the wreckage piled on her floor. She slipped to her knees and tried to see if any of her games could be saved. She began to sob in earnest as she picked up the broken pieces of her most treasured possessions, the things that had kept her sane in a house ruled by her father and his righteous ways. Only one had remained intact and she shoved it into her bag protectively. She wiped at her forehead to try to stem the flow of blood there and lifted up the hood of her sweatshirt to hide her battered face. She shouldered her duffel bag and then opened the bedroom window. She eased out onto the window ledge and gauged her drop to the bushes below. Without a backward glance or care for her safety, she jumped from the window and landed in the privet hedge. Her shoulder wrenched at the impact, but she ignored the lancing pain and was quickly on her feet and running as far away as she could go.

Trent shot bolt upright in bed, wrenched from sleep. She struggled to catch her breath while her heart pounded erratically in her chest. Wincing at the rawness in her throat, she came to the realization that she'd woken herself up screaming. Trent ran a shaking hand through her hair and squinted at the clock on her bedside. It read 3:55 a.m.

"Shit." She rubbed at her face, startled to find tears on her cheeks. "Goddamn it," she said and untangled herself from the bed sheets. She padded into the bathroom and turned on the shower. Trent stepped under the running water, gasping at the cold spray before it turned lukewarm. The tepid temperature did nothing to banish her shivers, but

Trent knew all too well that chill came from the nightmare and not the cool air of the summer night. She didn't stay long under the water. She toweled off roughly and found clean clothes to wear. For a moment Trent considered going back to bed, but the dream was still too fresh in her mind for her to settle back down. She checked the clock one more time and weighed her options. Someone, somewhere in the world would be online and willing to play. She bypassed her bedroom and headed for a door farther down the hall. Sometimes, in the quiet of the night, knowing that someone was out there ready to go into battle at her side, albeit in a game, was the only thing that kept Trent sane.

I'll sleep later. For now I just need to escape.

CHAPTER NINE

D ue to her restless night, Trent ended up sleeping late and was only awakened by the sound of her doorbell chiming. Disoriented, she got out of bed to open her blinds and look out her bedroom window. Monica was walking up her path to join Juliet at the front door.

"Fuck," Trent said. She opened her window and leaned out. "Morning, ladies."

Juliet stepped back from the doorstep and shielded her eyes against the bright midday sun to look up at her. "Are we too early?" she called.

"No, I'm running late," Trent said. She dangled a set of keys she'd dug out from her pants pocket. "Use these to open the side gate. I'll be down in a minute." She tossed the keys down and Juliet caught them. Then she shut her window and rushed to wash up and prepare to meet her guests.

Ten minutes later, tucking a T-shirt into a clean pair of jeans, Trent trotted down the stairs, slipped on her boots, and unlocked the back door.

Juliet stood out of the way while Monica trampled through some of the overgrowth. Trent couldn't help but admire Juliet in her worn jeans and short-sleeved pink shirt. She closed her eyes briefly at the way her body reacted to Juliet's presence.

"Did we wake you?" Juliet's voice broke Trent's quiet communion with herself. She had slipped her hands into her jeans back pockets, waiting for Trent to answer.

"No, I was just being lazy debating whether to get up or not," Trent smoothly lied and tried not to focus on the way Juliet's stance pushed out her chest or the way her lips curved even when she wasn't smiling. She took an involuntary step forward, determined to taste those lips again. She was rudely interrupted by Monica stomping toward her. Trent almost retreated at the fierce look Monica leveled at her.

"How could you let your yard go like this?" she said, sweeping her arm out to encompass the whole backyard.

"I wasn't interested in it, so I just left it to its own devices," Trent said, trying not to stare too much at Monica's idea of suitable gardening clothes. Her usual long hair was tied in two pigtails that hung low from a bright red skull-infested bandana. A red and black striped top was tucked into black cargo pants that housed a seemingly unlimited number of pockets.

"Do you have enough storage space there, Pirate Pete?" Trent couldn't stop herself.

"Yes, I do, Butch Cassidy," Monica drawled as she eyed Trent's worn cowboy boots, "but obviously not enough for the copious sticks of dynamite I'm going to need to blow this yard away to replace it with a thing of beauty." Monica stepped into Trent's personal space. "You are a defiler of nature."

"Actually, I'd say I was a poster child for the Green Party, letting this piece of nature choose its own path to follow." Juliet chuckled behind Monica, and Trent was glad she wasn't on the receiving end of whatever look Monica threw over her shoulder at her.

Monica balled her fists on her hips. "Don't you 'Greenpeace' me. You've been too damn busy banging away at mushrooms in your games to pay attention to the land outside your own back door."

Trent refused to blink under Monica's stare. "So can you fix it?" she asked.

"Fix it?" Monica's voice rose and Trent caught Juliet cringing in reaction. "This is not as simple as a game, my dear." Sarcasm dripped from her voice. "There is no *walkthrough* for this disaster."

Trent tried to school her features to look suitably contrite in the face of Monica's ire. "Can't you weave the magic that Juliet says you have when it comes to landscaping?"

Monica looked over her shoulder at Juliet. "She said that?"

Trent nodded. "That's why I wanted you to come see this. I think you're the only one who could resurrect this mess to something beautiful. And you'll get Juliet to help, which will, in turn, help her toward making a decision on joining you in your work."

Monica narrowed her eyes and seemed to consider Trent's words. "I'd document the whole dig. Everything would be photographed to prove that I transformed it from this dump to something worth looking at."

"Take all the pictures you need."

"Let me give this disaster area a good look over and see what I can suggest." Monica flicked a pigtail in Trent's direction and stalked off, pulling a pad and pen from her back pocket.

Juliet quietly edged her way over to Trent's side. "She's excited by the challenge. I can tell."

"Yes, I could see excitement bubbling underneath all that scowling." Trent's gaze traveled down Juliet's body unbidden. She wedged her hands firmly into her pockets to stop herself from reaching out to pull Juliet close. Swallowing at the sudden dryness in her mouth, she finally spoke. "You wear pink well."

Juliet took her own time looking Trent up and down. "And that T-shirt clings in all the right places."

Trent gritted her teeth, willing her nipples not to tighten at Juliet's obvious stare. "It was the first thing that came to hand."

"We *did* disturb you." Juliet pouted and Trent stifled the groan that rose as swiftly as the urge to kiss those lips and put that pout to good use.

"I thought about you last night," she said out loud, startling herself.

Juliet looked equally shocked, then a wicked grin spread across her face. "Glad to see I made you restless enough to forget we were coming to visit."

"If Monica wasn't here I'd kiss you senseless."

"Monica who?"

"Hey! How y'all doing?" Elton's voice cut through the moment as he came in through the side gate. "Thought I'd come and see how my favorite ladies are all getting along. You know, in case any of you needed rescuing from whatever lives in this…" He gestured toward the yard. "I think I just witnessed Peter Jackson drive off. He mentioned something about an ape?"

Trent made a face at him. "Very funny, wiseass."

Monica sashayed out of the foliage and gave Elton a dazzling smile. He reached out to tug at her pigtails and she giggled.

"So are you two really going to take on this challenge?" he asked, sweeping an arm around Monica's shoulders to hug her close.

Juliet nodded. "It will give me a chance to see whether I'm ready to work in both landscaping and with Monica."

Trent bit the inside of her cheek to hold her tongue in check. Monica caught it and cut her a look.

"I am perfect to work alongside, but the work itself is both demanding and very physical." She looked Juliet over critically. "You're not so flabby after sitting behind a desk for all those years, my friend. I think you could do it."

Trent had to agree that Juliet was a fine figure of a woman, with curves in all the right places. She stuffed her hands even deeper in her jeans.

"I just need to get some more measurements and then I'm all yours," Monica said to Elton, who swiftly made himself available to hold the tape measure while Monica plotted out the lay of the backyard.

"What do you have planned for the rest of today?" Trent asked Juliet while Elton followed orders like a docile lamb.

"I have a proposal that I am supposed to be getting ready for in a month's time to present before my bosses. Charts and graphs on ways and means to cut costs and save the bank money."

"Sounds enthralling."

"Oh, it's the highlight of my life. It's like applying duct tape to a sinking ship. What about you? What does the rest of this Sunday have in store for you?"

"I have a game on the 'net with some friends later tonight. I think Zoe and Nick will be online so I'll team up with them, and we'll go gang up on some poor unsuspecting players to shoot the bejeezus out of them."

Monica had finished writing everything down that she needed, then slapped her book shut. "I am done. Let me go and work on this and we'll plot out a plan of action." She gave Trent a considering stare. "You going to be okay with us camping out in your backyard?"

"It will be just fine. I'll give you the key to the side gate and you can come and go as you please if I'm at work."

Monica nodded. "Juliet, I'm going to go back to Elton's. I'll see you later?"

Juliet waved her off. "I'll use the time alone to work on that damned proposal."

Elton gave Trent a thumbs-up sign as they left.

"Something tells me our being here isn't something you'd usually tolerate," Juliet said.

Trent shrugged, unsure how to explain or if she could even begin to. She reached for Juliet's hand and tugged her toward the back door. "Come sit a while before you have to leave." She led Juliet to her kitchen table. They sat for a while drinking Pepsi.

"You don't spend much time down here, do you?" Juliet asked quietly, gesturing to the plain rooms and the empty feel they radiated.

"That obvious, eh?" Trent looked about her home and for the first time acknowledged what Juliet could see. "It does look pretty sparse, I'll admit. I tend to spend most of my time upstairs, so these rooms just never get used."

Juliet raised an enquiring eyebrow. Trent shook her head at the obvious silent comment.

"No, not like that! I don't invite women back here at all." She realized too late just how much she had inadvertently admitted.

"And yet, here I am," Juliet said softly.

"Yes, here you are."

"What makes me different, Trent?"

"You just are."

Juliet reached over to brush a stray lock of hair from Trent's face. "I'm glad."

"Me too."

❖

It had been a none too chaste kiss that Juliet had left Trent with at her front door. Now, over twenty-four hours later, Trent was still feeling the press of those full lips against her own.

"You've got that faraway look again," Elton said, handing her a roll of stickers and guiding her to a cart. "Price 'em up, partner."

Trent went through the motions, gaining comfort from the routine. She could sense Elton hovering nearby.

"Are you seeing Monica tonight?" she asked, hoping to deflect his concern.

"We're over at my place for pasta and a fine wine."

"Get you, Mr. Domesticated. Wine, eh?"

Elton leaned against her cart and threaded a finger through his beard while he mused. "I'm so glad she came to the tournament. What if we'd never have met? The most perfect woman in the world for me and I could have missed her."

"How she dresses makes her kind of hard to miss," Trent said and accepted the punch on her arm in good humor. "She complements you, my friend. You were obviously meant to be."

"And what of her guiding light of a roommate?"

Trent sighed. "She kisses like a dream."

Elton clapped his hands. "Now we're talking! No wonder you're all misty eyed and off the planet today. So could this be something serious?"

Trent wouldn't meet his eyes. "You more than anyone know I don't do serious."

"But Juliet isn't like any of the girls you used to hook up with." He leaned in closer. "You know, before you took the vow of celibacy."

"No, she isn't, which is why she is dangerous." Trent continued applying the sales stickers with a little more aggression.

"Trent, you deserve someone who will make you happy. You're way past due."

"I'm doing fine on my own."

"Sure you are, but your heart is yearning toward that pretty blonde whose eyes light up every time she sees you, and yours return the same signal. Like it or not, you're pulled toward her."

"She's too fine for me, Elton. She's way beyond my reach."

"Well, she doesn't seem to agree," Elton said cryptically, his tone making Trent follow his line of vision. She checked her watch.

"School's out already?" She wondered how she had sleepwalked through the entire afternoon in her job.

"Looks like little bankers are too." Elton sauntered over to where Juliet and Kayleigh were perusing the game-lined shelves.

Trent felt the tug on the invisible string that bound her to Juliet. Elton got a hug from both Juliet and Kayleigh and then Juliet sought out Trent.

Oh God, her eyes do *light up.* Trent took an involuntary step forward. *And like a sailor called forth by a siren's song, I have no course but to go to her.*

"Trent! Juliet brought me to see if anything new has come out."

Trent accepted Kayleigh's hug. "New games are released on a Friday, so you're too early to start spending your birthday money, kid. How about we go peruse the list that tells you what's out soon and see if we think any of the new releases will be of any interest to you?" She checked out Juliet's banking suit. "You're looking very somber there, Juliet. I think I like you better in your jeans." *For so many reasons*, Trent thought, remembering how the denim clung to Juliet's curves.

Juliet tugged at her jacket as if it were constrictive. "This is my power suit."

"Something tells me that's just one of the reasons why you want to look into changing vocations." Trent moved closer and noticed Juliet's added height. She looked down at her shoes. "Serious heels."

"Butt-kicking heels," Juliet said with a steely glint that sent a curious shiver down Trent's spine. She admired the length of leg Juliet was displaying. Kayleigh tugged on her hand and broke her from her musings.

"Trent, my money is burning a hole in my pocket here!" she whined.

Trent was suitably chastised by Kayleigh's tone. She tried to ignore Juliet's amusement and Elton's choking cough. "Sorry, kid. Your sister distracted me looking so girly."

"She always looks girly," Kayleigh replied as she was led to the counter. "She's pretty that way."

Trent couldn't argue with that and just reached for her list to start thumbing through the games. She could hear Elton and Juliet's conversation as they spoke nearby.

"Monica says after we've tackled Trent's yard that yours is next on her to-do list."

Trent felt a little less picked on now that she knew Monica had seen Elton's backyard and found it equally wanting.

"I've asked for a centerpiece shaped like a skull," Elton said.

"I've seen the preliminary sketches. You'll get your wish. She knows exactly which pebbles she'll use for the skull and what plants will be perfect for the eyes to make them 'glow' red."

Elton rocked back and forth on his heels in delight. "God, that girl is a genius. It's going to look so cool."

"Trent, I want this one."

Trent turned her attention back to Kayleigh to see what game she was pointing to. "An excellent choice. That will be a great game. I've seen some of the previews, and it looks amazing. Let me get you a pre-order slip and you can pick it up on its day of release." She reached under the counter for the necessary paperwork. "You going to leave a deposit on it?"

"How much?" Kayleigh said, obviously enjoying having Trent's full attention.

"Give me one hundred dollars and you can buy mine for me too." Trent gave Kayleigh a sly look and was pleased to see her laugh.

"I don't have that much!"

Trent pretended to be disappointed. "I'll buy my own game, then, penny pincher." She started to fill in the form for Kayleigh. "Give me ten dollars for a deposit and you're set."

Kayleigh whipped a bill out of her purse. "That I have."

"Excellent." Trent finished her form and ripped off Kayleigh's copy. She ran the money through the register and stapled the receipt to Kayleigh's form. Then she made sure Kayleigh tucked the slip safely away in her purse. "In two weeks' time, the game is all yours." Trent nudged her gently. "Or if you can't make it, have your sister call me and I'll bring it by after work for you."

"You'd do that for me?"

"Only for you." Trent found Elton and Juliet still deep in conversation. "What are they up to?" She figured if anyone would know, it would be Kayleigh.

"I think Elton's asking Juliet about Monica." Kayleigh cupped a hand to Trent's ear. "I think he likes her a lot."

Trent nodded. "I think so too."

"My sister says she's going to dig in your backyard when she's not in the bank. Can I come help?"

"I don't know. I don't think I'm allowed to go anywhere near it either while Monica is working."

"She's a landscaper. Juliet says that is way more important than a gardener."

"A lot more," Trent said. "And I think she's in charge."

Kayleigh frowned, then let out a pitiful sigh. "Guess I'll be told to stay at home, then."

"You can come see it when they're all finished. It will look better then."

"What will look better?" Juliet asked, coming over to join them at the counter.

"The yard once you and Monica have finished with it." Trent caught Zoe gesturing toward Kayleigh, and Trent nudged her so she would see what Zoe wanted. Kayleigh grabbed up her purse and left them alone.

"She just made a ten-dollar deposit for a game that's out in two weeks. It's perfectly suitable, and she's going to love it."

Juliet gave her a curious look. "I trust you, Trent. I don't think you'd steal Kayleigh's birthday money from her."

"I'm just keeping you informed. The receipt is in her purse so you can see what deposit she made."

"She was so excited about coming here today. Seeing where you all work. I managed to get off work early to go fetch her. She wanted to see you."

"And what about you?"

"I'm trying not to let my mind wander as to things I could do with you and that tie you're wearing."

Trent blinked at Juliet's casually spoken words; her face flamed as her own mind conjured up images. "Damn it, you can't say things like that to me here."

"Why not?" Juliet's voice was innocent.

"Because the storeroom isn't as private as I'd want, and you're testing my limits." She was pleased to see Juliet shiver at her words. She could smell her subtle scent as Juliet leaned toward her and spoke very quietly for Trent's ears alone.

"I deserve more than a quick fuck." She deliberately returned Trent's words to her.

A soft sound escaped Trent's lips at the sensuous tone in Juliet's voice.

"Monica wanted to know if she could start work at your place tomorrow, seeing as she has the day off work?"

Trent was more than a little thrown by Juliet's ease at changing the subject. She slipped the necessary key from her key chain and held it out for Juliet. "Tell her to just let herself in through the side gate. I'm in here from nine a.m. tomorrow. The yard will be all hers."

"I thought I might swing by after work to help her clean up."

"If I promised you a meal when you were done, would you eat with me tomorrow night?"

"I'd love to."

Trent didn't censure the words in her head before they tumbled out of her mouth unbidden. "Then it's a date."

Juliet's delighted look made her chest ache with the need to pull her close and kiss her. She looked toward the storeroom door and was caught by Juliet's-all-too knowing eyes.

"You drag me in there and the whole place would know what we were doing."

"Would I be dragging?"

"No, I'd be quite willing, but I don't want to give my little sister any more fodder for what she already tells strangers about her big sister."

"I'm not a stranger anymore."

"There's still so much about you I just don't know. Maybe tomorrow you'll open up and tell me about yourself."

Trent tried not to let her fear show. *You've already gotten closer than anyone has in years. I don't know how much closer I can let you get.*

CHAPTER TEN

Juliet Sullivan, tell me you didn't walk out of your tight-assed building dressed like that and didn't call me so I could come witness the resulting chaos?"

Juliet looked down at her ripped jeans and red V-necked T-shirt. "What's wrong with these? These are my rattiest clothes that you requested that I wear, but they're still decent."

Monica paused in her digging and rested on the handle of her spade. "Sweetheart, that T-shirt shows off the kind of cleavage I would kill for, and your jeans have very enticing flashes of flesh. Now, while in and of themselves your clothes are fine and very sexy on you, I just wish I'd been there to see your colleagues' reactions as you walked past them looking like the truly gorgeous woman I know and love."

Juliet cocked her eyebrow at her. "Next time I'll just borrow a pair of Dad's overalls and save you the show."

Monica reached over for the extra shovel and picked her way over toward Juliet. She handed it to her as if it were a prized sword. "It's not me who's going to want to explore those holes." She looked Juliet up and down admiringly. "Each and every tantalizing one of them."

Juliet caught her drift and waved her comments away. "I'm going to be covered in dirt and God knows what when she comes home. I'm not going to be in the least bit desirable."

"You really don't see it, do you?" Monica returned to her digging. "You are the quintessential femme, so perfectly suited to your studly gardening-impaired butch."

"Do you really think so?"

"Hey, if she doesn't want to rip those jeans off by that particular frayed hole in the thigh, then she's either crazy or too damn shy, and I don't think she's either, do you?"

Juliet considered divulging with Monica Trent's apparent restraint when a high-pitched voice shouted hello over the fence at them.

"Monica dear, you shouldn't have!"

Monica rushed over to the fence to speak with the old lady trying to peer over the fence.

"Mrs. Tweedy, you have the most beautiful Fryclimbdown Crimson Cascade that I've ever seen. How could I not help by cutting it back for you? It was wasting its gorgeous flowers over in this yard. Now they can be trained to bloom all in your own again." Monica reached over the fence to touch at a rose with its dark red petals. "They feel like velvet. It's the perfect rose for a Goth, the deep red splashed against the black of our dresses."

"But you're so busy, you shouldn't have."

"It was no problem, a five-minute job. Now it can continue flowering in all its glory for you." Monica gestured for Juliet to join her. "Mrs. Tweedy, this is Juliet. She's helping me in the yard."

Mrs. Tweedy eyed Juliet closely. "So you're another of Trent's friends? She certainly knows some pretty girls."

Juliet liked the old lady on sight. "It's lovely to meet you."

"So you're both working on that yard at last? I've told Trent so many times she needed to get it sorted. She can't have a nice young girl over and have a messy yard. How can you sit and watch the stars together when the yard is so overgrown?"

Juliet was startled at Mrs. Tweedy being so open about Trent's sexuality.

"Don't you think she's a handsome woman?" Mrs. Tweedy asked suddenly, her question directed straight at Juliet.

"Yes, she is."

"*You're* very pretty."

Juliet was taken aback by her bluntness. "Thank you."

Mrs. Tweedy nodded at Monica and uttered something like *perfect* under her breath. "Trent's coming home around six o'clock tonight, isn't she? It's a shopping night. She always brings me a cake when she goes shopping, and whatever else I ask her for. She's a good girl." Mrs. Tweedy disappeared from behind the fence. "Anyone deciding to hurt her would have me after them with my walker. I barely use the blessed thing, so it could stand a few dings!"

Juliet stood open-mouthed at the sound of retreating feet. She turned to Monica. "Why do I get the strangest feeling I've just been warned?"

Monica shrugged. "She already knows about me and Elton, so she must figure you're in the running for her neighbor's attentions."

"You've barely been here a day and already you've been gossiping with the old woman next door?"

"What can I say, I'm the friendly sort." She slipped down from the fence. "Do you know that Mrs. Tweedy very rarely sees anyone go into Trent's house?"

"So? She's private."

"She says she never seems to have friends over."

"Monica, she just lives next door. She can't know everything."

"She's the unofficial neighborhood watch. She sees all and reasonably hears all." Monica began digging at a very stubborn root. "There are already two lesbians living together across the road, with two dogs *and* a chicken." Monica paused. "Mrs. Tweedy gets free eggs from it. Can you imagine?"

Juliet found her own patch of dirt to turn over. "You two together are truly frightening."

"Want to know what I think?"

Juliet bit back her sigh. "I'm sure you're going to tell me anyway."

"I think you're either falling for a lean, mean, and downright sexy heartbreaker, or you have someone who is very careful who they let get close to them. From what I understand from the little Elton has revealed, I think you have the latter."

"She is a marvelous blend of contradictions. So sexy and passionate, yet so sweet and respectful. Kayleigh absolutely idolizes her."

"And what about you?"

"I'm falling harder every time she looks at me with those deep brown eyes." *But I'm not pushing. I want to get to know her without frightening her away.*

"Your sister and that games tournament have a lot to answer for."

Juliet had to laugh at the look Monica spared her. "You and Elton are perfect for each other."

"He's fiercely loyal to Trent. There has to be a story behind that because he loves her so much. Thankfully, I know it's nothing to be jealous of, but he's very protective. It does make a girl curious."

"They've been friends for years; friends are like that." Juliet was glad to hear Elton was the kind of friend that didn't spill confidences.

"I'm glad you came back to Baydale to us. I love having you

living with me. It's so cool to have you closer than just at the end of a telephone."

"I missed you too."

"Guess you coming back here was all fated. You come here and through you I meet the man of my dreams, and you…"

Monica's sentence hung in the air. Juliet knew what she was waiting for.

"Do you really want me to say it out loud?" Juliet said.

"No, I want you to say it to *her*. She's the one to hear it. I just want you to *realize* it."

Juliet continued to dig. She had already realized what Monica suspected, but realizing and doing something about it were miles apart.

❖

Trent let herself in through her front door and juggled her shopping bags in her arms to hurriedly turn off the alarm beeping out its few seconds' warning. With a well-placed heel against the door, she pushed it closed. Heading into the kitchen, Trent tried to clamp down on the excitement she could feel simmering away inside her. She laid her bags down and looked out the kitchen window. She saw Monica wrestling with a large overgrown bush. Then Trent's breath caught in her chest. Juliet was nearby, bending over to tug at something fixed firmly in the ground. Trent's eyes lingered just a little too long on Juliet's shapely rear encased in denim. A piece of pale skin was peeking out on Juliet's thigh. *It's official. She's trying to kill me!* Her elbow hit the bowl in the sink with dishes left in and they clattered together, startling Trent from her pensive staring.

She forced herself to do something responsible and quickly stored the perishable items in the fridge and laid out the makings for the meal she had to prepare. Trent was excited and yet nervous she was about to see Juliet again. *Damn, this woman throws me off balance.* She smoothed a hand down her tie and made sure her shirt was tucked in smartly, then she ran a hand through her hair. It fell back across her forehead where she left it. Trent unlocked the back door's multiple locks and then stepped out into her backyard. She was astounded by how much work had already been done. There was more visible light pouring into the yard and it seemed so much bigger. Trent sought out

Juliet first and was the recipient of such a welcoming smile that she forgot everything but the need to kiss her. Trent took a step but found her path impeded by a gathering pile of yard debris blocking the path. She kicked at it in frustration.

"Hi, Trent, mind you don't ruin your clothes on the thorns hidden in that mound."

Trent dutifully stepped back at Juliet's warning and had to settle for just looking at her over the pile. Juliet was smudged and grubby and had loose bits of foliage in her hair, but to Trent's eyes she looked so happy that she could have hugged her, dirt and all. "You've done a lot of work. I didn't expect you to get so much done in such a short space of time."

"Monica's done all the hard work. I've only been here for an hour or so." Juliet held up her filthy hands. "But I got stuck straight in to earn my keep."

Trent wrinkled her nose at the sight of Juliet's dirt-covered hands. "You can take a shower if you like before I feed you. I'm sure I can find something for you to wear to save you having to put your banker's garb on again."

"Are you politely telling me that I smell?"

"No, I was merely pointing out that you might prefer to sit for our meal refreshed from a shower after your exertion in this warm sun." Trent folded her arms across her chest at the urge to reach out and wipe away a particularly tantalizing droplet of sweat that was traveling toward Juliet's cleavage. "I'll even let you loose with the rubber duck in there."

Juliet wiped at the sweat on her forehead and inadvertently smeared a streak of dirt across her skin. "Sold." Juliet paused in what she was doing and ran her eyes up and down Trent's body until Trent had to shift under the concentrated gaze.

"What?"

"We're not exactly the same size. You're so tall and lean and I'm…"

"Smaller yet much more voluptuous," Monica said.

"Thank you, Monica, for your observation." Juliet gave her a look.

"I have some things that will be suitable, so don't worry," Trent said.

Monica checked her watch. "Time to quit. We'll start clearing up and I'll get going." She picked up her shovel. "We can leave the tools in the shed."

"I have a shed?" Trent said.

Monica pointed a sharp finger at her. "You…go inside now! Get back into your house and hang your head in shame! Yes, you have a shed. It was buried behind all the trash in that corner."

Trent looked over to where she gestured, and sure enough, there was an old wood-paneled shed revealed.

"Well, would you look at that?" Trent turned to Monica. "I have a shed."

Monica just scoffed at her. "Yeah, like you're ever going to use it."

Trent winked at her as she backpedaled toward her door. "Doesn't mean I'm not excited to have one." She leaned against the frame lazily, giving Juliet her full attention. "I'll go start cutting and chopping, Juliet, so I'll see you shortly." She caught Monica's attention. "Monica, keep the key so you can just come and go as you please back here. And thank you for what you have accomplished so far. It looks so much better already."

"Thanks, Trent, I'll do that."

Trent reluctantly stepped back inside and took off her shoes out of habit. She raced up the stairs to find Juliet some clothing. *Though I like her in those jeans, especially that rip that just screams for me to go exploring there.* She couldn't help the length of the sweatpants she found, but she reckoned Juliet could be comfortable in a sweatshirt she had that was a "one size fits all" make that she'd won at a tournament and had never been able to wear. Trent laid out the items on the bed along with a clean pair of socks, then grabbed a clean T-shirt to change into. Loose jeans replaced her black suit trousers, and Trent trotted back down to the kitchen to start their meal. She had everything washed and diced and was just preparing to open a beer when there was a tentative knock at the back door. Trent opened it to find Juliet leaning against the wall tugging her boots off.

"Come on in." Trent held the door open for Juliet to enter.

"My jeans are filthy. I really don't want to walk through your house like this, but I didn't feel right taking them off outside in full view of your neighbors."

Trent went warm at both the thought and the wicked glint shining in Juliet's eyes. "If you'd rather leave your jeans down here I promise to avert my eyes so you can escape upstairs."

Juliet's hand went to her waistband and she began to undo the button. Trent was unable to turn away, mesmerized as Juliet slid the zipper down slowly.

"There are towels in the bathroom ready for you, and I've left clothing on the bed." Trent could hardly breathe. Her gaze was drawn to the bright flash of color being revealed beneath the denim. "I didn't think my underwear would be of any use to you." She swallowed hard as Juliet began to slip her jeans off her hips, and only then did she turn away to give her privacy.

"You not into lace, Trent?" Juliet's voice teased from behind her.

Trent had seen the intricate lace that covered Juliet's skin, and her mind had conjured up images of her running her fingers over it, tracing the patterns, before edging beneath them. "Not on me personally." Trent was grateful to hear her voice didn't sound as strained as she thought. "I wear boxer shorts. I didn't really see you wearing those, and I can see I was right.

Trent tried to dismiss the vision from her mind of Juliet dressed only in her underwear and bit back the groan that washed through her gut.

"Are you going to show me where your bathroom is?"

The sound of heavy material hitting the floor by the door made Trent clench her fists. "That would require me turning around, and I'm trying so very hard to be chivalrous."

"Trent, I have nothing I'm ashamed of, so you might as well turn around."

Trent did and her mouth grew dry as she took in Juliet's near nakedness. The T-shirt did little to cover Juliet's hips, so the pink panties were clearly visible. Trent studied the length of Juliet's legs. She immediately imagined them wrapped around her hips. "Please let me walk up the stairs in front of you because if I walk behind you looking like that, I'm liable to forget chivalry altogether."

Juliet waved a hand to let Trent past. "I need to remember next time that I'm going to sweat so a change of clothes would be advisable. Also, I need a sunhat. I can already feel where I got burned today."

"You need to be careful. Your skin is so pale it wouldn't take much to damage it. Apply plenty of sunscreen too." Trent forced herself to make simple conversation, but she could smell the heat on Juliet's flesh and still had the vision of those pale legs imprinted on her mind. She was thankful she didn't miss a step and stumble.

Trent reached for the bathroom door and pushed it open. Juliet slipped past her and stopped in her tracks. "Wow! That is some shower." She reached for the edge of her shirt and Trent beat a hasty retreat.

"My room is right next door. You can change in there."

"Thank you, Trent."

Trent barely caught the words as she reached the bottom of the stairs in record time. She wiped at the sweat that prickled on her forehead. She knew it wasn't due to the seasonal heat. She grabbed for her beer and drank from it long and hard. Hearing the shower go on, Trent sat with a thump at the table at the image of a naked Juliet separated from her by just a floor. Trent ran the cold bottle against her forehead and groaned.

Will this wanting never cease?

Juliet luxuriated under the spray of the water, washing off the sweat from her labor and the accumulated dirt. Squeezing out a handful of shower gel, she recognized the familiar scent she associated with Trent as it filled her nostrils. She lathered the soap all over her body and washed it off under the jets. Then she searched the shelves in the shower for something to wash her hair with, squirted some out, and massaged it into her hair. The suds drifted down her body like gentle fingers and Juliet recalled Trent's unabashed staring when she had stood pants-less before her. Juliet liked how Trent looked at her, how a mere look from her was almost a physical caress. She quickly rinsed out her hair and turned off the water. She reached for the towels thoughtfully placed within easy reach and rubbed at her long hair before sweeping it up in the towel. She tucked the other towel between her breasts and padded out of the bathroom to find Trent's bedroom. She pushed the door ajar and peeked inside. Her jaw dropped at the room. *No wonder she spends all her time up here instead.* Juliet slipped inside and just stood looking around the room in astonishment. Unlike the downstairs rooms, the bedroom was fully decorated. A light blue paint covered the walls. The large bed that dominated the room had a contrasting blue spread. Dark wooden shelves took up a wall and were filled with books and DVDs, all lined up just so. A large screen TV was positioned at the end of the bed. *That's why I didn't see a TV downstairs*, Juliet thought, wondering at the screen's actual size, as it took up a great deal of space. She realized that Trent had closed the blinds for her sake, so she slipped the towel from her body and began to dry herself off. She caught sight of a photo frame on one shelf, a picture of a much younger Trent with a clean-faced Elton. She guessed they were barely in their teens when the photo had been taken. They were grinning at the camera, arms about each other's shoulders. Next to it was another photo of them, only they were older. Trent was more serious and Elton was starting to get his facial hair. Juliet leaned closer to see a photo from a newspaper of the Baydale Reapers winning their first tournament. Elton was wearing his Reaper makeup while Trent held up the trophy. *Elton's never far from your side, is he?* Juliet wondered at their closeness and the reason behind it. She slipped into the sweatpants and rolled up the excess leg material, chuckling as she did so. Then she pulled on the light sweatshirt. It was just big enough to have her chest not be constricted. She sat on Trent's bed to pull on the socks. She was highly conscious of the fact she was now bra-less and panty-less, but the items were soaked through with sweat, and she really didn't like the idea of putting them back on for modesty's sake. She rolled her clothes and the towels into a ball and tugged a hand through her hair to try to dry out the tangles in its length. Finally, she called down to Trent.

"Do you have a comb I can borrow, please?" Footsteps came up the stairs immediately.

"Sorry, I just carry it with me." Trent waited on the landing and Juliet opened the bedroom door so she could pass the comb over.

Trent eyed her in the sweatshirt. "Trident Games has never looked so good emblazoned on someone's chest."

"This has to bury you."

"I'm too slender for it, but it suits you perfectly." She looked down at Juliet's legs. "Sorry about the trousers, though. I can't do much about the length."

"They're on and not slipping off. Besides, rolled-up cuffs are very fashionable these days." Juliet began to run the comb through her hair. "Trent, your bedroom is beautiful."

Trent shoved her hands in her pockets and looked almost shy at Juliet's praise. "You think so?"

"It's restful, and you have an amazing array of DVDs. Some I've never even heard of." She ran through some of the titles until she named one that made Trent cough slightly.

"That's not exactly a mainstream film," she said.

Juliet reached out to slip the DVD from its slot. The naked women on the sleeve gave away its contents.

"It's one of the best lesbian erotica films available."

Juliet blinked and looked at the DVD in her hand. "I see." She could feel her face burn as she realized she had found Trent's collection of porn.

Trent was obviously glad she wasn't the only one embarrassed. "I can't recommend them highly enough. But if you prefer big budgets and more aliens to your movie watching, then I'd suggest something totally different from another shelf."

Juliet chuckled softly at Trent's wry comment. "I'm sorry, Trent."

Trent just shrugged. "No apology necessary. We're both adults. We know how sex works." She rocked back on her heels. "I may be considered a geek in some circles, but I'm no virgin."

"That's all a myth, then?"

"You might want to double-check with Eddie, who is the stereotypical gamer geek who still lives with his mother, but as for the rest of us, we all manage to reasonably function in polite society."

Juliet was once again drawn to the photographs on the shelves. "These are wonderful pictures of you and Elton."

"He's the only guy you'll ever find in my bedroom and only then in photos." Trent moved closer to lean over Juliet's shoulder. "Look at him without all that facial fuzz he sports now. He looks like a baby."

Juliet leaned back just a fraction and touched Trent's chest. She was warmed by the way Trent immediately wrapped her arms about her and held her gently. Juliet was drawn closer. Trent's chin brushed against her hair and her breath caught in her throat when Trent pulled her even closer. For a moment they were silent.

"I have your meal waiting for you. I hope salad is okay. It's too hot for anything else lately."

"Salad is fine." Juliet was loath to have Trent move from her hold. She caressed Trent's hands where they lay laced across her stomach. She traced the long fingers and solid palm. Trent's chest hitched behind her.

"Would you believe me if I said you're the first woman who's stepped foot in my bedroom?" Trent began to rub Juliet's stomach in tiny circles through the material of the sweatshirt.

"I'd be surprised. You don't strike me as a woman who would lack for feminine company." Juliet felt Trent shift behind her. "You're way too gorgeous to be celibate."

Trent sighed against her hair. "To be honest, it's been a while."

Juliet hugged Trent's arms around her. "No pretty girls to turn your head lately?"

"No inclination to play the games the women I usually come across want me to play."

"So, you're not *that* much of a player?" Juliet twisted in Trent's arms to look over her shoulder at her, intrigued despite herself at what Trent would answer.

"Only in the games I want to play." Trent nuzzled her lips against Juliet's neck.

Juliet shivered as Trent's warm lips trailed up and down her skin. The warmth of her tongue skimmed over Juliet's pulse point. Juliet bit her lip as Trent's sharp teeth tugged gently at her sensitized skin. After each nip the sting was soothed away by a swipe of her tongue, and Juliet was conscious of her breath sounding shakier with every exhalation.

"I don't know what it is about you that makes all my good intentions fly out the window the minute I get too near." Trent buried her forehead into Juliet's shoulder and sighed softly. "You do strange things to me, Juliet."

Juliet ruffled Trent's dark hair. "Good strange things, though?" Trent nodded.

"We need to go downstairs before I break another first."

Juliet all but moaned at the loss of warmth as Trent stepped away from her and headed toward the door.

"I never bed women in my own bed," Trent said as she started down the stairs.

Juliet remained still for a moment, her eyes inexplicably drawn toward the large bed in the room. "First time for everything," she whispered and smoothed a hand over the sheets before leaving, quietly shutting the door behind her.

CHAPTER ELEVEN

The table was laid out as best as Trent could manage, the food looking bright against the stark white of the kitchen table and plain white plates. Even to Trent's eyes the room looked lifeless and empty. She was frowning when Juliet came down the stairs.

"What's wrong?"

Trent's head shot up at being caught evaluating her living space, and she shrugged as she gestured around her kitchen. "I was thinking I could do this room up next, maybe add a little color." She took the towels from Juliet and stuffed them into the washing machine. "Your clothes will be ready for you tomorrow. I won't put the washer on while we're talking."

"You don't have to wash them. I could have taken them home and done it."

"It's the least I can do." Trent pulled back a chair and directed Juliet to sit. She padded back to the fridge. "What would you like to drink?" She pulled open the door and displayed the contents to Juliet.

"Beer will be great, thank you." Juliet's eyes widened as she looked at the meal laid out before her. "Are you seriously expecting us to eat all this?"

Trent sat down opposite and looked a little embarrassed. "I may have overestimated the portions for two eating, but I figure what we don't eat tonight I can use as leftovers for work tomorrow." She busied herself reaching for the tomatoes. "It will stop me from heading to the food court and buying food that isn't healthy for me."

"It's a pity salad doesn't last. You'd have enough for a week here." Juliet forked some of the food onto her plate.

"We'll eat enough. I haven't eaten properly today anyway. I

worked through my breaks." Trent began to grate cheese over her meal with a heavy hand. "I love cheese."

Juliet obviously couldn't help the smile that formed as she watched Trent liberally spread the cheese out. "You're entitled to your breaks at work."

"I know, but it's Zoe's birthday soon and her mom wanted to take her to look at suitable gifts for a twenty-one-year-old. Today was the only day her mom could get free from her work. They needed longer than an hour to choose a new laptop for Zoe, so I gave her my hour too so they wouldn't be rushed."

"You really are too good to be true sometimes."

Trent blinked in surprise. "I am anything but good."

"Every time I see you, you're looking out for your friends, putting them first, making sure their needs are met."

"That's what friends do; they look out for each other. Besides, I get to use the time I worked to leave early one of the days so it all works out."

"Who looks after you, Trent?" Juliet's voice was gentle.

"Elton always has had my back. We've looked out for each other for years."

"How long have you known each other?"

"We met when we were both ten years old, so that was an amazing twenty-two years ago." Trent lost herself in the memory of a tall and skinny Elton starting at her school, the new boy who invariably stood out. "It seems like just yesterday. How did you and Monica meet? I mean, you're not exactly like drawn to like."

"We met at college. We had a few filler courses together, and we just hit it off really well, despite the fact we have very few things in common. We shared an apartment for a year or so before I graduated. We stayed in touch all the time I was posted from one division to another until I finally settled in Chicago for the past few years. When I was being transferred back here Monica told me she had a free room with my name on it, and she welcomed me in just like we'd never been apart. It's exactly like it used to be, except she's even more certain now that landscaping is her vocation. She's very driven, knows exactly what she wants, and goes for it without deviation. She knows her path in life." Juliet popped a small piece of cucumber into her mouth. "I want to support her in that. It's nice to know someone who knows what she wants to do with her life and is willing to work hard for it. She's always asked me to consider working with her. Before I moved back here, what she was saying really began to strike a chord in me, and I started to give it serious thought. I've had so much fun today with it too. I didn't realize how involving it could be."

"Can you afford to switch careers?"

"I've been savvy enough to invest and save while working. Although how much there will be left once the dust settles on the problems the world economy is facing is another matter." Juliet let out a sigh, pushing back her hair from her face.

Trent was charmed by Juliet's nervous habit. It was so at odds with the confident face that Juliet usually projected.

"I just know I'm disillusioned every time I have to sit behind my desk and face another 'make us rich at the expense of our customers' round of meetings."

Trent could tell Juliet was unhappy; it was written clearly on her face. "I've loved my job from the start. Surrounded by games every day, working with like-minded colleagues, and I get to recommend what folks should buy and watch them leave happy."

"It's perfect for you," Juliet said. "In fact, I've never seen anyone so well suited to a job. Although, I'd better warn you, Kayleigh has her sights set on working with you all when she's older, so you might want to start creating a position for her."

"Maybe we can get her a Saturday job when she's a little older." Trent rubbed her hands together gleefully. "We can't let true gamers slip off to another branch. Baby Reapers grow into Baydale Reapers."

Juliet pushed her empty plate away and picked up her beer. "Changing the subject a little, I have to admit I'm slightly curious."

"Curious about what?"

"There's no sign of your games anywhere in this house. I expected to find them in your bedroom, but there was nothing."

Trent reached for their plates and began putting them in the sink. "Well, you haven't seen all that this house has hidden behind its closed doors." She moved over at the sink when Juliet came to wash her hands beside her. Juliet's hip nudged hers, and it was comfortable sharing the space with her. Trent marveled at the fact she didn't feel threatened by that.

"So do you aim on being here all week to give Monica a hand?"

Juliet retook her seat. "I hope to be. I really enjoyed this evening. It's nice to see some progress being made and know that I'm the one that did it. Although I have to admit, I'm looking forward more to the planting of your new flowers. De-weeding and digging up roots is all well and good, but I like the pretty flowers better. The blisters I'm feeling from using the fork might take some getting used to too."

Trent snorted. "You are such a girl."

Juliet narrowed here eyes at her playfully. "But still butch enough to do more digging in that yard than *you* have tackled."

Trent clutched at her chest playfully. "Madam, you wound me!"

Juliet just laughed. She looked at her watch and sighed. "Can I mention that sometimes I really hate my work?"

Trent was disappointed to realize that the evening was ending. "You have things to do?"

Juliet nodded. "I'm still working on that proposal, gathering all the information I can from other companies." She stood and stretched and her sweatshirt molded to her figure. Trent longed to run her tongue along the edge of flesh that had just been exposed. "So I need to call it a night."

Trent walked her to the door. "Your laundry will be here ready for you tomorrow. I'll be sure to fold your undies just right." Trent couldn't help the devilish grin that escaped at the thought of handling Juliet's lace panties.

Juliet's cheeks turned a delicate pink. "I'll have you know I don't leave my underwear just anywhere."

Trent's heart sped up at the coyness Juliet displayed. She could barely temper the rush that burst through her, wanting to devour, wanting to claim. Instead, Trent gently brushed her lips against Juliet's. Her tongue explored and traced, committing to memory the shape and feel of Juliet's mouth beneath hers. She backed Juliet against the door, resting her hands on Juliet's hips then sliding them around to cup her rear through the sweatpants to all but lift her closer. Juliet's hands slid to Trent's shirt front and rose to touch her breasts, but Trent swiftly pinned her hands in place. Juliet pulled back from their kiss to stare at her in confusion.

"You don't want me touching you?"

Trent kept her eyes lowered to where their hands were stilled on her chest. She didn't know how to answer. *I'm not used to being touched, I haven't been touched intimately since...* Trent couldn't find the words to quell the confused look in Juliet's eyes.

"You're not stone butch, are you? All give and no take?" Juliet asked with a disappointed tone. "I've had enough of those, and frankly, it's no fun not being able to reciprocate."

Trent burned with a flare of jealousy that lanced through her gut at the thought of someone else touching Juliet. "I'm not stone," she said gruffly. "I'm just...more used to doing the touching, taking the lead..." She groaned silently at how pathetic that sounded when voiced aloud.

"If we're going to see each other, Trent, I'm going to want to do more than lie back and let you fuck me." Juliet slipped her hands from under Trent's and placed them on Trent's shoulders. "I want to know that I can give you pleasure too."

The answering shudder to those words shook Trent's body visibly and Juliet's hands tightened in reaction. "I think you've been hanging out with the wrong girls if all they've wanted was for you to do your thing, then they left you high and dry." Juliet paused at her own words and a saucy glint lit in her eye. "Or not so dry if your porn collection is anything to go by."

Face flaming, Trent's breath came out in short pants as Juliet scrutinized her.

"It's a pity I have to go home," Juliet said softly and brushed her fingers down Trent's cheek. "Otherwise, I'd show you *exactly* where I intend to touch you."

Trent pressed a kiss in Juliet's palm, her voice silent, her body trembling. She was so unsure what to say or do. No one moved her like Juliet did.

I am in so much trouble.

CHAPTER TWELVE

When the nightmare returned, it wrenched Trent from her sleep, her ears ringing with the sound of her own screams. Shaking, she looked in every corner of her bedroom until she realized she was safe. She ran a trembling hand through her hair and searched her fingertips for any blood visible in the pale dawn light. Her fingers were clean.

"Fuck" slipped from her lips as she willed her heart to calm its frantic pace. Swallowing hard against the rise of bile in her throat, Trent resigned herself to getting up. Unsteady feet carried her into the bathroom, where she waited until the wave of nausea eased. She searched her face in the mirror, seeing only strained features instead of the battered visage that had been in her nightmare.

"I don't care what time it is, I need a beer," Trent told her reflection and headed downstairs to the kitchen. She caught the time on her kitchen clock: 4:33 a.m. "This is getting old fast." She popped the tab on her can and drank half of it down in one swallow. Hands still shaking, Trent ran her fingers over the scar that lay partially hidden under her hair. She paced the length of the kitchen and back, draining her beer can. *Seventeen years ago, and I'm still ruled by that day, terrified by his anger and bearing the scars.* Trent slammed the can into the sink. "You have no control over my life now, Dad, so stay the fuck out of my dreams!" She flung open the fridge and grabbed a bottle of water. Taking the stairs two at a time, she ran back up to her bedroom where she hastily dressed in workout clothes. "Time to hit the Wii Fit, and if yoga doesn't help me relax, then I am switching to boxing so I can beat the shit out of someone."

❖

It was still too early for the mall to be open to the public when Trent flashed her pass at the security guard manning the door. She walked the length of the mall to where Gamerz Paradise resided. At her banging on the shutters, Elton raised them to allow her to slip under and get in the shop.

"Christ, Trent, you look like shit," he said. "You pull an all-nighter with the guys?"

Trent headed toward the back of the shop. "I wish. Damn nightmares are back."

Elton let out an angry sigh. "Dammit. What brought those on again?"

Trent shrugged. "Guess I was long overdue a visit from the ghosts of a lifetime past. It's been a while since the last bout." She tapped on the keypad to go back into the staff quarters, Elton hard on her heels. Stowing her messenger bag in her locker and taking off her jacket, Trent was all too aware that Elton was watching her like a hawk.

"Do you think it's because of Juliet?" he finally asked, putting Trent's fears into words.

She leaned against the lockers and sighed. "Which is why I choose never to get close. Women are a nightmare in more ways than one."

"You like this one, though. Maybe your subconscious is fighting while your heart is trying to draw you closer."

"You are way too profound for this ungodly hour of the morning." She moved to walk past, but Elton deftly stepped in her path.

"You look like crap, little sister. I'll go get you some coffee and a doughnut from the food court, but first…" He put his arms around her shoulders and just held her close. Trent relaxed into the hug and willed herself not to cry. After a long moment, Elton let her go. "There, all better now."

Trent coughed at the emotional lump that had lodged in her throat. "Thank you, Uncle Elton."

"Hey, my hugs have healing powers, and all my nieces and nephews think I'm the coolest thing on the planet."

"Second only to me." Trent slipped past him back to the shop floor while he blustered. "I'd like a frosted doughnut, please. Heavy on the sprinkles."

Elton bowed at her request and raised the door shutters again. Leaning back against the counter, Trent closed her eyes briefly. *I can't live my life like this, haunted by the past and not getting beyond it. Always being in control so I'm not caught off guard again. Yet Juliet's touch makes me want so much more. Can I really let my guard down now? Can I let go of it all with Juliet?* Trent was still considering this when Elton returned.

"I could hear your mind working overtime from out there. What are you plotting and planning?"

Trent gave him a tired look, her mind made up. "I'm going to ask Juliet to accompany me to Zoe's birthday party."

Elton handed her the coffee and doughnut. "Like in a date?"

Trent nodded, quickly taking a big mouthful of her doughnut.

"Good for you. Do you realize that Zoe has invited my family as well?"

"Mama Simons will be there?"

"Yes, Mother is gracing us with her presence along with a sibling or two. You know how they love a party, and Zoe invited the whole Simons clan."

Trent's tightness in her chest eased. "I'll do it. I'll ask her this week. Maybe she can bring Kayleigh along."

"A little chaperone to keep you two in line?"

"That woman just bowls me over, Elton. I've never experienced anything like it."

"You need it, Trent. You're too wonderful to be alone in this world."

Trent held out her doughnut to share, and Elton took a sizeable bite. "You're slightly biased."

"I know you better than anyone. My word stands."

"I suppose you want a share of my coffee too?"

"Just some of the whipped cream off the top. You can have the rest."

Trent dutifully handed it over and experienced her first peace in hours.

❖

Managing to find a quiet spot in the day, Trent tucked herself away in the locker room to text Juliet. She hesitated only for a second before sending the message. She sat staring at the screen for a moment, then raised her eyes heavenward. "She's working. She isn't waiting for you to call." She was just slipping her cell phone away when it announced an incoming text message.

Yes 2 bday. Will CU tonight.

Trent left the locker room with a massive smile on her face. Elton instantly sidled over to her.

"The fair Juliet said yes, I take it?"

Trent nodded, both nervous and excited and at a loss to explain either feeling. "Now what do I do?"

Elton patted her on the shoulder comfortingly. "Welcome to the dizzy world of dating for dummies."

The yard's overgrowth had been ripped out and the bareness was quite a contrast to what Trent had been used to seeing from her window. She sat on the back doorstep, handheld console in her grasp as she split her attention between the game and the women in her yard. One woman in particular, Trent had to admit, as she paused her game for the umpteenth time just to watch Juliet move something or reach to push a branch aside.

"Are you really playing that or just using it as cover to ogle my coworker?" Monica spoke so only Trent could hear.

Trent jumped at being caught staring. "I was not ogling, merely admiring her dedication and commitment to the work in this yard." Trent shaded her eyes to look up at Monica. "She's really taken to it, hasn't she?"

"She's marvelous in the yard, as I knew she would be. But your eyes aren't following her every move because you admire her work ethic."

Trent stared at her. "Haven't you got something to dig?"

"I'm too busy tripping over your line of vision going straight to her ass."

"Monica, I can't lift this slab up." Juliet's voice cut through Monica's taunt. Trent gave her a toothy grin.

"I'll be right there. Don't pick it up on your own." Monica turned her attention back to Trent. "The party this weekend, Zoe's birthday bash? Elton tells me his sisters will be there."

"Stevie and Anne and their assorted kids plus husbands, no doubt." Trent realized Monica was uncomfortable. "They're going to love you. The family needs another splash of darkness so it's not all on Elton's shoulders to carry the Goth banner."

"Thank you for that reassurance. I've met his mother. She's a sweetheart, but siblings are…" She searched for the right words.

"Judgmental, overbearing…nosy?" Monica nodded at Trent's assessment. "They're all that and more, but you'll do fine. Once they understand you like kids, they'll just foist their offspring on you and go enjoy the party." Trent considered for a moment. "Or is that just me they do that to?"

"So I shouldn't be nervous?"

Trent turned back to her game. "They give you any grief, you come straight to me and I'll tell you tales about them as teenagers. But I assure you, they won't be any problem. They'll love you as much as Elton does."

Monica blustered. "We haven't got that far yet."

"*Yet*," Trent said simply. "Just enjoy the party. Your friends will be there if you need us."

"Monica," Juliet called again. "Needing help here, please."

Trent immediately went to get up but a hand stopped her. "You're in your work clothes. You're not stepping anywhere off your back step and touching stuff that could damage those game-playing hands." Monica pushed her back down. "I am reliably told your hands are like a surgeon's, not to be damaged or else." Monica stepped away. "Personally, I think that's your and Elton's excuse to get out of any hard work."

"I could go change," Trent said.

"Yeah, like you'd be any use whatsoever. All I'd hear is how you got a splinter and then Elton would start grumbling, and it's not worth the hassle." Monica walked away to aid Juliet.

Trent kept an eye on them while still playing her game, but she lingered too long on Juliet's face set in concentration, and the level she'd been working so hard on in her game slipped from her grasp. Trent stared at the screen as the taunting "Game Over" message played. "Well, that was unfortunate." She started the level again. The level wasn't as difficult as Trent's inability to keep her eyes from Juliet, so she saved her progress, switched the machine off, and conceded defeat for now in both playing and observing.

❖

The nightmares mercifully stayed away for a few nights and Trent got to catch up on her sleep. She was still wired, edgy, and almost hyper by the time the weekend drew close.

"Geez, will you turn it down a notch? You're like a ten-year-old who's been force-fed additives and fizzy orange pop!"

Trent skidded to a halt in front of Elton. "What? I'm just stocking the shelves with the new releases."

"It's your way-too-happy face while you are doing it that's going to scare the customers away."

"I can do serious." She hardened her face, but the grin soon broke free. Elton sighed and swatted at her playfully. "I can't help it. I've actually slept three nights in a row, my yard no longer looks like the Amazon, and I have a date this Saturday."

Zoe and Rick seemed amused at Trent's unusual giddy enthusiasm. "Dad's getting the barbecue all fired up," Zoe said. "It's going to be a great party."

"She's invited all the neighbors so no one can complain if we get too rowdy," Rick added.

"So you're bringing Juliet? Actually bringing and not just tagging along with?" Zoe leaned back against the counter, regarding Trent with a fond look. At Trent's confirmation, Zoe beamed. "Good, we like her. I wonder if Kayleigh would like a sleepover with Sam? That way you wouldn't have to worry about getting her home and having to leave early."

Trent grasped Zoe's face between her hands and placed a loud kiss on her forehead. "I knew there was a reason why I liked you so much."

Zoe laughed at Trent's silliness and looked over her shoulder at Elton. "Keep her away from the doughnuts." She got her cell phone and began typing away. "I'll get Sam to invite her. They've been e-mailing each other daily since Kayleigh's birthday party."

"So you gonna use not having the kid to worry about as an excuse to get all up close and personal with this woman when the stars come out?" Elton asked.

Trent just shrugged. "Who needs an excuse when the lady is so damn hot?"

CHAPTER THIRTEEN

The weekend arrived without a cloud in the sky and the temperature in the upper seventies. Trent had no problem dressing for this party. She pulled out a pair of surfer style shorts in camouflage grays and matched it with a T-shirt emblazoned with a character from a war game. She picked up her solid silver dog tags that Elton had brought for her, suitably inscribed with her name and rank from their favorite game. Then gathering up her sunglasses, she hung them from the neck of her T-shirt. Finally lifting the large present that was Zoe's gift from the Gamerz Paradise employees, Trent set her house alarm and closed the front door behind her.

"Trent, you're doing some gallivanting these days. It's a blessing to see."

Trent peered over the fence at Mrs. Tweedy, bedecked in a wide-brimmed hat that dwarfed her head. "Mrs. Tweedy, I'm not always stuck in the house. I do venture out to work."

"I know you do, dear, but now you're accompanied by that pretty blond girl. That's different."

Yes, it is, Trent admitted to herself.

"You look happy, my dear."

Trent peered over the fence. "Thank you, must be the weather making me smile."

Mrs. Tweedy snorted. "Of course it is, not the thought of your sweetie whose car I can hear turning into the top of our road."

"Why is it you can hear that but not the cats fighting on your front lawn ripping up your pansies?"

"Selective hearing, my dear. You're automatically equipped with it once you hit seventy years of age."

Trent looked up as, sure enough, Juliet's car pulled up at the bottom of her drive. "No loud parties now, Mrs. Tweedy. You know the neighbors will talk."

"Back in my day, I'd have given them something to talk about, mark my words," she replied.

Trent returned Kayleigh's wave as she got closer to the car. Juliet leaned over to open Trent's door. It afforded an all-too-brief flash of cleavage that Trent immediately grew hot over. *And so it starts.*

"Good afternoon, ladies," she managed to utter as she slipped into the car. "Are we ready to party?"

"I'm staying over at Sam's house tonight," Kayleigh said. She held up her bag. "I've got my pajamas and everything."

"But have you brought your DS? I know Sam has one too."

"She never goes anywhere without it," Juliet answered. She looked Trent over. "You look like you're ready for battle. Is the line for the barbecue going to turn into a skirmish?"

Trent managed to fasten her seat belt under the large box she rested on her lap. "I'm ready for any battle in order to get my share of Zoe's dad's spare ribs." She smacked her lips loudly. "He does the best barbecue ever, and we would fight over it. War is never pretty." Trent cast an eye over Juliet. "Now you, on the other hand…" She admired the pale skin that emerged from thigh-length shorts. "Nice weather for shorts, isn't it?"

"It's too hot for anything else." Juliet pulled away from the curb.

"That's a very big present, Trent," Kayleigh said. "What is it?"

"You'll see when Zoe opens it, squirt. It's a big present because all of us from work chipped in to get her something she really wanted. I think she'll be pleased." Trent settled back to watch Juliet drive, her eyes firmly fixed on the way Juliet handled the steering wheel in her hands.

"Stop looking at me," Juliet whispered from the corner of her mouth.

"I can't help it," Trent whispered back. "That shirt looks really good on you."

Juliet glanced down at her pale lilac top. "Zoe said it was strictly casual."

Trent nodded. "Barbecue parties are for letting your inner scruff out. You just know whatever you wear is going to get covered in drippy sauce."

"Trent, you have lots of muscles in your arms," Kayleigh said matter-of-factly from the backseat. She leaned forward and lifted the cuff of Trent's T-shirt. "And you have a tattoo! Juliet, Trent has a tattoo!"

"And before you even ask, no, you're not old enough to have one," Juliet said swiftly, her eyes on the traffic as she drove up the main road.

"Did it hurt?" Kayleigh asked, keeping Trent's T-shirt lifted so she could see the pattern that ran around her upper arm.

"No, I was very brave," Trent answered, then said under her breath for Juliet, "and more than a little drunk thanks to Elton." Kayleigh poked at a muscle.

"Did you get this strong playing games, Trent?"

Trent coped with Kayleigh's endless stream of questions. "I work out, Kayleigh, with weights and stuff, but the Wii has some fitness discs that I use too to keep me in shape."

"She looks great, doesn't she, Juliet?" Kayleigh asked.

Juliet's eyes left the road for just a moment and seared Trent with their heat. "Yes, she does, Kayleigh." Trent's stomach clenched at the husky cadence to Juliet's voice and she swallowed hard. It was with some relief that Juliet pulled into Zoe's road and parked her car on the street outside the house.

Kayleigh was instantly getting out of her seat belt. "There's Sam!" She scrambled from the car, leaving Trent and Juliet behind.

"Good thing you'd put the parking brake on," Trent said as the girls met in the middle of the pavement and squealed their hellos. She jumped as warm fingers touched her skin. Trent's eyes followed Juliet's fingers as they traced the tattoo that was inked into her skin.

"What's with the Space Invader theme, Trent?" Juliet's fingertips traced the familiar blocky artwork of the alien characters as they wound their way around Trent's bicep in a band. "Is this your favorite game?"

"No, just the one that survived with me." Trent knew she was being evasive, but she didn't want to explain now. "Maybe one day I'll tell you the story behind the tattoo, but for now I just want to go enjoy the party with you by my side." She met Juliet's eyes. "Please?"

Juliet leaned forward and kissed her, slowly but with a gentle pressure that promised of passion to come. Trent's whole body shivered when Juliet finally drew back.

"I like how you say please," Juliet said, touching her lips with her tongue as if tasting Trent there.

Trent couldn't look away as Juliet reapplied her lipstick. She followed every sweep of the color as it was spread on Juliet's mouth. It only served to make her want to kiss it all back off again.

"You ready to go join the rabble I can hear from here?" Juliet asked.

I'd rather spend the day kissing your lips Passion Pink free. "Sure, like I don't see them enough at work." She forced herself from the car, away from the temptation of Juliet's lips.

❖

Juliet was startled when Trent shifted the large box in her grasp and reached out with her free hand to hold on to Juliet's. Trent led the way up the path toward the front door that had been left wide open by the two younger girls. Juliet loved the feel of Trent's strong hand in her own. It was comforting and she liked what it signified. She was *with* Trent. Juliet wondered if Trent realized her own actions. She was letting everyone know that Juliet was with her, staking a claim. Entering the house, Juliet spotted a small woman bustling her way from the kitchen and making a beeline toward them.

"You're here at last!" The woman imperiously waved a hand for Trent to dutifully lean forward so the woman could pat her on the cheek in welcome. Her gaze fell on Trent's occupied hand and her eyebrow rose.

"Miranda, this is Juliet, Kayleigh's big sister," Trent said.

"Glad to meet you, sweetie. Everyone is out in the backyard." She guided them through to where there was already a crowd growing. "Go make your presence known, Trent."

Juliet felt Trent's hand tighten on hers as they walked out into the backyard. Everywhere was strung with balloons, streamers, and Happy Birthday banners. Zoe came bounding up and gave Juliet a sideways hug seeing as Trent still hadn't released her hold.

"Happy birthday, Zoe," Trent said, brushing a kiss on Zoe's forehead.

"Yes, happy birthday." Juliet handed over her gift.

"You didn't have to get me anything. It's just cool you and Kayleigh are here." Zoe looked pretty in her sparkly shorts and top, her eyes shining from all the attention. She held the small present to her chest. "Thank you, though. Can I open it now?" At Juliet's nod, Zoe tore open the wrapping and exclaimed over the necklace Juliet had picked out for her. "This is gorgeous." Zoe quickly swept up her hair and handed the chain to Rick. "Fasten it on me, honey." The gold chain rested just below her neck and the attached pendant shone in the sunshine. "Juliet, thank you. I love it."

Juliet was thrilled to have her gift so well received. She'd taken a long time choosing the exact piece she'd wanted for someone she didn't know all that much about. But she knew Zoe liked Juliet's jewelry from the things Kayleigh had said via Sam so had sought the perfect piece.

"Where is the littlest Sullivan? She came in with us, then disappeared with Sam." Trent looked around the yard but couldn't see either girl.

Zoe rolled her eyes at them both. "She and Sam are upstairs making sure Kayleigh's stuff is put just right for tonight."

Juliet could see all the Gamerz Paradise crew converging toward them, Elton included. They circled around Trent, and Juliet was disappointed when Trent finally had to let go of her hand.

"Now that the gang is all here." Trent seemed to be counting heads, then obviously satisfied, took a deep breath. "Happy birthday, Zoe, from all your friends at Gamerz Paradise who all chipped in to get you this present." She held out the box for Zoe. Zoe tested the weight of her present, then lifted her eyes to Trent.

"You didn't?" she asked hesitantly, her voice barely above a whisper as she clearly recognized the shape and weight of the box.

"Open it and see," Rick said, urging her on.

Zoe ripped off the paper and her face told them all how pleased she was with her present.

"Your old Xbox succumbed to the red ring of death. I'm not facing the online clans without my best sniper beside me."

Juliet saw tears well up in Zoe's eyes at Trent's declaration. Zoe flung her arms around Trent and squeezed her as tight as she could while still holding onto her new console.

"Group hug," Elton bellowed and everyone piled in to clutch Zoe close. When the group finally broke, Trent placed a hand on Zoe's shoulder.

"Just tell me you backed up all your save files."

Zoe nodded and Juliet was amused at how everyone let out a collective sigh of relief.

"You got me the Resident Evil red," Zoe said, running her hands reverently over the box. "You guys are the best!"

Elton flipped a thumb in Trent's direction. "She phoned around all our stores after that one. We never even got one in ours. Trent pulled in some pretty big favors to get it for you."

Zoe blew Trent a big kiss. "You are my hero."

Juliet was captivated by Trent's shy discomfort. It made her look sweet, not that she'd ever tell her that.

"Well, it's for all of our sakes because when a console dies it's said that a star goes out in the sky," Trent said mournfully, inciting a round of sniggers around her. "I got an extra controller thrown in so that Rick here can play too."

"You guys are the best," Zoe said. "I couldn't have wished for a better present."

"Next Friday night, mark your calendar; we're all going hunting," Trent said. "Our sharpshooter will be back online." Zoe nodded enthusiastically and the others all high-fived each other.

"Games night cometh!" Elton roared and laughed maniacally. He grabbed for Trent's arm. "Come here a minute. Someone's been asking for you." He caught Juliet's eye. "I promise I'll send her back."

Trent tossed Juliet an apologetic look as she was pulled away.

"I can't believe they did that," Zoe said to Juliet, hugging her present to her chest like a precious child.

"Trent sorted it all for you," Rick said. "The minute your machine died she started making phone calls."

"I'm beginning to realize that anything game related means a lot to all of you," Juliet said, amazed by how serious they all seemed to be about a machine.

"For some of us, it's all we have, our friends online, the competitions, proving that the hours we spend on the machines are worth it. You hone your skills and climb up the leader boards. I'm lucky that when I met Rick, I got to share it all with him. It's more than just playing, it's a whole social network. And our team is showing that we are very good at what we do. It's what we live for, the next big game to pit ourselves against."

Juliet laughed. "It's weird, but for a moment there I could distinctly hear Trent's voice."

"She's brilliant, and could and would wipe the floor with all of us in any game she plays. But she uses her skills to encourage the team, and she never puts us down if we lose."

"Not even Eddie," Rick muttered.

"Elton would have killed him by now if it wasn't for Trent," Zoe said. She paused a moment, looked around surreptitiously, then back to Juliet. "Trent has never brought a girl to any of our get-togethers before."

Juliet's eyebrow rose and she wondered how she should answer.

"You must be very special," Zoe added.

"*She's* special."

Zoe drew Juliet's attention over to where Trent was surrounded by people slapping her on the back in welcome.

"Yes, she is and she doesn't realize it at all. We all love her. She's part of our families because she doesn't have one of her own and because, quite honestly, we want her with us. I can tell you care for her too."

"It's that obvious, eh?" Juliet's eyes followed Trent as she was gathered into the crowd.

"She looks at you in the same way, when you don't notice it, when you're not looking," Zoe said. "Like she can't believe you'd be with her. Even now, while she's doing the meet and greet with my family her eyes haven't strayed far from you. She's making sure you're still here, that she can see you, that you're safe."

Juliet's chest swelled. "Ever the protector. She seems to watch over a lot of people."

"Yes, she does. She's a very good friend." Zoe leaned in closer to speak confidentially. "But she doesn't look at any of us the same way she does *you*."

Juliet blinked at Zoe's confident tone. "Thank you."

Zoe just smiled at her. "I'm going to take my new baby inside now. No one is messing with my new Xbox. It's strictly hands off except for the birthday girl!" Zoe giggled and bumped her hip into Rick. "You can look. I'll let you. I still can't believe she got me the red one."

"I take it that's a special one?" Juliet asked, not sure why it was such a big deal.

"It's a limited edition, produced for a specific game promotion," Zoe gushed. "I have the game but couldn't have afforded the machine as well. Trent rocks!"

"I don't think anything would stop her from getting something she wants."

"You'd better heed your own words, because I think *you're* top of that girl's wish list!"

Juliet's smile broadened as she watched Trent being picked up off the ground by Elton and spun around. "I like the sound of that."

"Go help yourself to anything you want, Juliet. We have every kind of meat available, or vegetarian stuff if you are inclined." She beckoned Rick to follow her. "I'll be right back after I go check in on the girls and get them down here to eat."

Left alone, Juliet searched the crowd for familiar faces. She could just make out Monica on the fringe of the yard but couldn't attract her attention and was reluctant to move seeing as her vantage point afforded her a direct view of Trent, still in Elton's grasp as he teased her in front of their friends. Trent finally managed to disentangle herself from Elton's roughhousing and made her way back toward Juliet. The look in her eyes made Juliet's knees quiver. She admired the long, lean length of Trent's body as she sauntered toward her, her handsome face and her cheeks red from all the attention she'd received. Juliet was just about to reach out a hand to grasp Trent to pull her close when Trent was bowled into by a small child.

"Upt upt!" a little boy demanded, his arms wrapped about Trent's knees.

Trent dutifully picked up the child and held him out at arm's length as if he were contagious. "Do I know you?"

The child giggled. "Higher, Unca Tent, higher."

Trent lifted the boy over her head and settled him on her shoulders.

"King de castle!" he crowed and patted Trent's hair roughly. "Higher, Unca Tent."

"We've got to get working on you sounding your Rs, Craig," Trent said and tried again to rejoin Juliet. "Come and say hi, little man."

Juliet looked up at the child perched on Trent's shoulders. "And who might this be?" There was something vaguely familiar about his features.

"This little guy is Craig Anders, one of Elton's nephews. Say hi to Juliet." Craig put his hands on Trent's hair and leaned forward to shyly say hello. Then he scanned the yard, obviously making the most of being literally head and shoulders above the crowd.

"Unca Elt's here," Craig shouted, pointing over to where Elton stood.

"Yes, he is," Trent said. "Why don't you go see him while I go get a drink for Juliet?" She lifted him off her shoulders and put him down. He hit the floor running and darted off through the legs of the adults.

"He's adorable." Juliet heard his high pitched voice calling to Elton as he pushed his way through. "And he calls you *uncle*."

Trent shifted uncomfortably under Juliet's amused eyes. "We've tried to disabuse him of that, but he just won't say *aunt*. I think he's so used to seeing me with Elton that he links us together so I'm an honorary uncle. But if it means I get hugged every time I see him I don't care. I love him to bits. He's one of Anne's kids. Elton's older sister, but the younger of the two girls."

"Speaking of which," a voice said from behind them, and Juliet turned to see the owner of such a sultry voice. Anne was as dark as Elton, not quite so tall and carried a bit more weight, but the resemblance was startling. She held a tiny baby in her arms. With a practice born of years, Anne reached up and tugged Trent down to give her a kiss on the lips. "Glad you finally made it, tall, dark, and brooding." She turned to face Juliet. "You have to be Juliet." She kissed her too, but with more propriety on the cheek. "It's wonderful to meet you. I've heard so much about you from my brother." She gave Trent a scathing look. "I got nothing from this one because she hasn't visited for a while."

"I've been busy working, Anne," Trent said, suitably contrite.

Anne huffed at her. "Yes, yes, I had to hear all about your recent victory on the gaming circuit too." She shrugged a shoulder at Juliet. "Believe me, growing up with two gamers in the house was a nightmare."

"Anne, you were away at college by the time I was there," Trent said.

"And look where getting a degree got me." Anne jiggled the baby in her arms. "I need to go find Craig so he can nap. Make yourself useful, Trent." She handed Trent the baby and a bottle of milk, then gave Juliet a hug. "Lovely to meet you, Juliet. You and I will talk later." She shot Trent a sneaky look. "The stories I could tell you…"

Trent growled at Anne as she walked past and received a friendly slap on her arm in retaliation.

"Hey, holding the baby here!" Trent stared at the wriggling child in her arms and let out a big sigh. "You can see I am used and abused by Elton's family."

"I think you love it, as they obviously adore you to pieces." Juliet leaned in to get a look at the baby. "Oh, she's just beautiful."

"This is Gilly, she's only four months old."

Trent tested the temperature of the milk on the back of her hand before easing the nipple into Gilly's mouth. She looked perfectly natural standing there with a baby in her arms, while dressed in army fatigues and looking so butch it twisted at Juliet's heart. *Trent Williams, you're so damned gorgeous.* She reached out to touch the baby's hand and enjoyed the way Gilly's fingers wrapped around hers.

"You seem very comfortable around children."

"Elton's family is full of them. You learn to love them or hide. And I'm kind of a kid magnet." She shrugged. "I don't know why. You'd think looking like I do I'd scare the little buggers off."

Juliet caught something underlining Trent's words. She wondered at the obvious pain that Trent voiced so calmly. "You are the most beautiful woman I have ever laid eyes on. That dark and moody look you wear does curious things to my insides that I am not going to mention while you stand there holding such an innocent babe and looking so damn hot doing it." She was warmed to see Trent's face color.

"My dad used to say I was a poor excuse for a woman, looking so much like a man."

Surprised by Trent's quiet disclosure, Juliet couldn't help but be disgusted at a comment so cruel from one who was supposed to love his child no matter what. "He was wrong. You're gorgeous, and masculine features do nothing to detract from the fact you are undeniably a woman." Juliet pressed into Trent's side and wrapped an arm around her waist. "I love how you look. It drew me to you, and I love that for all your big bad butchness, you're not hard. You wouldn't have so many people drawn to you if you were." She ran her hand soothingly over Trent's tense back.

Trent placed a kiss on Juliet's forehead and let out a sigh. "You're too good for me."

"Maybe we can find out just how good I can be *for* you?" Juliet snuggled in close as the baby wriggled contentedly in Trent's arms.

"Well, well, isn't this a picture of domestic partner bliss?" Monica said dryly, skipping toward them and linking her arm through Juliet's. "This kid yours, Trent? You kept that a secret."

Juliet felt Trent's body quake with silent mirth. "Darn it, the truth's out. She's actually mine and Elton's love child."

Juliet caught sight of Elton heading their way, choking on his beer at Trent's comment. He laughed after wiping his face and beard free of foam. "Like I would leave you high and dry with such a beautiful baby." He brushed a tender finger over Gilly's fine hair. "I hope she gets to keep this amazing orange color. We haven't had a Titian in the family before."

"We do need a fiery redhead to disrupt the dark haired-balance your family has," Trent said. She lifted the baby up onto her shoulder over the cloth Anne had kindly furnished her with. She rubbed at the baby's back gently. Elton moved behind Trent to add encouragement.

"Come on, kid, burp it out!"

Gilly did so, loudly. Elton cheered. "Definitely a kid from the Simons gene pool."

"Yes, she sounds just like her uncle Elton," Trent said in Juliet's direction.

The flash of a camera startled Juliet and she looked up to find an attractive older woman waving the camera at them all.

"Wasn't that a beautiful moment to savor? Now which one of you two is going to make an old lady happy and actually give her a grandchild?"

Elton groaned. "Mom!"

"Mama Simons!" Trent mimicked his tone.

Juliet was entertained by their discomfort. Mrs. Simons immediately reached out for her hand and gripped it tightly.

"You have to be Juliet." She looked her over, but Juliet didn't feel anything but amusement at the obvious scrutiny. "Are you managing to keep our Trent in line?"

Juliet purposely didn't look in Trent's direction. "Hardly."

Mrs. Simons nodded. "You'll learn. She's a pussycat. Don't let that handsome face fool you. She's a good girl at heart."

"Mama," Trent said, shifting the baby from her shoulder and handing her off to Elton, who rocked her close to his chest. Monica immediately gravitated over to him and began cooing at the baby. Trent's hand sought Juliet's and Juliet made sure to hold it tight.

"Have you eaten yet?"

Juliet shook her head at Mrs. Simons's query.

"Trent, go fetch this beautiful girl a drink and then escort her to the barbecue pit before Stevie's husband eats the whole lot."

"The Hog is here?" Trent craned her neck to look across the lawn. "Juliet, you've got to see this guy eat."

Dutifully, Juliet followed by Trent's side as she led her through the people, enjoying the excuse to hold on tight and stay close.

"See you later," Mrs. Simons called after them and Juliet turned, only to receive a wink from the old lady.

"I'm sorry about Mama," Trent finally said, not meeting Juliet's eyes.

"What for? She's wonderful."

Trent slowed her steps and looked down. "She took me into her family. She's been like a mother to me, the best one I could have had."

"What happened with your family, Trent?"

"Not now. Soon, maybe." She lifted Juliet's hand up to her lips. "Not here on a happy day."

Juliet read the pain in Trent's expressive eyes and capitulated. "Feed me. I'm suddenly ravenous for meat."

Trent's face lit up. "How do you like your barbecue?" Trent pulled her along toward the marvelous scent coming from the large barbecue pit.

"Well-done and plentiful," Juliet replied, her mouth watering at the smell that tantalized her nostrils.

Trent tugged gently at Juliet's hand. "Then you've come to the right place."

❖

Trent finished off her last plate of meat, then settled back in her chair and groaned. "I may never move again." She caught Juliet licking at her fingers, and her stomach trembled at the sight of her pink tongue chasing after the remnants of spicy sauce. Trent bit back another groan that was more to do with arousal than a full belly.

Monica sat back in her seat and shaded her eyes to look over toward the designated play area. "Kayleigh has found lots of new friends today."

Trent spotted Kayleigh and Sam, along with the ever-present Wade, playing with many of Elton's nieces and nephews, cousins and friends. "They're a great bunch of kids. She's in good company. It's good to see her enjoying herself." Trent turned her attention lazily to Juliet. "How about you, big sister, how are *you* doing?"

"This is a great party with excellent food that I have eaten way too much of, and I've met some very chatty people." She cast Trent a sly look. "Some with a few interesting stories to tell concerning you."

Trent closed her eyes. "I knew I should have kept you miles away from Stevie. She's such a blabbermouth. Five minutes in the same food line and she's spilling tales about me."

"Elton, your family is really lovely," Juliet said.

Trent gave him a poke. "Yeah, kind of makes you wonder where you came from." He swept a backhand in her general direction but missed. He was far too busy soaking up the sun with his eyes closed and a very content look on his face after his meal.

"Children, no fighting or there'll be no dessert for either of you." Mrs. Simons appeared behind them and ruffled at their hair.

Without moving a muscle or opening his eyes, Elton asked, "Mom, did I mention that Monica is doing Trent's yard and that Juliet is helping her?"

Mrs. Simons tried to smooth Elton's wild hair down a little. "Yes, you did and I look forward to seeing what these talented ladies have done to that wilderness Trent called a yard." She reached over to pat Trent. "About time you made that house a home, my girl." That said, she sauntered off at the call from a grandchild.

Trent stretched and rested her arm along the back of Juliet's chair. She played with the fine blond hair that her fingertips could reach. She couldn't remember ever having the need to touch someone so much. She liked the silky feel of Juliet's hair as it wound through her fingers. She loved the quiver she could feel every time her fingers brushed Juliet's neck and Juliet reacted. In turn, Juliet had placed her hand on Trent's thigh and was rubbing slowly. Trent's heart began to beat a little quicker as Juliet's hand strayed closer to the top of her thigh, then swept back down slowly. On one such foray Trent captured Juliet's hand and kept it in place. Juliet raised her eyebrows at Trent's action but acquiesced with a smile at Trent's warning frown.

"Hot enough for you?" Juliet asked innocently.

Trent was amazed at how cool Juliet looked while Trent was almost ready to burst into flames at the delicious friction Juliet had been generating. Usually the one who dictated the pace with a woman, Trent found Juliet's boldness exciting, if a little unnerving. Trent's need to be in control finally pushed her out of her chair on the pretense of stretching her legs. She immediately headed indoors for the bathroom and was grateful to find it unoccupied. Once inside, Trent quickly splashed cold water on her face, hoping to cool herself down. She examined herself in the mirror over the sink. *I really need to get a handle on this because she's driving me crazy with those sly little touches. She's making me yearn for things I've never considered before.* She shook her head ruefully at the direction her thoughts were going. *Like a life, with her, someone I can actually stand to be with for longer than an hour.* Trent physically shook at the enormity of her realization.

My father said I forfeited every right to a family life when I chose the path that led away from his beliefs. Mother said my deviant lifestyle would cause me nothing but grief and pain. My sisters didn't even bother to speak to me. I was already cast out in their eyes. Why the fuck would I want to open myself up to more hurt? Trent's thoughts shifted to Juliet, and her chest eased its tight constriction. *I don't do relationships, and yet suddenly, I want all that and more besides with her. To be with her, to make love to her, finally, possibly, have a family to call my own.* Trent stared at her reflection in the mirror again. *I don't recognize myself anymore. I want things I never let myself dream were possible of having.* She doused her face again roughly. "I have no idea what I'm doing. I'm bound to screw this up somehow. And what if she's uninterested? No strings she said, and I agreed. It's safer that way, no one gets hurt. Especially *me*."

Leaning against the sink, Trent willed her mind to stop its racing. Only when her breathing had slowed down did she make her way downstairs to step back into the party. Music was playing and people were up dancing. Juliet wasn't in her seat and Trent immediately searched the yard until she caught sight of her dancing with Monica. Trent was amazed that Monica apparently knew all the dance moves to a peppy pop song that played from the stereo.

"You look lost in thought," Anne said, sliding up behind her and linking her arm through Trent's.

"Just enjoying the party and seeing everyone here."

"It's not like you to turn up with someone on your arm. You usually stag it and end up carrying Elton home."

Trent looked over to where Elton was dancing beside Monica, his moves fluid and skilful. "You'll notice that Elton has a lady of his own present and he's steering clear of the beer seeing as he's too busy paying attention to her." Trent shrugged. "He won't be in need of my help anytime tonight."

"I can't honestly remember a time I've seen you with a woman. I know you're a lesbian, but I did wonder if you were celibate."

"Not celibate, merely…cautious."

"You're a long time out from under your father's roof, Trent."

"I know. But some things are hard to shake." *And the fear never eases. I can't lose everything again. I've been so careful not to let anyone too close and give them that power over me.*

"Rumor has it you're not even a love 'em and leave 'em kind of gal."

"There hasn't been much love, if truth be told." Trent heard the wistful tone in her own voice and bit back a sigh. She really didn't need Anne digging too close in the wounds Trent knew were a long time from healing. "And I don't do things like love and intimacy. I'm not capable of them."

Anne shook her gently. "That's bullshit and you know it. Look around you, Trent. Your friends adore you whether you recognize it or not. And you love them back with that fiercely loyal way you have about you. You've loved Elton better than any of his women have ever gotten close to. Admittedly, it's a platonic, friendly love, but it's still a strong emotion and you feel it even if you don't want to acknowledge it."

Trent couldn't look at Anne. She was too exposed and it frightened her. "I could lose so much if I let myself care, Anne."

"You didn't lose anything before that you haven't regained in another form. You're surrounded by family, Trent, a family of *your* making. You need to let go of the past." Anne nudged Trent's attention out into the crowd. "You care for this one, don't you?"

"She's the first I've let in my house."

"The fact that she's actually been in your house says a great deal. For her *and* you."

Trent just nodded, her eyes unerringly finding Juliet again in the mass of people dancing to the song still playing. "She's finding her way into more than just my home."

"And you're scared. I can see it written all over your face."

"Terrified," Trent said in a whisper.

"You going to invite her upstairs?"

"She's already been in my bedroom." Hastily, she added, "To change clothes, nothing more." The music switched tracks and Juliet held Kayleigh's hands in hers to dance with her. "But there's one room she hasn't seen yet."

"The make-or-break room." Anne chuckled. "That's what Elton calls his, and I hear it's nothing compared to yours."

"The room that I can't explain even if I tried to, but I think I need to, for her. She deserves to know what she's getting into. If she wants to, that is."

"She'd be a fool not to. You know, there were times I wished I hadn't been straight. You were always too good a catch to go to waste." Anne hugged Trent to her and mercifully changed her focus. "Elton's new girl seems the perfect choice for him too."

"She's exactly what he needs, and they complement each other so well. And she's incredibly talented. As well as being a landscaper, she makes all her own clothes." Dropping this bit of information deliberately into the conversation, Trent slyly waited for Anne's swift mind digest this fact.

"No kidding? I need a few alterations to a skirt I have post-baby that needs to be let out." Anne mulled this over. "Do you think she'd have time to do it? I'd pay her for her work, of course."

Trent regarded her wryly. "Go ask her. I think she'll love the fact you're ready to exploit her talents just like you would any other member of the family that can do something you can't be bothered to do."

"That's what family is for. Just because your last name is Williams doesn't mean I can't expect favors from you like I'd expect from a blood relative Simons."

"I consider myself fortunate," Trent said. Anne pushed her away forcibly. "Hey!"

"Now go ask that girl to dance, for God's sake."

"You and I both know I can't dance worth a damn."

"Women love a hopeless case. Make her feel sorry for the fact that you may have been blessed with fingers that can manipulate a control pad, but that God left you in the back of the line for dancing genes."

"You just want to see me make a fool of myself to give you more fodder for your rumor mill," Trent grumbled.

"You forget, I knew you as a teenager. Been there, done that with both you and Elton. I have enough fodder for years to come to make your lives uncomfortable at the dinner table."

Trent made a face at her and eased her way through the dancers. She dodged the flailing arms and overenthusiastic steps until she reached Juliet's side. The look in Juliet's eyes that she received lifted her heart.

"I got dragged onto the dance floor," Juliet said, obviously enjoying herself.

"Trent, dance with us!" Kayleigh expertly twirled Sam in a little twist that Trent knew she'd never master.

"Wow, I am surrounded by dancing queens."

"Who you calling a queen?" Elton said.

Juliet wound her arms around Trent's waist and swayed to the beat. "Word is you're way too cool to dance."

Trent gave Elton a swift look and he slyly winked at her. Trent reminded herself to treat him to a doughnut next week. She looked into Juliet's sparkling eyes and couldn't lie to her. "I wouldn't say too cool, exactly." She leaned down to whisper in Juliet's ear. "I have two left feet. I'm severely dance-impaired."

Juliet just regarded her closely. "Then I'll just hold on to you and you can follow my lead." She rested her hands on Trent's hips and swayed in her arms. Trent was mesmerized by Juliet's energy and contagious joy.

"Aren't I supposed to lead?" Trent said.

Juliet pulled her a little closer until their legs touched and their bodies pressed together. "We can take turns. Makes for a more interesting dance that way." Juliet rested her head on Trent's chest and they moved in time to the music, never shifting from one spot. Trent thought it was the perfect moment: Juliet in her arms, a slow song playing, and being surrounded by family and friends. She held Juliet a little tighter and luxuriated in the feeling of Juliet's lush body pressed intimately to her own.

"See, you can dance after all," Juliet murmured, rubbing her face against Trent's T-shirt just above her heart.

"Who'd have believed it? Must be the woman in my arms working miracles." Trent rested her face on Juliet's hair and breathed in the fresh scent. "But if they start playing country, I'm sitting it out. I don't line dance for anyone."

Juliet chuckled against her chest. "I'll agree with you on that."

Trent let herself relax for a moment then bit the bullet to ask, "Would you come home with me tonight? There's something I'd like you to see."

Juliet searched Trent's face closely, obviously seeing the strain that Trent feared was all too plainly written there. "I'd like that," she said simply.

Trent nodded, her fate sealed. She'd asked, Juliet had agreed. There was no turning back. She pulled Juliet close once more and hoped she was doing the right thing. But Trent couldn't see a way forward until she'd shared with Juliet the most important thing in her world. Trent's hold tightened a fraction more and she willed away her fear of the unknown.

"You're trembling," Juliet said softly.

"Too much sun, I guess."

"Do you want to sit down?"

"No, I like where I am right this minute. Dance with me just a little longer, Juliet." She relaxed as Juliet snuggled closer.

"It would be my pleasure."

Trent rested her chin on Juliet's hair and savored their bodies touching. She feared pleasure didn't even begin to cover what she was feeling.

❖

The party looked set to go on well into the night, but Trent had other ideas. She checked her watch again and Juliet caught her.

"That's the fourth time in as many minutes you've checked what time it is. Do you want us to leave now?"

Trent nodded, grateful that Juliet had instigated their departure. "I'm not going to settle until I get you home," she said, blurting out the truth, then belatedly realizing how it sounded. Juliet's slow blink made some of her nervousness abate, and she shrugged awkwardly at the stare she received. "Believe me, Jule, I would use a much better pick-up line if I were attempting to seduce you back to my place."

Juliet's face creased into a beautiful smile. "I like how you shorten my name. You haven't done that before, and everyone else calls me Jules."

"But you are a jewel, something rare and eminently precious." She forced herself to sit back in her seat before she did something more than just tease Juliet.

"Do you have any idea what you do to me?"

"The feeling is mutual, I can assure you." Trent cast a look around the party. "They won't miss us. They're gearing up for the next phase— drink the party dry." Trent held out a hand to help Juliet to her feet. Elton stirred beside them.

"You guys leaving already?"

"Heading home, dude." Trent stretched and yawned. "Damn, Zoe throws great parties. I don't think I'll need to eat for at least three days after the feast her dad prepared for us."

Elton rose and hugged Trent in farewell. "See you Monday. You're on the early shift, don't forget." He pulled back and regarded her. "You okay?"

"Make-or-break room," Trent said under her breath, and his eyes widened in realization.

"Whoa. You're that serious, then?"

Monica was busy saying good night to Juliet and nudged Elton in his ribs. "What are you two whispering about?"

"Nothing too important." Elton hugged Trent to him again, whispering in her ear, "You'll be fine. She looks like a keeper."

Yes, but will she really want to keep me? *And can I let go long enough to be kept?*

CHAPTER FOURTEEN

The journey back in the car was strangely silent until Juliet spoke. "Trent, I don't think I've ever seen you so nervous, so will you please just tell me what's going on so I can stop worrying?"

Trent rubbed her hand over Juliet's thigh in apology. "I didn't realize I was broadcasting. Sorry."

"What is it? Have I done something?"

"God, no! No, it's nothing you've done, Juliet, it's just…" Trent closed her eyes and tried desperately to arrange her thoughts so she could explain. "I've had the best time with you today. Having you meet my family, seeing you fit right in with everyone, watching the guys trip over their tongues at the sight of you."

"They can all keep their tongues to themselves. Yours, however…" She let her words linger in the air. "I loved meeting the Simonses. Even though it's not through blood ties, it's painfully obvious you are as much a part of their family as they are yours."

"I want to tell you about that, explain some of it."

"You don't have to if you don't want to. I'll understand."

"I know you would, which is why I want to let you in—" Trent stopped in mid-sentence as her own words rang loud and clear. *Let her in.*

"That's not something you do very often, is it? Let people get close. Let *women* get close."

"No, you'd be the first for a long time."

"Thank you."

"Don't thank me yet. You haven't seen it all."

"I've seen enough to know I'm drawn to you like no other woman I've ever met," Juliet said wistfully. "I saw you today, surrounded by your friends and work colleagues. I recognized some of the people from the tournament, people you competed against and beat, yet they congregated around you asking your advice about anything and everything. It surprises me. I've worked for the same company in different branches for years, and I have no one from any of them that I can truly call friends. Everyone is looking out for their own interests. It's an old saying but true; you can't mix business with pleasure. I never once felt I fit in. Yet you're friends with everyone, from the older folk to the little kids. And, it has to be said, you looked so damned sweet cradling that baby."

"*Sweet?*"

"Yes, sweet. You can be big and butch holding a baby and still be the sweetest thing I've witnessed in a long time." Juliet pulled into Trent's street. "You're so sexy I could hardly stand it all day, being near you, touching you, but not being able to do what I wanted. Even in those crazy surfer shorts you're wearing that only serve to make you sexier, though don't ask me how. I lost count of the times I wanted to grab you by your dog tags and drag you off to a corner somewhere and lick the sweat from your neck."

Trent swallowed hard against the tide of arousal that rushed to engulf her. "What stopped you?"

"I wouldn't have stopped at just your neck."

The air in the car grew charged and the silence lengthened.

"Have I shocked you?"

"No, I'm trying to remind myself that you need all your attention for the road and that I need to keep my hands off you."

"Just for now, though, right?"

Trent swallowed hard. "God, you're like no other woman I've ever known, Juliet."

"How so?"

"You're so damn beautiful you make my chest ache. And you're funny and fucking sexy with it. And you have a rocket scientist brain."

Juliet snorted with amusement. "I work in a bank, Trent. That doesn't make me overly smart, it makes me a glorified bean counter."

"Did I mention the beautiful part?" Trent worked her hand into Juliet's hair, unable to hold back any longer from touching her. "Your hair is so soft."

Juliet pulled the car to the curb outside Trent's house. The second she applied the parking brake, Trent undid her seat belt and reached for her. It wasn't a gentle kiss. It was raw and passionate and almost desperate. Juliet moaned as Trent ravished her lips; the sound vibrated against her mouth and set her body tingling. She traced her tongue over Juliet's full lips, slipped inside to caress and deepen the kiss. Juliet clung to Trent, one hand reached up to spear through her short hair and tug at it gently. Trent shuddered, the gentle eroticism of such a simple act nearly undoing her. She pulled back gasping for air, her eyes searching Juliet's bruised lips and dazed face. Juliet touched her lips with a shaking hand.

"Next time, I'm just dragging you away by the dog tags, I don't care where we are." The hand in Trent's hair tugged her down so that Juliet could rest her lips against Trent's. "Your lips are so soft," she whispered, causing a shudder to race through Trent's body, then purposely flicking her tongue against Trent's lips. Juliet's satisfaction was noticeable when Trent reacted again.

Trent angled her head so that Juliet's fingers could continue their foray through her hair. "Your touch drives me crazy."

Juliet's hand drifted down to cup Trent's face. She kissed her again, a fleeting press of her lips that touched Trent deep inside.

"We'd better move inside before we give Mrs. Tweedy a heart attack should she catch us steaming up the car windows." Juliet unfastened her seat belt and pulled away from Trent.

Fumbling one-handed for her keys, Trent led the way up the path to her front door, all the while firmly holding Juliet's hand. She gestured for Juliet to precede her once she got the door unlocked. Trent closed the door and swiftly turned off the annoying alarm that sounded way too loud in the silence. She turned to find Juliet right in front of her, barely a breath between them.

"Why do I get the feeling this isn't a simple social call, Trent?"

Trent took a deep breath to quell her nerves. "I want to show you something. I need to." Chewing at her lip nervously, Trent reached out to snag Juliet's hands.

"Whatever it is, it's okay," Juliet said, searching Trent's face.

Trent looked straight into Juliet's concerned eyes. "I had the most amazing time with you today, and I'm not used to doing that."

"Having fun?"

"Spending time with a woman outside of what I take from them and what they want from me. I don't do what we appear to be doing."

"And what are we doing?"

"I think we're dating, and I never do that. It's too complicated and difficult, but with you it's so easy to fall into." Trent focused on their hands, linked between them. "You said no strings, but there are already more strings than I'm used to." She let out a low moan as the strength of her feelings threatened to engulf her. "You're tying me in so many knots, Jule."

"Are you saying you don't want to see me anymore?"

Trent flinched at the misery in Juliet's voice, knowing she was the cause. "What? No! I'm trying to say I want to spend more time with you, and I'm screwing it up just like I knew I would." The air was knocked out of her lungs as Juliet launched herself into her arms and gripped her tightly.

"Jesus, Trent! You really do suck at this, don't you?" Juliet grumbled against Trent's breast.

"I know, but I haven't had much practice so bear with me." Trent knew she was pleading but didn't care. "I'm set in my ways, Jule. I'm solitary and my sex life before has consisted of no fuss, no ties, no swapping numbers. You're the first woman I've wanted to spend time with, to get to know. I told you before, you were worth more than a quick fuck no matter how hot you make me or how desperate I am to hold you down and make you mine." A flash of fire ignited in Juliet's blue eyes. Trent's body reacted by growing tight. "I need to show you something first, then you can decide."

"Decide what?"

"If I'm worth it."

❖

Juliet could almost feel Trent's trepidation radiating off her as she led Juliet up the stairs. Instead of heading toward the bedroom, Trent walked a little farther down the landing to another door. It had an elaborate lock system on what was obviously a reinforced door.

Juliet leaned against the wall as Trent unlocked it. "If you're going to show me a highly personalized S&M dungeon set up in your spare bedroom, I'm going to be more than a little perturbed."

Trent pushed open the door. Leaning against the door frame, she regarded Juliet steadily.

"I can't believe I'm going to do this, but there's a lot I'm doing that I don't believe where you're concerned." Trent's eyes rose heavenward as she seemed to search for words. "This house is my refuge, my one safe place, my home, and, for some reason I just can't fathom, you seem to fit right in." Trent reached out to stroke Juliet's cheek.

"I wouldn't betray anything you show me or tell me, Trent."

Trent pushed the door open farther and stepped back to allow Juliet to enter. Curiosity getting the better of her, Juliet took a few steps, then stopped dead in her tracks. Her mouth dropped open.

"Oh my God, I've died and gone to gamer heaven!" Trent released a soft snort behind her, but she didn't follow Juliet inside; instead she left Juliet to explore on her own. Juliet looked all around the room. The blinds were drawn, but a bright white strip light bathed the room in a clean, crisp illumination. Center stage in the room was a padded chair, beside it a small table covered in various games controllers all laid out in neat rows. A huge-screen TV dominated the room. Juliet estimated its screen was at least sixty inches. "That's some TV."

"You should have seen Elton and me getting it up the stairs."

Juliet continued looking around. The wall behind the TV was a massive bookcase lined with game cases. Juliet edged closer and noticed everything was organized by console and then alphabetized. "You have your games listed by name?"

"Wouldn't you with that many to sort through?"

Juliet had to agree. She was fascinated by the endless array of older games in their big boxes sitting next to games in newer plastic cases she was familiar with as ones now littering her sister's room. One box, an old Space Invaders box, stood out among the rest. Juliet acknowledged its implied importance by the way it was positioned so prominently. On the wall to the right was a smaller bookcase housing consoles. Some of them Juliet didn't recognize, but they were of every size and system. She noticed a few were the same machine, only in different colors.

"You have two of some?" Juliet asked.

"Limited editions."

"Like a Resident Evil red."

"Exactly. I forgot you were talking to Zoe for a while."

A small love seat sat under the window and Juliet moved to seat herself there, aware that the chair in the room was undoubtedly Trent's. She moved aside a few of the gaming magazines that lay on the cushions and sat back to take it all in. Her eyes fell on Trent hanging back in the doorway.

"This room is amazing."

Trent stepped inside and Juliet saw how her posture shifted. *You feel safest in here. Why do you need to feel safe, Trent? What scares you so much outside this room?*

"When I first moved in, I did this room and my bedroom first. It took me a while to get it like it is now, and it's only been recently that I could afford the bigger screen." Trent's eyes shone with her excitement. "Sixty-two inches, HDTV, plasma screen. You wouldn't believe how cool it looks seeing all your soldiers in high definition when you deploy them on this baby."

Juliet was enthralled by Trent's obvious glee. "You sound just like a guy commenting on size. Does Elton play here with you?"

"No. No one plays in my room except for me."

Juliet wondered at the emphatic answer. She just waited until Trent seemed ready to explain more. Trent finally sat in her chair and swiveled it to face her.

"I know it sounds crazy. *My* house, *my* room, *my* games, but it's just how I am."

"I understand. I had my own place in Chicago and loathed to share it with anyone else. I had everything where I wanted it and hated it when someone came over and disrupted my order. Sharing with someone again has been hard."

"Elton and I keep our homes separate from work. He does have occasional parties. He's not quite as bad as I am." Trent made a wry face. "If it was known I had this much space, I'd have Eddie sleeping on the living room floor every other week because his mother has kicked him out again." Trent ran her hands over the arms of her chair. "This is my place. I grew up never having privacy. This is my chance to do whatever I want, when I want."

"Tell me about this room." Trent's eyes sparkled as she warmed to having someone to share her treasures with. Her pride was obvious at what she'd accomplished with the room.

"I practically live in here, which is why downstairs is a little desolate." She pointed to the shelves. "Those are every game I own. I rarely trade in. Sorry, but that would be too much like giving away my children."

Juliet loved Trent's exaggerated horror at the mere thought.

"I have nearly every console available from past to present. Some of these machines are no longer in production so are rare and very valuable."

"No wonder you have security on the door."

"And the high-tech security system I have on the house." Trent pointed to her side. "These are the consoles I use for my general playing and my online gaming." She shifted in the chair and pointed beside Juliet. "And then there's my computer, which is also gamer friendly." Trent sat back and faced the screen. "I compete from here. I have everything set up for easy access, and I can just sit back and play with anyone from anywhere in the world." She looked back at Juliet. "I love this room; it's where all the fun begins."

"It's the perfect reflection of you, this and your bedroom." She studied Trent quietly. She had to ask the question that was gnawing at her brain. "Why am I the first person invited into your house? And more importantly, into this room?"

"I need you to see how much this all means to me. This is me. I play games for hours on end. Yes, it's a part of my job, but mostly it's because I love games. This isn't like me coming home hours late from work. This is a dedication to something most people think is a waste of time."

"I'm beginning to realize just how much this world means to you and the others who play in it. I'm glad you've chosen to share all this with me. I want to get to know you, Trent, all of you. Because you are the most fascinating woman I have ever come across, with or without a game in your hands."

"I could just be a big kid with a room full of toys."

"No, you're a grown woman with exceptional skill at playing these games. That requires dedication and I admire that. You forget I've seen you in action. You're amazing."

"So if I missed a meal or two because I was trying to finish a level, it wouldn't annoy you? What if I didn't come to bed for hours because I was playing online with a few buddies? Are you saying you wouldn't get mad?"

Juliet sat back and gave her such a long, considering look it made Trent's face flush as the silence lengthened. "Are you trying to use your game playing as an excuse for us not to get involved?"

Trent's mouth opened, but no words came out. She finally had the grace to look sheepish. "I guess I am."

"At the moment, I work long hours in an office, can be called in at any moment because of some crisis or another that they feel needs my hand directly on it to put it right. Would you be able to understand my dedication to that?" Trent mulled this over. Juliet enjoying Trent being so unaware of the transparency of her expressions that she could almost read what was going through her mind.

"I understand what you're saying," she finally replied.

"How many women have told you to put down the controllers and just play with them instead?"

"What relationships I have had haven't lasted that long for it to be a problem. I don't usually meet someone who wants more than a quick fuck at a games convention."

"You score girls at tournaments?" Juliet voice rose and she cursed the fact that her jealousy rose another notch at the thought of other women touching Trent.

"I did when I was much younger. I don't bother now." She ran an agitated hand through her hair. "I got tired of being worth nothing more than a quick fumble. I didn't want to be the notch on a gaming groupie's belt."

"Gamers have *groupies*?"

Trent raised her hands behind her head to lean back in her seat with a seriously smug grin. "What can I say? In some circles we're superstars."

Juliet narrowed her eyes at Trent's amusement. "So these bimbos you'd 'service,' they never touched you in return?"

Trent flipped a thumb in the direction of her bedroom. "Hence the extensive DVD collection for my own amusement." The humor slipped from her face. "I have the reputation of being stone butch, which I'm not, but it stuck. My looks don't exactly help, and I guess I got disillusioned early on in my pathetic sex life when I realized not everyone likes to give as much as receive."

"I've known some die-hard stone butches, Trent, and believe me, you're nothing like them. The posturing, the aggressiveness, the unwillingness to be touched, that's not you at all." Juliet moved forward on the sofa and touched Trent's knee. "I love how you melt in my arms when I kiss you, how you react to my touch. You were meant to be held and touched and loved just like any woman." Juliet moved again, this time to straddle Trent's lap. Trent's hands immediately clasped Juliet's hips as she settled onto her. "You're letting out your fears, Trent, one by one for me to see. I'm not going to be turned away or off by them." Juliet pressed her lips to Trent's forehead and a shudder ran through the body underneath her. "You've opened your secret places to me." She let her lips trail soft kisses toward Trent's ear. "Now, let me in."

CHAPTER FIFTEEN

Juliet's kiss was fierce and Trent instantly returned it with twice as much passion. She groaned loudly as Juliet's tongue pushed past her lips and began to tease her. Tightening her hands on Juliet's hips, Trent managed to keep her anchored as she leaned forward to ravish Trent's mouth.

"God, you're so hot," Juliet murmured, kissing a line along Trent's jawline and nipping at her skin before returning for another kiss. Her hands slid over Trent's T-shirt, working under the sleeves and gripping the muscles there.

Trent's hands wound their way under Juliet's shirt and explored her naked back. She scored her nails softly on Juliet's flesh and Trent thrilled at the way Juliet arched into her touch. She ran her fingertips up Juliet's spine and complained at the separation of Juliet's lips from hers when Juliet had to pull back to gasp for air. Whatever words Trent was about to utter died in her throat as Juliet sat back and begin to unbutton her shirt. Her heart raced as the material was tossed to the floor with little concern.

"You're so gorgeous," Trent said with a rasp. Her fingers found the soft skin of Juliet's stomach to touch and trace patterns upon it. Her breath stopped when Juliet reached behind her to unfasten her bra. "Fuck," Trent mumbled when Juliet's ample breasts were released. "They're more beautiful than I even imagined."

Juliet threw the scrap of clothing on top of her shirt. She leaned closer into Trent. "You've been imagining my breasts, have you?"

"Every damn minute I could get," Trent said, reaching up to hold them in her palms and brush her thumbs gently over the rigid tips. She kissed each breast reverently, trying to keep her desire in check for fear she'd hurt Juliet if she let loose what she was feeling.

"I won't break if you touch me, Trent," Juliet whispered. She took Trent's hands and pressed them tighter to her body. Trent's whole body trembled in reaction. She already knew her hands were shaking. She savored the feel of flesh spilling over her palms. She sucked a nipple into her mouth, running her tongue around the hard knot. Then she licked the areola and marveled at how tight the skin raised and was pressed more fully into her mouth as Juliet crowded even closer.

"Your mouth feels wonderful. Suck me harder."

Trent swiped her tongue over and over the pebbled skin, at first sucking, then flicking, enjoying every sound that came from Juliet's lips. Turning equal attention to the other breast, Trent repeated her ministrations and relished the fact Juliet began to rock on her lap.

"You're driving me crazy," Juliet said. When her breathing began to get more ragged, Juliet pulled Trent away and kissed her hard.

Trent began tugging at Juliet's shorts, anxious to reveal more flesh.

Juliet wagged a finger at her. "Not before you get naked too." She tugged at Trent's T-shirt, so Trent quickly dragged it off. Juliet's hands were instantly all over her arms and shoulders.

"You're so powerful. I love your muscles." She put her mouth on Trent's shoulder and bit down gently. It ricocheted straight to Trent's clitoris, and she released a long, shaky moan. Juliet pulled at Trent's bra but ended up just tugging it down so that Trent's chest was bare.

Trent knew she was nowhere near as endowed as Juliet was, but by the look in Juliet's eyes, it didn't matter. Not as cautious as Trent had been, Juliet swiftly rubbed Trent's nipples to hard points with the palms of her hands.

"You need to stop. I'll be coming in my shorts if you keep that up," Trent panted.

"No problem, lover, we won't be stopping at just one tonight." She gently pinched Trent's nipples, forcing her to close her eyes as the pleasure ignited deep within her belly. Trent dragged Juliet down for another kiss, her mind fast losing track of where her hands were while Juliet's roamed over her skin with a vengeance.

"Slow down, please," Trent said. "You're going to give me a freakin' heart attack!" Trent stilled the hands caressing her breasts to distraction.

Kissing her gently, Juliet relented. "Okay, but don't think I'm letting you off lightly." She rose on her knees and popped the button on her shorts. The sound of her zipper being lowered was loud in the room.

Trent was surprised she could hear it over the sound of her own sharp breaths. Juliet stood to divest herself of shorts and underwear, then settled back in Trent's lap. Trent managed to catch a fleeting glimpse of pale hair framing the top of Juliet's legs before Juliet was once again in her arms and their breasts were pressed together. Trent ran her hands over Juliet's buttocks, squeezing the round cheeks, and then lifted Juliet higher into her lap. With Juliet's legs spread wide open across her, Trent let her hands ease up the soft thighs and soon found where Juliet was wet and wanting. She touched gently and Juliet moaned in her arms.

"Do it," she whispered against Trent's mouth.

Trent circled her fingers through the rich moisture covering Juliet's lower lips. She explored the soft, puffy flesh, gathering moisture as she slid her fingers around, learning the contours of Juliet's sex. She brushed gently at the hood covering Juliet's clitoris and delighted in the gasp it drew from Juliet and the way her hips pressed forward for more. Trent spread a line of kisses along Juliet's jaw, down her neck, licking at the beating pulse point. She pushed Juliet upright, all the time keeping her fingers roaming between her legs. Trent's own body throbbed in unison. She could feel her clitoris rubbing against the seam of her shorts, and every move Juliet made tightened the fabric and only served to increase the ache.

"You are so sexy." Trent was filled with desire. She withdrew her hand and brought it to her lips to savor Juliet's arousal. Juliet shivered and grabbed to push Trent's hand back where she needed it. Resisting, Trent licked at her fingers, watching the flush of red cover Juliet's breasts as she witnessed the act. Juliet's eyes darkened when Trent returned her fingers to the source. "I told you, you were worth more than a quick fuck, but I don't think I can wait any longer to have you." In one swift movement, Trent slipped a finger inside her, and Juliet's back bowed. "Fuck, you're tight." Trent growled and grabbed for a swaying nipple. She caught the red tip between her teeth and sucked on it. Juliet's hips began to buck in earnest as Trent's thrusts deepened.

"More," Juliet said.

Trent inserted two fingers, and Juliet's resulting keening cry was the sexiest thing Trent had ever heard. Her own sex clenched in sympathy. Trent had never been so turned on by touching another woman. Nothing came close to how she felt now with Juliet in her arms and her fingers pressing inside Juliet's body. Juliet's pleasure was Trent's, and this time, Trent could feel everything; it wasn't one-sided. She pressed in harder and was rewarded with a rush of moisture. Juliet grabbed for her shoulders, and the sharpness of her nails was a pleasant sting. Looking up from Juliet's breast, feasting on her flesh, Trent could feel Juliet's warm walls welcoming her deeper inside. She pressed her thumb to the exposed head of Juliet's clitoris and rubbed. Juliet's body jerked in her arms.

"Oh God!" she yelped and pumped erratically against Trent's fingers.

Trent rubbed harder still and Juliet's head fell back. She pumped faster, closed her teeth around Juliet's right nipple, and bit down gently. The answering scream was enough incentive for Trent not to stop. She curled her fingers inside Juliet and rubbed at her secret spot. Juliet cried out Trent's name in a strangled sob and came hard, her body jerking in Trent's lap, drawing out every last shudder as the orgasm raced through her body. Trent gathered Juliet close when she slumped forward, spent. It was a new experience for Trent to cuddle after sex. Nuzzling into Juliet's hair, she decided she liked it and couldn't help relishing the fact.

"Good God," Juliet said shakily, her face buried in Trent's neck. "I've never come so hard in my life."

Trent was glad Juliet couldn't see how smug she was feeling.

"You are amazing." Juliet sighed and tried to sit back up, shuddering with a long, drawn-out moan as Trent's fingers slipped from inside her.

Trent took her time taking in every freckle and mark visible on Juliet's skin, committing them to memory. Juliet sat upright and Trent licked her lips at the glorious sight she was afforded.

"Your eyes just went an incredibly dark chocolate color."

"I want to watch you come again, only this time using just my tongue to set you off."

Juliet shivered and gave Trent a smile that melted her heart. "You're too damn good for me," she said softly, touching Trent's cheek reverently.

"I think that's my line, Jule."

"No, you're perfect for me. You know exactly how to touch me and leave me desperate for more."

"My thoughts exactly." She reached for Juliet again. Trent was puzzled when Juliet evaded her grasp.

"No." Juliet slipped from Trent's lap slowly and sensuously to rest on the floor between Trent's knees. She pushed Trent's legs apart.

"Now it's your turn." Her hands began to run playfully up Trent's legs to the edge of her shorts.

Trent swallowed audibly. Her head was filled with the sound of her heart beating out a nervous rhythm so loud it was almost deafening. She was certain she could hear music too. From the look on Juliet's face, she could hear it as well and was less than pleased.

"Damn it, that's my cell."

"Leave it," Trent said gruffly, her body tight and desperate for its first touch in years from someone other than herself.

The music stopped. Juliet's lips curved into a sensual smile. "I want you so bad."

Trent was still as Juliet's hands slipped over her shorts and aimed higher. She moaned deep in her throat as the sound of the cell phone began again. Juliet grumbled under her breath and reached for the pocket of her shorts to draw the offending phone out. She flipped it open to see who was calling.

"If this is Monica, I'll kill her slowly and painfully." She looked at the screen and frowned. Juliet's eyes lifted to Trent's. "It's my boss."

Trent's nerves were stretched to their limit, but she nodded anyway. "Answer it."

Juliet's frowned deepened. "Why would they be calling me at this time of night and on a weekend too?"

"To screw with me so you can't," Trent said and listened in as Juliet took the call. The play of emotions that raced over Juliet's face told Trent it wasn't good news.

"I understand the need for urgency, but can anything really be accomplished at this time of night?" Juliet listened to the voice on the other end of the phone and made a face. "I see. We need to rally the backers before the stock markets get wind of anything." She rolled her eyes expressively. "Yes, sir, yes. I'll be there shortly." Juliet slammed the phone shut and flung it back on her shorts. "This is why gardening seems so much better as a career choice."

"Problems?" Trent feared the worst by Juliet's reaction.

"One of our foreign partners has just declared bankruptcy, throwing bankers into a tailspin and my offices into a state of extreme panic. They want me to go in to do damage control before the news hits the wires and the rest of the banking community gets wind of our shit hitting the fan."

Trent could still feel Juliet's wetness on her hand, could taste her on her lips. "You have to go *now*?" For the first time in years, Trent didn't want a woman to leave.

Juliet rested her hands on Trent's spread knees. "Believe me, I don't want to. I want to take your clothes off and climb inside you as deep as you were in me until you scream my name."

Trent clenched her hands as she tried to keep from reaching out to grab Juliet to her. Her insides had melted, her shorts were soaked from just having Juliet come in her arms. Trent was curiously lost. She was unable to move from her chair for fear her legs wouldn't be able to hold her up. Juliet reluctantly began to get dressed. As she buttoned up her shirt with jerky movements, Trent managed to get to her feet, pull up her bra, and scramble for her T-shirt. She brushed Juliet's hands away from where she was fastening everything wrong and completed the task for her. Juliet looked up at Trent. Her eyes were shiny with tears.

"Jule?"

"I don't want to go," Juliet said, wrapping her arms around Trent's waist and holding on tight.

"I don't want you to either."

"I hate my job."

At this moment, I do too. Trent took Juliet's hand and led her from the game room. Juliet pulled her to a stop at the top of the stairs.

"Thank you for sharing your room with me," she said sweetly, reaching up to kiss Trent gently.

"I'd say it's well and truly christened now." Trent ran her fingers together, the slight stickiness of Juliet's passion remained, and Trent was loath to lose it.

"I'll phone you tomorrow, I promise. Just as soon as I know what's happening." Juliet hastened down the stairs.

"Guess Monica will be gardening on her own." Trent couldn't stop the disappointment in her voice and she winced at how pathetic she sounded even to herself. Trent reached to open the front door and was startled when Juliet pushed her against it and pulled at her to deliver a kiss so sweet and passionate it made Trent's knees buckle.

"My decision was made a while ago concerning the question you asked me earlier." Juliet let Trent go but didn't release her gaze. "You're more than worth it."

Juliet left the house and ran down the path toward her car. Trent closed the door behind her. She ran her hand down her chest, feeling the swell of arousal still thrumming through her. She set the house alarm and wandered back upstairs in the direction of game room. It looked oddly undisturbed by what had just transpired in there. "I've just lived every gamer geek's dream. A hot blonde naked in my lap while I took her in my gaming chair." She hovered in the room for a moment trying to decide what to do next. She was restless, agitated, too turned on to try to distract herself with a game.

She turned off the light, locked the door up out of habit, and walked the few steps into her bedroom. She lay on her bed with a loud sigh and rested her hand over her eyes. Trent was instantly assailed by the scent Juliet had left on her flesh. She breathed it in deep and an answering tug sparked low in her belly. She slipped her hand down to her crotch. She knew a few good tugs would be all she needed to rid herself of the ache pounding through her clitoris. Surprisingly, Trent didn't want it to be quieted by the touch of her own hand. Only Juliet's touch would truly satisfy this need. She rested her hands on her stomach and stared at the ceiling. For the first time, she hadn't been the one to fuck and walk away. She'd been the one left behind, leaving Trent very alone. She lazily lifted her hand to her face and breathed in again the lingering scent of Juliet. Her stomach clenched in reaction. "I've got a girl who has me take her in my game room and then she leaves me high and dry." She shifted her legs uncomfortably. "Or not so dry." She ran her tongue over her lips. "I can taste her."

With a deep growl Trent leapt from her bed and headed to the bathroom. She scrubbed at her hand, trying desperately to erase the sweet stickiness. Satisfied all she could smell was soap, Trent changed out of her shorts and found her sleep attire. Finally, she padded back down the hallway. Trent pushed open the door to the game room and a now-familiar subtle scent assailed her nostrils. "Goddammit! I can smell her everywhere!" Trent switched on her TV, picked up a controller, and found a game to go online with. Waiting for a connection to be established, Trent sat back in her seat and was instantly overwhelmed by the erotic images she'd just played out in reality in that chair.

"Boys, I am bringing a healthy frustration to the field tonight," Trent said before she was linked in with other players. "I'm going to frag each and every single one of you that dares to get in my way!"

CHAPTER SIXTEEN

Juliet resisted the urge to slam the receiver down in a fit of exasperation. Instead, she purposely laid the phone back gently in its cradle and pushed away from her desk. She dragged her hand through her hair as she stared out of the one window her office afforded. The surrounding buildings were darkened. Only their security lighting was on in selected windows. Juliet didn't bother to look at her watch. She didn't want to know what time it was. The night sky was dark, dawn still hours away. *What the hell am I doing here*, she wondered, catching the reflection of her computer in the window, its flashing denoting the frantic e-mails coming to her thick and fast. She looked out blindly into the night. *I could be with Trent, right this minute, touching her, holding her, feeling her inside me again.* Heat burned low in Juliet's belly, and she tugged at her work blouse, loosening the collar in the hope of cooling herself down. She jumped when someone knocked on her door. Carnie Warner, one of the managers, stuck her head in, then stepped inside furtively, closing the door behind her and leaning against it as if barring against intruders.

"How bad is this, Juliet?" she asked.

"As bad as it can be with the bankruptcy of one business setting off others to topple like dominos after it."

"We're safe though, aren't we?"

Juliet fought the urge to roll her eyes at Carnie's preoccupation for self-preservation. She knew this particular manager only looked out for herself, sometimes to the detriment of her staff. "For now, but who knows how far this will reach?"

"As long as it all blows over without touching my paycheck, I don't care."

Juliet was amazed by her selfish attitude. "Carnie, companies are losing money all over the world, and the people whose money is in those banks are going to be affected too. How can you not care?"

Carnie shrugged. "I don't get paid enough to care for everyone." Juliet's surprise was obviously visible because Carnie turned defensive. "Don't give me that look. I'm not like you, young and talented, being put on the fast track to head office. I'm nearer retirement than I am a promotion now," Carnie snapped. "And I'm way too old to use sleeping with the boss as a means to get higher up the corporate ladder."

Juliet bristled. "That's a path I have never chosen."

"I know that. I wasn't talking about you. You have competition, though, Juliet, and that particular female will use everything at her disposal to get your job. Stacy Atkins isn't above anything to secure that corner office they've designated for you, my dear."

Juliet dropped into her chair, suddenly tired of it all. "And what if I don't want the corner office?"

"But you're Mr. Castle's biggest and brightest star, the jewel in his crown."

The only jewel I want to be is Trent's Jule. "Well, maybe I don't want to shine in this line of work anymore."

"And instead you'll do what? Try your hand at gardening?" Carnie laughed at Juliet's face. "Do you really think you've skipped the rumor mill with that one? One comment, innocently made, can do the rounds to every floor before the last word has left your lips."

Juliet forced herself to take a deep breath, realizing more and more why she was becoming disillusioned working for such a company. *I'd much rather be out digging up a dirt patch than sitting in here dealing with Carnie. God, when did my priorities change from the good of the company first and foremost? Not to mention I could be with Trent right now, exploring all that life has to offer me with her beside me.* Not for the first time since she'd left Trent's home did she wonder what Trent was doing and hoped she was missing her half as much as she was missing Trent.

"I'm looking forward to your presentation." Carnie was oblivious to Juliet's distraction. "Though I hear Stacy is chomping at the bit to get some of her ideas put forth."

Juliet eyed an e-mail that came up on her screen and grimaced at the news of another company making its announcement of failure. "Then I suggest she goes through the proper channels." Dismissing Carnie from her thoughts, Juliet scanned her screen.

"Problems?" Carnie asked.

"You might want to go make sure your corner office is still there," Juliet said, reading the rest of the mail she'd received in just five minutes and feeling queasy at the sinking feeling settling in her gut. "Our flagship investor has just started to sink." It was with little satisfaction that Juliet watched Carnie scurry back to her own office. She grimaced as her phone started ringing again.

I should have stayed with Trent. I need her more than I need any of this. Putting that realization on hold, she picked up the phone, readying herself for whatever bad news was on the other end this time.

❖

Juliet tried to open the front door as quietly as possible, but caught sight of Monica already at the breakfast table. Monica looked up at her entrance.

"Get you, just rolling in at breakfast time." She stopped her teasing when she registered Juliet's clothing. "You changed into your work clothes?" Monica gave a frown. "Just how kinky *is* Trent?"

"Would you believe I got called into work last night?" Juliet said, tossing her briefcase on a chair and reaching over to snag a piece of Monica's toast.

"What was so bad they needed you in at midnight on a Saturday?"

"Active Banking declared bankruptcy, and the resulting crash was felt around the world. I've been on the phone most of the night to various countries trying to ensure them that their money is safe and we will weather this storm." Juliet sat with a weary thump at the table.

"And the real truth is?" Monica reached for another cup and poured Juliet some tea.

"That there'll be redundancies in every building from Tokyo to Germany, and here at home."

"I told you that banking was a foolish endeavor. You need to get out among the flowers, pour your energy into growing things. Not watching your fat cats grow fatter on other people's money only for them to lose it all because of their greed."

Juliet sipped her drink gratefully. "I know. I hear you. And once this damn presentation is done I can decide more clearly what I need to do. I just need this done and dusted. I've worked on it too long now to let it go. People are counting on me." She took another piece of toast from Monica's plate. "And, if I do say so myself, I think I have a damn good proposal to offer."

Monica was quiet for a moment, then changed the subject. "So how did your night go before you were called hastily away? Did you see Trent's sanctum of sanctums?"

Juliet blinked at her. "I beg your pardon?"

"My man Elton got the word from a very reliable source. Trent told him herself she was going to show you something special."

Juliet shrugged. "She might have," she said mysteriously.

Leaning over the table, Monica gave her a look. "You know that Elton thinks Trent showing you her game room is like her proposing marriage to you, don't you?"

Juliet choked on her toast and was grateful for Monica's hand pounding on her back. "I'm sure it's not that serious," she gasped, though that didn't stop her from yearning for it to be true.

"Come on, think about it. You've been let into the most private place of the Baydale Reapers' most renowned of players. I'm led to believe that room is everything from the Lost Ark of the Covenant to the bloody wardrobe that houses Narnia!"

Juliet was highly amused at Monica's fanciful ideas. "It's a game room. It has in it what you'd expect to find in there." She would never be able to explain how every picture on the wall or the small figures dotted around the room all were a piece to Trent's whole.

"But it's Trent's game room and no one is allowed in. That much I could glean from Elton's cryptic comments that I tortured out of him with a flash of a well-placed tattoo."

"You need to stop using your butt art in leverage with him. It will lose its power all too quickly once the novelty has worn off." She got up from the table and stretched. "Damn, I can't believe I have to sleep part of my Sunday away because they kept me fielding calls all night from major clients." Juliet picked up her cup. "This is not how I envisioned spending my Sunday after such a great party."

"It was fun, wasn't it? The gamer geeks sure know how to throw a decent shindig." Monica leaned back in her chair to regard Juliet steadily. "Although you two left early enough that you missed Rick and Elton's renditions of classic tunes sung with explicit lyrics."

"Damn, there's actually a part of me that wishes I'd seen that. Rick seems so quiet."

"And my Elton isn't? And what about the other part of you that skipped out on us with her handsome woman in tow?"

Juliet recalled how marvelous her evening had been up until the interruption of business had dashed her plans. "The other part of me had more fun than I could ever have dreamed of."

"Oh my God! You slept with Trent! Tell me you slept with her."

"No, I didn't." She pulled out her cell phone and turned it off deliberately. "This stupid thing spoiled any plans I might have had about seducing her."

"Oh, Juliet. I'm sorry."

The saucy look Juliet tossed her was answer enough. "I didn't *sleep* with her. That isn't to say things didn't get *very* heated before banking reared its ugly head." Monica rushed after her as she headed to her bedroom.

"How was it? Is she as good as she looks? Is she too butch to touch?" The questions tumbled from Monica's lips. "Details please, enquiring minds need to know."

Juliet shed her work clothes and slipped into her robe, aware that Monica was in the room with her but had seen it all before. Living with someone who designed her own clothes and always needed a model to "just try this on" left no room for modesty in the apartment. Juliet sat on the edge of her bed and regarded Monica fondly.

"Do I always tell you what my women have been like?"

"No, because most of them didn't make your eyes sparkle like this one does, so I'm curious as hell. Even I have to agree she's gorgeous in that handsome studly way only a butch girl can be. So spill!"

"It was mind-blowingly awesome. She is a fantastic lover, gentle, passionate, and so sexy she makes my chest ache. And she's not too butch to be touched by me." Juliet paused. "But we got interrupted before I could have my way with her."

Leaning against the door, Monica just stared at her.

"What?"

"I've never seen you so…excited over someone. If I didn't know better, I'd say you were head over heels in lo—"

Juliet raised a finger in warning. "Don't you dare tease Trent about this today, and no telling Elton either. Trent's not used to how you can be." She wagged a finger at Monica's playful wounded gasp. "I mean it. You only see the side she shows everyone else. I've seen the other side, Monica, and she's so sweet you'd move heaven and Earth to make sure nothing hurt her."

Monica was silent for a moment. "You know, Elton said pretty much the same thing to me when he was asking me last night if I thought you would deliberately hurt Trent. What do you think happened to her to make everyone so damn protective of one who looks like she could take on the world single-handed?"

"I don't honestly know. All I know is I want to be with her more than anyone I've ever known."

"That's some statement from you."

"They're the truest words from my lips today."

"I've got to go carry on my work at her house. You going to come by later?"

"I'd like to."

"I won't expect you to work." Monica pushed away from the door frame. "But don't think I'll always let you off so light when you work for me, young lady."

Juliet flopped back on her bed with a groan. "I'll bear it in mind, boss." She could hear Monica call out, "And don't you forget it," as she disappeared into the living room.

❖

Trent met Monica at the back gate and helped her carry stuff in from the car.

"You're up early," Monica said as she handed her a bucket to carry.

"Couldn't sleep," Trent replied.

Monica favored Trent with a sideways glance. "Juliet's disappointed she couldn't work here today."

"She got home safely, then?" Trent was desperate to hear Juliet was okay. Her feigned nonchalance didn't fool Monica one bit.

"Yeah, she came walking in at seven this morning, not in the least bit happy she spent the night at the office."

Trent nodded absently. "I guess work comes first."

"She'd rather have been here with you. I know that for a fact."

Trent's heart lifted at Monica's sincere words.

"They've promised her a day off this week for going above and beyond the call of duty for them."

"I've got Tuesday off."

"Really? I'll be sure to mention that to her. I have that day off too this week. Maybe we can all go and pick out some foliage for this naked yard of yours to start bringing it back to life."

"You want me to pick flowers?"

"You must have some idea what you'd like to see growing in your backyard?"

Trent shrugged. "I hadn't really thought about it. I just expected you to bring something bright and leafy in and plant it everywhere."

Monica's condescending stare almost made Trent shrink under its weight.

"You really are clueless, aren't you?"

Trent hoped to deflect some of Monica's growing irritation. "It's just not my area of expertise like it is yours."

Waving an imperialistic finger before Trent's face, Monica said, "Don't give me that look. It may work on Juliet, but it won't work on me." She turned away, only to look back over her shoulder at Trent. "You know exactly the look I mean, the one where you could give that damn cat from *Shrek* a run for his money."

Trent laughed at being compared to Puss in Boots, who used his wide-eyed innocent look as a weapon.

"Now that's a sound I like to hear." Elton swung open the gate and made a beeline for Trent. He hugged her swiftly, then set after Monica, his hug for her lingering, and their good-morning kiss would have lasted longer had Trent not started whistling.

"Where's your lady, Trent? I expected her to be here, you know, still in those tight shorts of hers." Elton's breath whooshed out of his lungs at the weight of the heavy bag Monica pushed into his arms.

"Juliet's not here. She got called into work last night." She pushed him in the direction she needed him to go.

Elton followed her lead, but his eyes never left Trent's face. "Bummer, dude," he said.

Trent agreed. "Totally."

As soon as Elton had deposited the bag Monica shooed him away. "Go play with your friend. You're standing in the way of my creativity." She kissed him on his cheek, then pushed him toward the slabs where Trent stood.

Trent eyed Elton warily. She knew he couldn't keep quiet for long.

"So did you show her your game room?" he whispered comically from the side of his mouth.

"Yes."

"And?"

Trent shrugged. "And it wasn't as big a deal as I thought it would be. She was really cool about it."

Elton edged closer to her. "Cool as in frosty?"

"No, cool as in she didn't judge or make sarcastic comments." Trent stared at her boots for a minute, replaying the night in her mind. "She was wonderful, Elt."

"That's good, right?"

"That's better than good."

The inflection in her tone must have given something away because Elton's eyes narrowed and he looked her over. "You're mighty mellow this morning." His eyes widened and his jaw dropped. "You got laid last night!"

Trent cringed at his words. She tugged sharply at his beard, making his head snap forward. "Will you hush? No, I did not get laid." *Not exactly.*

Elton rescued his facial hair from Trent's grasp and rubbed at his chin. "Did *she*?" he asked slyly and Trent turned red. "Oh my God, you did it. You fuc—" Elton didn't get any further because Trent slapped her hand over his mouth to shut him up.

"Will you keep your voice down?" She tossed a swift look in Monica's direction in case she could hear Elton's crude remarks. Elton mumbled something from behind Trent's hand, and with a resigned sigh she removed it.

"You had sex with the fair Juliet," he said excitedly. "Way to go, Trent!"

Trent understood his excitement and pleasure for her. It had been a *long* time. "Yes, and then she left."

Elton made a show of gathering up his beard. "A first for you. You're usually out of there before the last 'Oh, Trent' has been uttered." He mimicked a breathy female voice calling her name and even Trent had to grin despite herself.

"Stop that," she grumbled weakly, recognizing the truth in his teasing.

"Fuck and flee, that was usually your modus operandi," Elton said.

Trent shivered as she remembered Juliet coming in her lap. "Well, this time I had no intention of going anywhere. Instead, she did."

Elton bent his knees a little to rest his head on her shoulder in commiseration. "So, even though you didn't get to spend longer than you usually would with a woman, how was it for you?"

Trent closed her eyes and let the memory loose. "As damn near perfect as I could ever have imagined." The burning need to be with Juliet again suffused her soul.

"Sweet," was Elton's simple reply. "How about I take you for a drink while Monica works her magic on the soil? That way we won't make her nervous with our whispering and you can give me more details."

"Details?" Suspicious, Trent eyed Elton's innocent face.

"Yes, Trent dear, details." He cupped his hands against his chest and waggled his eyebrows suggestively.

"I am not divulging anything concerning vital statistics with you, you letch!"

"Come on, you know you're dying to share." Elton danced back from Trent's glare. "You've seen them up close and personal by now, I'm sure. Just how big are—"

Trent took a threatening step forward and hissed at him under her breath. "If you dare mention Juliet's breasts one more time in my earshot, it won't be just your beard I'll make a grab for."

Elton winced and backed off, hands held up in surrender. "Never could get you to share anything too intimate."

"And I'm not going to start now either, so quit asking."

"This one's special, eh?" Elton asked softly, switching from friend to his big-brother persona in an instant.

"I think so," Trent replied then added with more conviction, "No, I know so."

Slapping her on the shoulder, Elton cheered softly. "Glad to hear it. You can buy the first round, because I never thought I'd see the day you'd find someone to settle down with."

"Who said I was ready to settle down?"

"Trent, you're so damn sweet on this woman already. Tell me you haven't thought of forever."

Trent stayed silent so long that Elton hugged her to him. "Thought so," he said. "About time too. She'll be lucky to have you."

"She hasn't had me yet," Trent muttered into Elton's chest.

"Something tells me that won't be long in coming. No pun intended."

Trent prodded him lightly in his side and stepped back, struggling to hold back a smile at his blatant amusement at his own joke.

"What is he laughing at?" Monica asked, stopping her work and looking over at them both suspiciously.

Trent sighed and shook her head at Elton who was now wiping at his eyes.

"Same as usual, *me*."

CHAPTER SEVENTEEN

Trent hid herself away for the rest of the afternoon, leaving Monica working in the yard alone and in peace. Elton had long since wandered home after extracting a promise to see Monica later. Trent sat playing a game offline when her cell rang. Eyes still fixed on the screen, Trent didn't bother to look at the caller ID when she answered it.

"What are you doing that's keeping you from hearing me knock at your back door?"

"Juliet?" Trent paused the game, put down her controller, and rushed down the stairs. She flung open the back door and was met by the most beautiful smile. Juliet made a show of closing her cell phone.

"Hey you." Juliet reached up for a kiss.

Trent groaned into her mouth, allowing Juliet's tongue in to explore, holding on to her tight because she couldn't ever get close enough.

"Don't mind me preparing the soil all by myself over here while you two get down and dirty."

Trent ignored Monica's teasing voice, her attention fixed solely on Juliet and how much she wanted to do more than just kiss her. "Do you have to go back into work this weekend?" She checked her watch. It was well after four p.m.

"No, thank goodness. I had more than enough with last night bleeding into the morning." She cradled Trent's face gently. "Sorry I didn't get to call you like I promised. Work was hectic, and by the time I got home it was way too early to wake you just so I could hear your voice."

"I wouldn't have minded." Trent pressed a kiss into Juliet's palm.

"You're here now." She was delighted to see her. Trent hadn't expected to after the night before. "Are you here to help Monica?"

Juliet spared a look over her shoulder. "No, actually I'm here to see if I can take you out to pick up some food and then take you to my place for a change."

"You're inviting me back to your place?"

"You've let me into your home, now let me return the favor." Juliet turned to seek out Monica. "Hey, Monica, are you still seeing Elton tonight?"

"Straight after I've finished up here, so the apartment is all yours."

Juliet turned back to Trent. "I haven't been up long and I'm starving. For food," she added, depositing a swift kiss on Trent's curved lips. "And I want your company because last night ended all too abruptly."

Trent tugged her inside. "Come sit a moment while I go save my game, then we can go wherever you want."

"How does Nando's sound? I'm in the mood for some peri peri chicken."

Trent nodded and her stomach grumbled at the promise of food. "Sounds good to me. I only had a sandwich at lunchtime." She guided Juliet to a chair, kissed her, and then raced back upstairs to close her console down and switch everything off. Once back in the kitchen, Trent slipped on her Nikes and reached for her wallet. She stuffed it into her jeans pocket. "I just need to set the house alarm and we're good to go."

Juliet waited at the back door while Trent keyed in the combination and the house beeped out its signal that the alarm was being armed. Trent locked the back door behind her and then followed Juliet as she shared a few words with Monica. She didn't listen in to what they were saying. Instead Trent marveled at the transformation that Monica had worked from the wreck of her yard.

"What are you thinking?" Juliet nudged Trent gently, both women watching Trent's preoccupation.

"I can see my neighbor's house at the bottom of the yard. I can't remember seeing that before. And I have a shed, and there's dirt leveled out instead of tangled bushes, and…" Trent's excitement was tangible. "I'm getting a yard!"

Monica snorted. "You'd better still be excited Tuesday when we take you to every nursery in Baydale."

Juliet linked her arm through Trent's. "I'm going to ask for Tuesday off too. Someone has to keep you two in check."

"She won't know an alchemilla from a zantedeschia," Monica said, returning to her work.

Trent frowned. "She just made those up, didn't she?" she said to Juliet.

"No, one's a lady's mantle and the other is an arum lily."

Trent was impressed. "I guess you're going to be well-versed in your new job when you cut ties with the banking fraternity."

Juliet led Trent to her car. "You can't help but get drawn in when Monica starts talking plants. And believe me, the past few months, it's been our main topic of discussion." Their footsteps crunched on the gravel of Trent's driveway. Juliet reached for Trent's hand. "I missed you today. But I could feel you everywhere on my body, like you'd burned a trail across my skin."

"Tell me about it."

Once settled in the car, Juliet turned in her seat. "So did you put your extensive collection of DVDs to good use last night once I'd gone?"

Trent's face burned at the implication. "No, I didn't. I used my vast frustration to beat three clans who never knew what the hell hit them when I stepped online."

Juliet stared at her for a long moment. "You played games instead?"

Trent couldn't turn away. "I didn't want to waste what you'd made me feel by watching someone else have sex and come alone. If you weren't there to touch me, then the idea of jerking myself off just wasn't going to satisfy me. If you're going to set my soul on fire, I want you and only you to be the one to put it out."

Juliet's face softened. "I couldn't stay away from you today. I should be spending all my free time I have on my proposal; my deadline is approaching. I just couldn't keep away. I needed to see you. Especially after last night."

"I'm glad you did. I missed you too today."

With a heartfelt sigh, Juliet said softly, "So much for no strings."

Trent could only look at her, marveling at how beautiful Juliet was bathed in the light from the afternoon sun. She'd never experienced such yearning for a woman, and her growing need was even more unsettling. But as Juliet smiled Trent's heart tripped over a beat. *I am so lost and I really don't care anymore. She's kind, and I've never had that before in my life, not from a lover. She could kill me with kindness and I'd probably be a willing victim.*

"You are so beautiful," Trent said.

"And you are such a sweetheart." Juliet started up her car, her eyes sparkling at Trent's compliment.

"I say what I see, and I see the most beautiful woman I have ever laid eyes on sitting beside me. And then I see, in my mind's eye, how you were last night naked in my arms, and you make me ache so damn much to feel you like that again." Trent took a deep breath and blew it out shakily. "This is all new to me."

Juliet's eyes shifted from the road. "But it feels good, doesn't it?"

"Very good," she said, her eyes closing as she replayed what she had done to Juliet the night before. "So good and it feels so right."

"Why has no one snatched you up before now?" Juliet said, laying her hand on Trent's thigh as they waited at a traffic light.

"I didn't want them to." With the words out of her mouth, Trent finally realized the truth in them. She caught sight of the restaurant and was silent while Juliet pulled into the parking lot and found a free space. As Juliet turned off the engine, Trent slipped out of her seat belt and reached out for her. "I didn't want anyone. I was perfectly content being alone. And then I met you, and you turned my safe little world upside down and inside out."

"I didn't mean to," Juliet said softly.

"I know, but I'm getting to like the view from this new perspective." Trent got out of the car, then walked around to open Juliet's door gallantly. "How about we go get takeout, then you can show me where you and Monica live when you're not hanging out in my yard digging through to China?" She took Juliet's hand. "And maybe you can divulge how bad this banking situation really is and advise me on whether I should go remove all my savings before the banks go belly up."

Juliet put on her business face. "I cannot divulge company policy, but I think I can safely recommend that you keep your money in the banking institutions and not hidden instead under your mattress for safekeeping." She paused. "At least for now."

Trent was impressed by Juliet's smart reply. "Well, if we're not going to talk business, then we have to talk personal. You know, get to know each other by trading information." Trent was pleased to note Juliet's intrigued look.

"Information?"

Holding open the door to the restaurant for Juliet to pass through,

Trent continued. "Twenty questions, everything from favorite color to favorite sexual position." She caught the startled look on the maitre d's face as he stood waiting to direct them to a table. She pretended he hadn't overheard her last comment and gestured that they were headed to the counter for takeaway. He nodded swiftly and turned back to the other customers baying for his attention.

"He heard what you said."

Nodding, Trent just headed for the counter. "Yes, and think how disappointed he is that we're not taking a table so he could be ever so attentive to our needs in the hope of hearing you tell me how you like your loving best."

Juliet leaned in close to Trent's side to whisper. "But I haven't tried everything with you yet, so I can't possibly comment until then."

Trent feared she'd swallow her own tongue at the look Juliet flashed her before nonchalantly giving her order to the girl behind the counter. Trent managed to name something off the menu, but her head was spinning with the possibilities Juliet had hinted at. *Can I finally let go with this woman? Will she be able to push through the defenses I've built up over the years? Can I let her take the control that I so desperately hold on to?*

"You look lost in thought."

Juliet's soft voice brought Trent back to the restaurant. "Just weighing the possibilities life is offering me."

"You're having an epiphany in the middle of Nando's?"

"It's a today's special, comes with a side order of fries."

"I love your sense of humor."

"Glad to hear it." *Because I'm falling in love with you*, Trent realized as she looked at Juliet's face alight with laughter. *Completely head over heels, crazy out of my mind over you, and I wouldn't change this feeling for the world, no matter how much it terrifies me.*

❖

Trent washed down her last mouthful of chicken with her beer and sat back contentedly. Her eyes traveled around the cozy living room Juliet and Monica shared.

"I expected more coffins," she said, noticing that there weren't many Goth knickknacks around the living space.

"Monica saves that for her bedroom and her clothing," Juliet said as she pushed aside her own plate.

"She does make amazing dresses. Have you reached any further decisions about joining Monica in the landscaping business?"

"I've been checking into the courses and qualifications that I'd need. And I've already started to design the spreadsheets Monica will need for keeping a check on income and expenditures. We've been working out the fine print, but I think it's safe to say I'd be balancing the books so that every penny is accounted for. If I make the move I'd be giving up too much for this to be a *hobby* job."

"What happens next?"

"I need to see this presentation through. I've invested too much on it to just leave it. But I'm feeling the need to leave. I'm getting bored and frankly frustrated by all the politics that go along with rising through the ranks. I think I've done all I can do in this line of work that I'm capable of achieving or want to achieve, except maybe become a big boss in the city, and I really don't want the responsibility that comes with that position." Juliet stretched, affording Trent the sight of a strip of midriff that made Trent's hands itch with the need to reach out and explore.

"So." Trent was glad her voice didn't sound as strained as it felt as she dragged her eyes away from the tantalizing skin. "Everything hinges on your presentation being done, and then you can start getting your hands dirty in a new job."

"It's a big step I'm thinking of taking. For a start it will be a huge drop in pay, but I need the change and the new challenge."

Trent raised her beer bottle and toasted her. "To change and challenges."

Juliet leaned back in her seat beside Trent, wriggling to get more comfortable. "You mentioned twenty questions, my dear Trent. How intimate can these questions be?"

Trent swallowed hard at the husky timbre of Juliet's voice. "How intimate do you want them to be?"

Juliet's hand roamed down Trent's arm, raising the hair there, making Trent twitch. "I've already been naked writhing in your lap. I'd say that was pretty darn intimate already."

"I remember every single fantastic second of it." Trent's body burned as that night replayed itself in her mind's eye. Juliet bit her lip as if holding back her questions. "You can ask me anything."

"I have just three questions, and I'm not sure if you're ready to share the answers with me."

Trent frowned at the seriousness of Juliet's tone. Her chest started to tighten as an all-too-familiar fear started to steal away her breath. She had a feeling she knew what was coming. Trent surrendered. "Ask."

"What happened to your family? What's the real reason for all the security for your game room and home, and what's the story behind your tattoo?" At this last question, Juliet ran her fingers along the skin of Trent's arm, touching the artwork there.

Trent remained silent for a little too long as she tried to breathe around the sudden constriction in her chest. She was immediately light-headed and queasy. She was startled when Juliet put her hand to her face and kissed her softly on the forehead. "If you can't tell me now, I understand, but I hope one day you can. I want to know you, Trent, all of you, and I can't help but think that your being alone is a big part of you that you don't reveal." She traced the symbols on Trent's arm again. "But it's etched in you. This tattoo is more than just a favorite game. I've seen the symbols on your clothes, seen the game prominently placed in your room. There's obviously more meaning to it." Juliet stilled her touch. "Or am I just reading too much into it all?"

"The answers to your questions are all one and the same." Trent ran her fingers over the bold tattoo on her arm. "This game was the only thing I managed to escape with," she said finally. "Trust you not to just ask my favorite flavor of ice cream." She held up a hand to silence Juliet's apology then took a deep breath. "Years ago, my father smashed all my games and my console as punishment for my disappointing him. The Space Invaders cartridge was the only thing left intact when he had finished. Everything else was smashed beyond salvage."

Juliet gasped. "What had you done to warrant such a thing?"

Carefully placing her beer bottle down before her tightening grip smashed it, Trent stalled in replying. Did she really want Juliet to know what kind of life she'd had? She looked into Juliet's compassionate eyes and saw her answer.

"You don't have to tell me," Juliet said, stroking Trent's hand with her own.

"My father walked in on me and my girlfriend Corrine when I was fifteen years old," Trent said in one breath, wanting the words out.

"He didn't know you were gay."

"No, but he got a swift introduction due to the fact that Corrine had her head between my legs and was bringing me to what would have been an earth-shattering climax just as he walked into my bedroom." Juliet whispered a soft *Oh God*. Trent shook her head. "No, God *wasn't* there that day. My father was a good, God-fearing man. I was brought up to believe everything was a sin, and in my family, *I* was the most sinful."

"Oh, Trent."

Trent laughed without humor. "Even my name was a sign of his disappointment in me. He'd fathered two daughters already, good girls, pious and pretty. On the third try I was to be the son he dreamed of. Instead, I came into the world and my mother began to bleed so badly from the birth that they had to perform a hysterectomy. His dream for a son died as I lived. So he forced my mother to give me the name he'd wanted for a boy."

"What a bastard. But, truthfully, the name suits you."

"I grew into it." Closing her eyes, she unwittingly relived the anger visited upon her during her childhood. "You can guess the rest. I know not every family is perfect. Mine was no different to what other kids live through. When I met Elton, though, it was like he came from a totally different world. His family was *nothing* like mine."

Juliet leaned closer to Trent. "I'm glad you found him."

"He saved me, in so many ways. He was the one who explained to me that the feelings I had for other girls meant that I was gay. 'Homosexuality' was not a word used in our house in polite conversation. I was terrified. I knew my dad would kill me if he ever found out. I was pretty close to the truth on that outcome. I remember telling Elton that God would despise me for what I was. He just said, 'Then I think you need to find a new God who practices what his son preached—love for *all*.'" Trent could still hear the young Elton's voice from so many years past. A tear slipped from Trent's eye. She brushed it away swiftly, embarrassed by it.

"So I hid it from my family like so many other things." Trent paused for a moment, gathering her thoughts. "Elton had a console and we would play on it for hours at his house. I begged my dad for one and he finally agreed, after a comment about the devil making use for idle hands. I had to work for it, but it was a labor of love when I was able to go buy one. I'd play when everyone else was asleep. I loved the night hours where I got to be left alone, no preaching, no beatings for something I had done, just me and the games."

She caught Juliet's eye. "My being gay was going to be just another part of the long list of failings I had where my dad was concerned. I turned out to be more like the son he'd wanted than he would ever have imagined. I met Corrine at school and we'd steal kisses in the playground. Sometimes she'd take me to her home, and she was my first in everything. Until I made the stupid mistake of bringing her to my home when I thought everyone would be out." Trent fell silent as the cold press of fear slipped through her. "I've never witnessed so much hatred from a man who claimed to follow a God of love. I dimly remember hearing the front door close, but I was pretty preoccupied at the time, then Dad called my name out as he barged into my room and found us on the bed." Trent shuddered as the memories poured back. "I was trying to get my trousers pulled back up and Corrine was hastily wiping her face on her school shirt. God, we must have been a sight to behold. Corrine grabbed her clothes up and got out fast, but she wasn't the one Dad was furious at. I got the full force of his righteous indignation." She unconsciously rubbed at the scar in her hairline. "He was a big man and usually circumspect as to what punishments were visible. This time he just laid into me, and I think he must have knocked me off the bed because I remember blacking out for just a moment before coming to and finding him smashing my room to pieces. My console was thrown to the floor and stomped on. He did the same with my games, ripped the boxes apart and smashed the cartridges under his heel. All the time he was telling me he'd have me *cleansed* of my sinful soul. I knew what that meant. I'd learnt enough from the congregation he'd drag me to that people got *counseled* from their sinful paths. I knew the whispers. You toed the line or were physically punished. My dad would have me be humiliated rather than bring shame on the family and him. He'd make sure I saw the error of my ways, and if he had to use the strong arm of his church, then so be it." Trent smiled a little and let out a breathy laugh. "Fuck, it all sounds so melodramatic!"

Juliet hugged her tightly. "No, it sounds terrifying. I can't begin to imagine what you went through."

"Once he'd mentioned the council of elders, I knew I had to run. Screaming at me that I had sinned for the last time, Dad locked me in my room and went back to work. Wouldn't it just figure that the day I choose to take my girlfriend home for a quickie was the day he passed by on his lunch break and needed to pick up some papers he'd left that morning?" She shook her head. "I immediately scrambled into some clothing, stuffed what other clothes I could grab into my school bag, and grabbed anything else that wasn't wrecked. Unbeknown to my dad, I had a bank book hidden under the floorboards. My uncle Stan had given it to me, told me to hide it and never mention it to my family. 'You're going to need to be away from them one day,' he'd told me. 'I'm making sure you'll have the means to do so.' I found out he'd had a savings account set up for me. He never gave a penny to my sisters and he left me everything when he died. I swear he knew what was going to happen and gave me a way to never have to ask them for anything again. His doing that was a bone of contention between me and my sisters once the will was read, but I didn't care."

"He sounds like a sweet man."

"He was the best, and thanks to him I had a very handsome deposit for my house when I bought it and a little to set aside for emergencies." Trent took comfort from the feel of Juliet holding her close and was able to continue. "I got my bank book, then spotted a box half-hidden under my bed. The one game Dad had missed destroying. That in hand, I opened my bedroom window and climbed out. I hurt my shoulder jumping to the ground, but I just ran as fast as I could. I must have looked a right sight. My face was covered in blood and my eye was closing up, but somehow I got to Elton's house. Mama Simons took one look at me and gathered me inside. She cleaned me up, took me in, and made sure I never had to see my family again."

"What about your mother? Didn't she have anything to say?"

"She'd never stood up for me a day in her life. She wasn't about to start now over something as controversial as me being gay. My sisters turned their backs too. It would be safe to say I never saw eye to eye with my siblings." Trent laid her cheek on Juliet's head. "I had one last conversation with my dad over the phone where he informed me that I had lost all rights to ever having a family, seeing as I had chosen a vile and disgusting road to travel. He told me he'd known all along that I would bring shame to his name and that he was disowning me."

"You got a better family given to you, one that truly cares for you."

"I got a great adopted family of Simonses that keeps growing with nieces and nephews for me to love. But deep down I know they're not truly *mine*."

"Family comes in all manner of ways, Trent, adopted or otherwise. You make your own family with the people you love and who love you." Juliet leaned up to kiss her gently. "No wonder you have such a marvelous game room that you fight to keep safe."

"Those games kept me sane while I lived under my father's roof. With them I was able to escape the world around me and just be *in* the game. It was safer in there."

"I understand." Juliet touched the tattoo again. "This is a badge of survival, isn't it? A lasting reminder that some things remain untouched no matter what hell they have come through."

Trent stared at Juliet in amazement. *She understands.* "I wasn't as untouched, though." *I lost everything that day, my family, even my girlfriend. Corrine was never the same. She still cornered me for sex, but it was in secret places. Quick and uncaring fucks that she felt I owed her. It became the only way I thought I could be with women. Until you. And you, Juliet, scare me like no one else ever has. You make me feel and you make me want to be much more. I don't know if I can give you what you deserve.*

"For all you went through, it made you the person you are today, and that is someone who is kind and gentle to little lost kids. Someone who demands fair play and promotes fun in everything she does. Someone who is fierce and loyal to her friends and their family. Your own family had no idea what a marvelous woman they had in their midst. Their loss was everyone else's gain."

Trent shrugged uncomfortably. "Yeah, well." She comforted herself in the steady rhythm of stroking Juliet's hair. It calmed her after leaving herself so open and vulnerable. She sighed when Juliet snuggled into her arms and held her tight. "No one outside of Elton's family knows what happened to me."

"No one will ever hear it from my lips," Juliet said, then asked softly, "Do you want to stay here tonight?"

Trent thought about the invitation for a moment, but her feelings were too raw. "I think I'd rather go home if that's okay." Juliet shifted as if to get up, but Trent held on to her tightly. "But can we just stay like this for a while? I don't want to go home yet. I just want to stay here with you."

Juliet moved so that Trent's head was against her chest. The hold made Trent feel protected and safe. "For as long as you want, Trent."

I'd like forever. If I'm worthy of it ... with you?

CHAPTER EIGHTEEN

Trent was busy unpacking the new delivery of boxes when Elton joined her in the stockroom. Without a word, he began helping her.

"Aren't you supposed to be on the shop floor?" Trent peered at him suspiciously.

"I just wanted to see how you were. You've been rather quiet since you came in."

"I didn't realize my being less than gregarious on a Monday morning was a cause for concern." Trent leaned back against the shelves she'd been putting games on and waited for Elton to explain.

"Are you still having those nightmares of yours?" he asked gently.

"No, surprisingly enough I haven't. And I expected to battle that particular demon last night after I had regaled Juliet with the story of my childhood."

Elton's mouth fell open almost comically. "You told Juliet?"

"She asked about my family and I filled her in."

"Wow," Elton muttered. "You've never told anyone before."

Trent shrugged. "I think it's safe to say Juliet is different." *And she makes me feel different too, safe enough to talk about the things that no one has known about me in years.*

"If she gets you to talk, the woman is a certified miracle worker."

Trent waved off his awe and turned her attention back to her work. She dug into one box and let out a happy yelp. She held aloft a game case like she'd found the Holy Grail. "It's about time this was delivered. Dina said she'd sneak me a few copies before release date."

Elton sighed. "You reveal your deepest, darkest secret to someone and now it's 'oh look, a new game'?"

Trent held out the case to him. "Not just any game, it's *this* one." Her excitement was justified when Elton's eyes lit up too.

"Well, that's enough about you and your revelations. This *really* is more important!" Elton hugged the game to his chest, but his eyes belied his dismissive words. Trent knew he'd find her again later to make sure she was all right. For now, it was time to forget the past again. "I'd forgotten this was out this week." He began reading the back cover.

"You've been too busy making nice with Ms. Monica. Love has clouded your mind to the important things in life."

Elton snorted and pushed open the stockroom door. "Reapers! The call to duty has been sounded!"

Zoe and Rick dropped what they were doing and rushed to the open door. Zoe danced on the spot while Rick tried unsuccessfully to wrestle the game from Elton's hold.

"Nah ah ah," Elton said. "It's not supposed to be available until Friday, remember? What's it worth to you for me to allow you to even"—he dangled the case before Rick's face—"*touch* it?"

Trent punched Elton's arm gently. "Stop teasing the children. Let him have it."

"Oh, come on," Rick grumbled finally managing to get the game off Elton. "We need to practice this before we take our clan online." He shared the game with Zoe. They both pored over it, oohing and ahhing.

"When we close up tonight, have your money ready. Dina sent enough for the team." Trent smiled at the excited squeal Zoe let loose.

"Trent, you know the company policy about selling games before release." Elton's official company-line tone was negated by the fact he was digging into his wallet to check how much cash he had. "We'll send Dina her favorite chocolates again. She's a good girl and we need to keep her on our side."

Trent nodded. Dina always made sure they got certain games ahead of release so they could hone their skills. "This Friday night we go online prepared. We have a few days to learn the layout of the maps before this hits the shelves. I'm not stepping into the online community's sniper sights blind." She cut Elton a glance. "And company line be damned, they're quick enough to capitalize on our wins. They get free publicity for every trophy we raise."

"Eddie and Chris can have their copies when they come on shift tomorrow." Elton smirked in Trent's direction. "And I promise to text Eddie later to give him plenty of time to ask his mom for the money."

Zoe collected Rick's money along with her own. "We're all set." She gave Trent a sweet look. "And just think how beautiful this game will play on my brand-new, bright red pleasure machine." She mimicked cocking a rifle and taking aim. "Friday night belongs to the Reapers." She leaned forward to whisper to Trent while Rick and Elton were reading to each other all the new features the game had in store. "Want to join me in some multiplayer action tonight?"

Trent nodded swiftly. "I'd love to. Just promise you won't keep me up *all* night like usual."

Laughing, Zoe patted Trent on her arm. "Don't let Juliet hear you say that! Something tells me she's mighty serious about you and wouldn't take kindly to another girl getting near you." Her amusement deepened at Trent's unashamedly delighted grin. "Geez, you two have got it bad for each other. It's a pleasure to see and a long time in coming." Zoe's attention was caught by a customer. "Dang it, Rick, we need to get back to work."

As her colleagues rushed to deal with customers, Trent marveled again at what good friends they had all become. Elton invaded her space and nudged her out of her reverie.

"You've got tomorrow off. Are you really going to spend it traipsing behind two women picking out flowers?" Elton was rubbing at his mustache, trying unsuccessfully to hide his enjoyment at her expense.

"I'm told if I want my yard to look presentable, then I need to have some input into its decoration."

"But you haven't got a bloody clue about plants."

"I'll have Monica and Juliet holding my hand throughout the whole process. I'm sure it will be painless." Trent slipped back into the storeroom and began picking out the games for her colleagues and leaving them to one side.

"I'm betting you last an hour before you start dragging your feet like an errant four-year-old."

Trent was tempted to agree with him, but she brightened at a thought. "Maybe, but if I do fall behind, just think of the view I'll be afforded." Her sly wink made Elton laugh out loud.

"I love the way your mind works. And your fair lady has a very fine ass—"

"Elton, you're needed on the floor!" Zoe called out and cut off whatever comment he was about to finish. He waved at her and turned his attention back to Trent.

"I'm glad you've got someone to talk to, Trent. It does my heart good."

Trent waved him out. "It does mine too," she told the empty room. She looked at the last few boxes. "Guess I'll just unpack these myself, then?" No one answered her, so she ripped off the tape and continued where she'd left off.

❖

The kiss Juliet greeted her with when Trent opened the front door made her wish someone else wasn't waiting on them. Juliet's hand was cupping the back of Trent's neck as she pulled her closer and kissed her so thoroughly that Trent's knees actually buckled. Trent grabbed for Juliet's shoulders to keep both her balance and to stay upright. Juliet sucked Trent's lower lip between and then nipped it gently. Trent couldn't hold back her moan as the short, sharp pain was then soothed by Juliet's teasing tongue.

Juliet's lips curved with wickedness when she finally drew back. "Good morning," she said huskily, running a finger along Trent's swollen lower lip.

Trent's tongue slipped out to taste Juliet's fingertip. She let her tongue swirl along the length of it, then sucked the teasing finger into her mouth. She was satisfied to see Juliet's eyes darken a shade and her skin release a telltale flush. Slowly, Trent pulled back and let Juliet's finger slide from her pursed lips suggestively. "Good morning to you too."

Groaning, Juliet fanned at her face with her hand. "You have no idea what you've just done to me."

"If Monica wasn't getting ready to lean on the horn, I'd pull you in here to find out."

Frustration danced across Juliet's face and Trent forced herself not to just snatch Juliet inside to make good on her words. "If you want my yard to resemble anything like what Monica has in mind, we'd better get down the driveway before I…" Trent's words ground to a halt as Juliet licked her lips suggestively.

"Before you what?"

Trent leaned in closer to whisper in Juliet's ear. "Before I run my tongue around more than just your finger." Juliet's breath caught in her chest.

"Don't make me have reason to hate flowers," Juliet said, stepping back with effort and shoving her hands into her jeans pockets. "We have to go to the nursery. We have to finish your yard. God, but I want to finish what you've just begun!"

"What *I* began? You were the one who kissed me first, if I recall." She alarmed her house and locked the door behind her. She enjoyed the swing of Juliet's hips as she walked down the driveway ahead of her. "You have such a sexy walk for a banker."

Juliet paused and reached out a hand for Trent to hold. "You have to stop saying things like that. Monica is only going to need one look at my face to know how close to the edge I am."

Trent tugged at Juliet's hand and pulled her back until their chests pressed together. "How close?" she asked softly, watching the pulse in Juliet's neck flutter.

"Close enough that I wouldn't get as far as your gaming chair this time before I'd be writhing in your lap."

Trent bit her lip so hard she was certain she'd split the skin. "Like me picking flowers isn't going to be hard enough without that picture planted firmly in my brain now." *Like it ever left*, Trent silently admitted.

Juliet just laughed and pulled Trent after her down the driveway to the car.

"And here was I thinking I needed to get out of the car and come hose you two down." Monica sat in the backseat, her arm resting out the rolled-down window, eyes hidden by oversized sunglasses. "It's too early in the morning for you two to be so damn frisky."

Trent slid into the front passenger seat and greeted Monica. "Are you ready to show me the fascinating world of all things leafy?"

Monica huffed. "I'm just astounded you actually stepped foot out of the house. I got stood up last night with the excuse of 'I have to learn the ins and outs of this new game before we kick ass on Friday night.'" She gestured to herself grandly. "If *he* could turn this down for some *game*, then I'm even more surprised you've stepped away from your console."

"Believe me, I covered most of the terrain with Zoe until the wee hours of this morning. She has never heard the concept of 'just one last tour of duty.'" Trent shifted in her seat, angling herself so she could see Juliet. "I have the incentive of being out of the house in the company of two delightful ladies. I think I can manage to put my game on hold for that."

"Elton would faint on the spot if he heard you utter those words," Monica said.

"Yeah, I'm amazed to hear them too, but contrary to what everyone thinks, I'm looking forward to today. I want to know what it is about gardening that makes you two want to be up to your elbows in dirt."

"If you get too bored, just tell us, okay?" Juliet said.

"I've never been bored in your company yet," Trent replied. "Besides, this is your chance to show me why you're considering packing in a bigwig corporate job for something more"—she searched for the right words, then tried to keep a straight face as the thought struck her—"down to earth, as it were."

Monica groaned. "Something tells me we should have left her with her console."

"I can shoot the enemy online at any time. I'm here for you to enlighten me. So enlighten away." She settled back in her seat, eyes on the road ahead. "Think of this as a 'take your girlfriend to work' kind of day." She cut a sly look at Juliet and warmed at the delight on her face.

Monica chuckled darkly. "I so should have dragged Elton along for this too."

"When you do his yard you can afford him the same treatment," Trent said, "but today is *my* day out with the girls. Start the engine, Jule. We have plants to buy."

❖

Juliet unfolded the printed sheet that she and Monica had decided over the previous night. She caught Trent's expression as she looked from their high vantage point on the steps down to the nursery gardens. Juliet leaned into her gently, enjoying just being near her. Her body absorbed Trent's natural heat and it made her own temperature rise. "What is going through that head of yours?" she asked. Trent was taking in the seemingly endless rows of trees and shrubs.

"I'm thinking that's a whole heap of green."

Monica joined then, pushing a low riding cart in front of her.

"You're going to need some foliage. I thought small conifers to put along your fencing to give you privacy but not cut out the sunlight again. If you keep them tended you can manage their height."

Trent frowned at her. "But you could do that, right? I could pay you to keep the yard looking its best?"

"Geez, you aren't ever going to have a green thumb, are you?"

"I'd rather get the right people for the job than make an ass of myself and mess up your hard work. After all, I wouldn't expect you to be able to sell the right console to someone without knowing what you were selling. Each to their own talents, I always say."

"Something tells me we'll have a steady job where your yard is concerned." Monica tossed a look at Juliet. "Think we can manage?"

Juliet caught Trent's eye. "I think I can manage just fine."

Monica clapped her hands together briskly. "Okay, enough with the talking and the undercurrent of blatant flirting. Let's go see what they have that we can use to transform Trent's yard from the Wilds of Borneo to the Garden of Eden."

Trent's eyebrows rose. "Just what am I letting myself in for? A simple yard will suffice, thank you."

Monica's answering chuckle was dark. "Oh, Trent, hasn't Elton told you that I *never* do anything simple?"

Juliet's fingers curled around Trent's hand to hold on to it tightly. "Don't fret," she said. "I'm here to keep her in line and within budget." She felt Trent relax and return the squeeze with her own hand.

"I trust you, Juliet," Trent whispered out of Monica's hearing. "I'm sure you won't lead me astray."

Juliet decided she liked the wicked glint Trent had in her eye. It made her want to drag Trent behind the tallest trees on display and kiss her senseless. With a heartfelt groan at the burst of arousal burning in her chest, Juliet ground out, "Damn flowers."

Trent swiftly leaned down and quickly pressed her lips to Juliet's in a kiss that only served to make Juliet even more sensitive to her.

"Damn flowers indeed," Trent said. Juliet was comforted to see a dazed look on Trent's face that no doubt resembled the one she herself wore. "Come on, we'd better go before I drag you behind the bushes and end up scandalizing the nursery staff."

Juliet loved how Trent's mind worked.

❖

Monica took the printed sheet from Juliet's hands and slipped the pen from her unresisting fingers. She placed a check mark against one of the rows. "Conifers chosen. Now we move on to the flowers."

Distractedly, Juliet took the list back, her attention partly on what Monica was doing beside her with the remainder fixed firmly on Trent, who was standing a few steps away typing on her cell phone. Trent had excused herself briefly after receiving a text message.

"Do you think she's enjoying herself?" Monica asked, following Juliet's line of sight. "She seems like she is."

Juliet agreed. Trent had astonished them both by asking lots of questions and not being afraid to get in amid the branches to have a closer inspection of what Monica was pointing out. "She's enjoying seeing *us* happy. I think that's where she gets her greatest pleasure from, seeing others enjoying themselves."

"You've got yourself a rare one there, Juliet."

Silently agreeing, Juliet marveled at Trent's lean form as she walked back toward them. "Everything okay?" she asked, drawing Trent close to her side again, having missed her closeness and the clean tangy scent that was uniquely Trent.

"I was just texting Zoe back."

Juliet's eyebrow quirked. "Should I be worried?" Confusion colored Trent's face before she apparently caught Juliet's meaning.

"Zoe has somehow managed to wrangle the afternoon off so she can hone her skill at our game, she was asking whether I'd be online this afternoon so we can double team." Trent looked between the two women. "I said probably yes, seeing as I would only get in the way should I stay loitering in my backyard while you work."

"You do distract my workers," Monica muttered.

"Your *worker* is a distraction all of her own," Trent replied, looking down at Juliet.

"Don't you go blaming me. I'm just learning the ropes here." She regarded Trent with a keen look. "Are you ready to pick out plants now that you've sorted out your afternoon game plan?"

Seemingly relieved at Juliet's teasing, Trent made a show of bracing her shoulders. "Lead on. Show me what I need."

Handing over the cart to Trent, Monica took the list from Juliet again. "These are the flowers that Juliet and I worked out will fit in your yard and can be left to their own devices to flourish. You need flowers that bloom long, need little attention, and can pretty much look after themselves."

"And pansies," Trent added decisively. Monica stopped in her tracks and turned to stare up at Trent.

"Pansies?"

Trent nodded. "I like pansies; they have little faces. I'd like pansies in my yard, please. If they'll fit in with what you have in mind, that is."

Juliet tried not to react as Monica's face softened at Trent's hopeful tone.

"When you ask like that, how could I possibly refuse? Winter flowering pansies will be perfect for a vibrant splash of color." She gave Trent a radiant smile and carried on with a spring in her step. "We'll make a gardener of you yet, Trent."

Although Trent didn't need the assistance, Juliet helped her push the cart behind an excited Monica. "So," she said softly, "pansies, eh?"

"I like roses too, but the little ones, not the big ones. Do you think Monica will let me have some of those too?"

Juliet's heart clenched at the undercurrent of wistfulness just discernable in Trent's question. "I think if you show her what you like she'll let you have anything at all."

Trent gazed down at her. "What are your favorite color roses?"

Juliet thought for a moment. "I like the pink ones that are tightly budded."

Nodding, Trent called ahead to Monica. "Hey, Monica, we've picked out roses too. Pink ones, if you please."

Monica turned to walk slowly backward, giving Trent her undivided attention. "You don't strike me as a pink rose kind of girl."

"I like pink just fine. We want, maybe, the Bonica Meidomonac," Trent very carefully enunciated the last word and Juliet's whole being wanted to just hold her close and hug her. "Or maybe Pretty Polly, or even Sexy Rexy." She gave Juliet a saucy wink. "That one was really easy to remember!"

Monica raised an eyebrow at Juliet. "Have you been giving her crib notes?"

"No, she knows what she wants and isn't afraid to ask for it." Juliet laid her hand over Trent's fingers as they steered the cart after Monica. She hoped that Trent would never be afraid to ask her for anything because she knew, no matter what Trent wanted, she would move heaven and Earth to bring that rare sweet smile to her face. *My lover, and I'm here with her. So much for no strings attached. You're ready to tie yourself up in red ribbon and hand yourself over to this woman.* Her face heated as her thoughts raced ahead with that particular image.

"You've gone awfully quiet and very red," Trent said out of the corner of her mouth.

"It's hot out here," Juliet said, hoping Trent would just take her word for it and not question her blush.

"Huh-uh," Trent said with an amused air. "If I didn't know better, I'd swear you were thinking naughty thoughts."

Juliet's face flamed even more at Trent's low tone. "You bring out the worst in me." Juliet was flustered; she'd never had so much trouble keeping her hands and her libido in check around a woman. *Not just any woman: Trent.*

"That's strange, because you bring out the best in me."

Juliet stopped walking and just stared. "I do?" Her heart melted as Trent flashed a look that did curious things to her chest.

"I think you do." Trent set the cart in motion again. "Come on, try to keep up or Monica will make you push the cart on your own."

Juliet dutifully hurried to Trent's side. She hooked her finger through the belt loop on Trent's jeans and enjoyed the intimacy of being able to do something so simple yet intimate. "I'm glad you came with us today."

"Me too."

Curiosity getting the better of her, Juliet asked, "How did you know the flowers' names?"

"I Googled every type of flower going last night."

"You Googled about roses?"

"I didn't want your best friend to think I was a complete moron."

Juliet slipped an arm around Trent's waist and hugged her close. "You're no moron and Monica knows that." Her breath caught in her throat when Trent looked at her. She was drawn into the rich browns and golds that could see straight to her very core.

"And what about you?" Trent asked huskily. Juliet was mesmerized by how much Trent's eyes revealed to her. For a moment she was privy to all Trent kept hidden from view: the curiously shy soul desperately seeking acceptance.

"I think you're wonderful," she replied sincerely, her body warming and melting at Trent's closeness.

"I Googled other stuff as well. Find me some *Penstemons* or *Gypsophila cerastoides* and I promise to be the font of all knowledge."

"I can't believe you researched today on the Internet." Juliet was amazed by how much trouble Trent had gone to and at her obvious exuberance to show off what she had learned.

"I just looked on it as I would a game. You learn the basics, make sure you arm yourself with the best defense, and then position yourself among the foliage and come out fighting."

"No wonder Monica gave you full control of the cart."

"Probably the best place for me, to be honest. I could only memorize so much before my brain kicked it out for fear of losing precious gamer space."

"Each to their own." Juliet was still tickled by Trent's attempts to impress.

"Exactly."

❖

The backyard of Trent's home was littered with flower trays, compost bags, and trees waiting to be planted. Juliet struggled to help Monica hold a conifer upright as they settled it into the hole prepared for it.

"Only three more trees and then you can make a start on the flowers," Monica said as Juliet swore out loud when the tree shifted and nearly knocked her over.

"I think I'm less likely to lose an eye with a pansy than I am with this stupid tree that doesn't know where the hell to stick its roots." Juliet pushed the tree back upright again. "Just plant the bloody thing, and if it leans to the left who'll care?"

"I want this yard to be just right, so no leaning conifers are allowed, if you don't mind." She tugged the tree over a little more toward her and began to cover the roots with soil and stamped down to stabilize it. Once it was finally fixed, Monica and Juliet stood back to admire their handiwork. "There you go. Perfect." Monica brushed her hands together briskly. "Now, tell me this isn't more fulfilling than you pushing a pen around all day totaling up gains and losses."

"You've convinced me that this would be a more satisfying outlet for my energy. I am really enjoying what I am doing, it's rewarding. I haven't had that feeling in my job for years. But we still need something more than just passing out cards and letting people know we're here to change their yards for the better."

"I'm working on that. I have some contacts through the nursery that are getting in touch with me this week. And Mrs. Tweedy wants to see me later, says that someone has seen what we've been doing here and is very interested in talking to me. I won't let you give up your job for nothing, Juliet. I promise you. I'll have a solid base set up for us to work from."

Juliet stretched and winced as a muscle twinged in her shoulder. "Speaking of work, I just have to put the finishing touches on my presentation this week for Monday's big reveal." Mentally she counted off the days and what she had planned for each one. "Friday evening I need to just go through it all one last time." She caught Monica's stricken face. "What?"

"You've forgotten what this Friday is, haven't you?"

"What have I forgot?"

"I've got a movie night set up for my friends. Remember?"

Damn it. "I'd totally forgotten about that."

"I'm sorry, Juliet, but it's been planned for weeks now. I've got the girls coming over for Mexican, popcorn, and *The Lost Boys* on Blu-ray."

Juliet tried to temper the frustration she could feel cloying her chest. "I'll make other arrangements," she said, waving off Monica's hesitation. She thought briefly of going to her parents' house but knew she'd never get any peace there with Kayleigh all excited to see her. Juliet had the horrible feeling she'd be staying over at work Friday night working overtime to get the presentation over with. She caught Monica's apologetic look. "Don't worry about it. I'll sort something out."

"What do you need sorting?"

Juliet jumped at Trent's deep voice as she appeared out of the rear of the house bringing them fresh sodas.

"Nothing," Juliet replied quickly, her disappointment fading at the sight of Trent. She hadn't seen her for almost two hours and she'd been feeling oddly bereft. She drank in the sight of her now.

Monica reached for a can and swiftly popped the top. "Juliet forgot that the night she needs to finish up her life's work is the same night I have Goth-fest in our apartment."

"Ah yes, your Keifer Sutherland clan meet. Elton said he'd been invited as the token male, but that he'll be with *our* clan that night instead."

Monica narrowed her eyes playfully at Trent. "Yes, he'd rather be playing some game with his buddies than participating in the delights of young vampires in high def, Blu-ray glory."

"I'm surprised you haven't all switched your allegiances to *Twilight*." Trent popped the top of a soda and handed it to Juliet.

"That's for a different evening," Monica said.

Trent turned her attention back to Juliet. "So you need a place to work?"

Juliet shrugged. "Maybe I'll just try to fit it in over the weekend," she said. She had hoped to spend quality time with Trent this weekend, without the yard being her reason to be over.

"You could come stay here with me that night. It's not like I haven't got the room."

Juliet's eyes flashed to Trent's serious face. Trent obviously read her astonishment.

"I'm busy that night too, but I'll be upstairs playing my game so you can have the whole of the downstairs at your disposal. You won't disturb me, and I won't be moving much from my seat once the fighting starts so I'd say it would be the perfect solution to your problem." Trent's eyebrow rose in hope. "And I'd get to see you, which is always an added bonus in my book."

"I wouldn't want to put you out."

"You wouldn't be. You could sleep over too if you wish."

Juliet tried not to let the blush flame up her throat and rush to her cheeks. Hearing Monica's snigger, she knew she had failed abysmally. Trent held up her hands, laughing at both of them.

"It's a purely innocent offer. I won't sleep because we usually play until the early hours if none of us have a shift the next day. You can have my bed. If I need to, I can crash on the settee in my game room." Trent edged closer and Juliet had to tilt her head back to see her face. "You could get your presentation all done to your satisfaction while Monica parties with her friends."

Juliet was torn. She needed time to work on her presentation but to spend time with Trent was a gift she couldn't pass up. If Trent was caught up playing her game online then Juliet could put it to the test just how envious of the gaming community she should be. She nodded, mind made up. "Thank you, Trent, I'd love to come over."

Trent's grin was bright and she leaned down to plant a swift kiss on Juliet's lips. "I get to see you Friday, even if it will be fleeting while you work and I play. It's a win-win situation for me."

"Looks like your Friday is all sorted," Monica said, eyeing them both over the rim of her can.

Staring at Trent's happy face, Juliet couldn't hold back her own joy. "I promise not to disturb you."

"I won't hear a thing," Trent said. "I'll be wearing headphones, so all I'll hear is Elton yelling at Eddie to shift his ass out of the line of fire." She gave Juliet a measured look. "But if you needed me, I'd come running."

I know you would, and that's what makes you so damn precious to me.

CHAPTER NINETEEN

E lton sidled up to Trent as she was spreading sale tickets over a stack of games.

"Who are you and what have you done with my best friend?" he asked, first reaching out to touch Trent's forehead, then poking her as if testing something.

Trent continued with her task, purposely ignoring his teasing behavior.

"Come on, admit it. You've at least got to have been body snatched and switched because I know there is no way my oldest friend Trent would ever have a woman sleep over at her place."

Trent tried not to let a sigh escape. "News travels fast."

"You asked Juliet to sleep over in front of Monica. I'm going to find these things out from her. Besides, she told me in the middle of a protracted grumble about me playing games that night instead of being by her side at *The Lost Boys* fest." He ran his fingers through his long beard. "Vampires are cool and such if they come in the shape of Kate Beckinsale." His mind visibly wandered, and Trent waited patiently until he returned to his conversational thread. "But playing online with your friends with guns is so much better that watching the old Brat Pack play vamps." He mimicked taking aim at Eddie, who'd wandered into his eyeline. Eddie gave him a startled look, then took off swiftly just in case he was in trouble.

"Juliet needed peace and quiet to work. She wasn't going to get that with the Goth cinema club right outside her door. I did what any friend would; I offered her an alternative."

"And sleeping in your bed? How friendly is that?"

Gritting her teeth, Trent continued applying the stickers and willed her temper away. "You know and I know that we'll be fighting until at least four a.m. like usual. None of us have work that Saturday, so we'll stay up all night. That's why I planned it for this week. I can sleep in my chair if I need to." She started to get annoyed. "It was an innocent invite, not a means to get Juliet in my bed so I could just fuck her."

Elton leaned back against the shelf Trent was working in front of, effectively stopping her from stocking it. "What if she *wants* you to fuck her? What if she comes and stands in front of your TV and gives you a come-hither look while wearing only the skimpiest of undies?"

Carefully laying the last sticker down, Trent looked at him. "That's simple. Good night, fellow gamers, this game is over."

"You'd pick her sinfully sexy body over a rousing first-person-shooter experience with your buddies?"

"If she wants me I'm all hers. For however long she wants me."

"You've got it bad." Elton grinned. "I like how it looks on you. And Juliet is a stunner, with brains and beauty." He moved away from the shelf. "Just don't let her disturb you if we're winning. I want us to climb up the leader board and take that coveted top spot."

"I'll be sure to remain focused on my task, Clan Leader."

"Glad to hear it. No tits or ass should distract a gamer from their game." His missive delivered, Elton sauntered off. Trent stared after him for a moment, then turned back to her work.

"True, but she does possess a mighty fine set of tits and ass, so I could be forgiven for finding them a distraction and have to call off my game because I somehow lost my Internet connection."

She enjoyed the mental images she had of Juliet gloriously naked in her arms. She started counting down the hours until she could see her again.

❖

By Friday Trent was doubly wired. She was excited for the game night that lay ahead and the adrenaline rush that came with joining her friends in a test of their prowess against the other online players. But she kept looking at her watch for another reason. She was anxiously awaiting Juliet's arrival. Trent had forced herself to stay inside the house and not be found waiting at the end of her driveway like some love-sick puppy. She'd checked and double-checked her T-shirt and loose shorts umpteen times, dressed as always for a night of playing in comfort, but she was vain enough to want to know that Juliet would find her attractive in her casual attire. She flipped her wrist to check the time again just as a car pulled up outside. Trent flung open the front door to lean against the doorjamb. She drank in the sight of Juliet getting out of her car before reaching back in to gather up a small bag and her laptop case. The smile Juliet bestowed on her made Trent want to drag her inside and forgo any other plans she had for that evening.

"Hi," Juliet called sweetly.

"Welcome. Come get yourself settled. I've got a beer in the fridge with your name on it." Trent stepped back as Juliet walked past her. Breathing in deeply at Juliet's floral scent, Trent had to close her eyes against the rush of lust that poured through her. She pushed the door shut and followed her. Juliet had already laid her laptop on the kitchen table and her bag on the floor. Hands free, she stepped directly into Trent's waiting arms. Trent shivered as Juliet drew her close for a gentle kiss hello that threatened to undo her. Hands resting on Juliet's hips, Trent pulled her closer until she could feel Juliet's body pressed against her. Soft lips traced Trent's mouth. Juliet's tongue pushed inside and tangled with hers. Tugging her even closer, Trent ran her hands possessively up Juliet's back, down her sides, and then up to cup her breasts. She teased Juliet's nipples into hard knots, rolling them under her thumbs. Juliet squirmed at her touch, ripping her mouth away from Trent's, letting out a cry as Trent caught her nipples between finger and thumb and tugged.

"God, I've missed you," Trent said, taking Juliet's mouth roughly. She couldn't kiss her enough, couldn't get close enough. Trent needed to touch Juliet everywhere and mark her as taken. Her heart pounded in her chest as she kissed her way across Juliet's cheek and then moved to nip at the fragrant curve of Juliet's neck. The sound of a very loud beep broke through her passion.

"Shit," she grumbled and ignoring the sound slipped her hands around Juliet's bottom to lift her up. Juliet's back pressed against the wall and Trent kept her pinned there, wrapping Juliet's legs around her hips. Trent pushed into Juliet's body and pumped her hips just once. Juliet reared back and she gasped for air as Trent obviously hit the spot that ached for her touch the most. Trent's hips rocked, needing to be closer, wanting to push inside Juliet's warmth. She cursed the clothing between them, but it didn't stop Juliet's heat from warming Trent's flesh. Trent's breath hissed out as she licked a path down to Juliet's cleavage. The beep sounded again and Juliet managed to drag Trent's attention up from where she was buried.

"You're beeping every minute," Juliet panted softly, her eyes glazed and unfocused.

Trent laid her forehead against Juliet's chest. "It's the five-minute countdown to my game."

Juliet tilted Trent's face up and kissed her. Trent's hips bucked at the sensuous ravaging Juliet's lips wreaked upon her. "You need to go," Juliet said. "Your friends are waiting for you."

Trent didn't want to move from Juliet's hold. How had they gone from hello to this? She couldn't control herself around Juliet anymore. Carefully, she let Juliet slip back down to her feet. For a moment Juliet still clung to her, trying to regain her equilibrium. The watch beeped out its warning again.

"You need to go play and I need to go to my own work." Juliet pushed Trent away gently. "I'll see you later if you come up for air."

Trent kissed her again lightly this time, running her hand through Juliet's hair and marveling at her beauty. "You'll stay?"

"I'm not going anywhere. I'll be right here."

Reluctantly, Trent pulled back, licking her lips and almost groaning at the faint taste of Juliet that clung to them. "I didn't mean to ambush you. I've just really missed you this week."

Juliet ran her hand over Trent's chest, resting it on her stomach. "I'm glad. I'd hate for this to be all one-sided and it only being me desperate to strip you naked and make you mine."

Trent's insides clenched at the look in Juliet's eyes. She shook her head ruefully. "It's not one-sided at all, believe me." Her watch beeped. "I'd better go before they start phoning me to get me online." She gestured about her. "You have the run of the house, and you know where I am if you need me." Trent started up the stairs.

"Have a great night, Trent. I hope you beat them all."

"And I hope you get that presentation finished so you can forget it and concentrate on what's really important to you."

Please let me be included in that, Trent wished.

Once in her game room, Trent settled in her chair and picked up her controller. She logged in, put her headset on, and could soon hear her friends' familiar voices.

"About time you came online, Trent," Elton said. "I had visions of having to come around your house and drag you into the game."

"I was just making sure Juliet was settled, being a good host, you know." Trent ignored the sniggers from her other friends. "Shut the fuck up, all of you, and let's play," she grumbled playfully, taking their teasing well.

Elton's rich laughter was loud in Trent's ear. "You heard her. Time to face the enemy."

Like she had done so many times before, Trent readied for the game. She closed her mind to everything but the task ahead, conscious only of the voices in her ear and seeing only the soldiers on the screen. She prepared to do battle, to immerse herself in the thrill of the game. But for all that, Trent was still well aware of the presence downstairs in her home. For the first time ever, Trent was safe in the company of someone else in her space.

❖

Three hours into the game and Trent was directing her team out of a sniper's sights, her eyes quickly scanning the area as she barked out orders that everyone swiftly followed.

"I swear that guy moves the second we do," Zoe said as her counterpart on the screen crouched behind a sheltered wall.

"You need to get closer, target him, and shoot the bastard," Elton said. "He's beginning to piss me off."

Trent could hear the chatter of their opponents, Elton's cousin Dave among them and their gaming rival Evan. "You don't want him pissed off, guys," she said as Dave made a comment, "that's when he borders on genius." She could hear them all squabbling among themselves and moved her soldier forward, popping up from behind her cover and shooting Dave's soldier dead.

"Headshot!" Elton crowed as Dave let out a wail.

"Where the hell did you come from?" Dave said.

"Play or gossip. Either way, I'll shoot you down," Trent said as Zoe's sniper rifle expertly took out Evan's soldier. "Excellent shot, Zoe," she said, enjoying hearing the men good-naturedly complain about being bested by a woman.

"Damn it," Evan said. "How long have you guys been playing on this?"

"Long enough to put your clan to shame," Elton replied as his soldier followed swiftly after Trent's and they stormed into Dave's hideout and wiped them all out. "Game over!" Elton said, and everyone on the Baydale Reaper's side let out a cheer. Trent punched the air in delight, having enjoyed the competition Dave and his clan had given them.

"Good game, guys," she said once Elton's jeering had quieted to a dull roar.

"Up for a rematch?" Dave immediately asked.

"Definitely, after a toilet break and time to go grab a cool beer," Elton replied, giving everyone the signal that they had five minutes to get back to their screens.

Trent hurried to the bathroom, then bounded down the stairs before she realized that her less-than-quiet entrance might be distracting to Juliet. She skidded to a halt, bare feet squeaking on the kitchen tile. Juliet's amused face made Trent feel welcome.

"Sorry for the intrusion. I have five minutes before the next round starts. I need a beer and then I'll be out of your way." She opened the fridge and waved an extra can at Juliet.

"Please." Juliet took the can and popped the tab. "Have I mentioned lately how much I hate my job?"

Trent took a long drink from her can, taking in Juliet's disheveled hair. She surmised that Juliet had been running her hands through it as the presentation drove her to distraction. "Once or twice you might have mentioned it."

Juliet turned the laptop away as if she couldn't bear to look at the screen. "I take it by the exuberant yell of victory that your team is winning?"

Trent nodded. "Sorry if I was too loud. I have to compete with Elton and Chris to be heard sometimes."

"It was delightful. It's lovely to hear you having so much fun."

"I just shot Dave in the head," Trent said, still on a high from her expert shot. She grinned even more at Juliet's slow blink as she took this information in. "It's just a game. He's ready to do battle again, I promise."

"Glad to hear it."

Trent checked her watch. "Break time is nearly up. Gotta go steer our troops away from Dave's team's vengeful retaliation. I fear he'll be out for blood now."

"You be careful," Juliet said unnecessarily.

"I'm always careful. I'm careful, cocked, and ready to roll." She smartly saluted Juliet with her free hand and darted back upstairs. "I'd better go. I can all but hear Elton from here."

"I'll wait to hear a winning cheer," Juliet called.

"I'll do my best for you," Trent called back and flung herself into her seat and set her headset back on. "Trent reporting in."

"We're just waiting for Rick and Dave and then we're ready to try a new map," Elton said. "Everything okay in your world, Trent?"

"As good as it gets, Elt, and can only get better."

"Exactly what I wanted to hear, soldier." Elton's delight was audible in his voice. "Oh, I can hear Dave's heavy breathing in my ear, so I think we're set to hand him his ass again."

"Can I at least take a drink before we start?" Dave asked, sounding like he'd run.

"What were you doing in your five minutes, old man?" Elton asked.

"I have a wife I need to check up on. She needed something from me."

Elton's silence spoke volumes. "So that took care of one minute," he drawled and everyone burst into hysterics at Dave's expense.

Trent chuckled at their family banter. "Boys, play nice. Save it for the battlefield." The screen loaded their next scenario. "Reapers, prepare to reap."

"You're going down, Elton," Dave muttered.

"Funny, that's what your wife said the last time I saw her," Elton shot back.

Trent shook her head as the familiar bickering began. "If you two don't shut up, I'll shoot you both myself," she said, readying her weapon and scanning the area ahead. "Zoe, I think this is our war." She recognized one of the maps that she and Zoe had already fought through.

"Bring it on," Zoe said.

Trent ran her soldier into battle, the voices of her friends all around her and knowing that Juliet was close. *I love games night*, she thought briefly before heading into the fray.

❖

Juliet blinked tired eyes as her laptop powered down and finally shut off. She lowered the screen, then stood to stretch the kinks out of her back. She tidied everything away then looked at her watch. It was well past one o'clock and now, with her laptop off, she could hear faint noises coming from upstairs. *The war is obviously still raging*, she mused and padded upstairs to get her night clothes out. The bedroom door had been left open and Juliet stepped in, feeling a mixture of excitement and apprehension at sleeping in Trent's bed, even though Trent had made it clear she would be sleeping alone. She brushed her hand over the soft sheet turned back for her and mused at the sweet gesture Trent had made. She pulled her sleep shirt and shorts out of her bag, then went to make use of the bathroom. She brushed her teeth, washed, and changed, but still didn't feel tired enough to lie down and sleep. Cautiously, she edged her way along the hallway and peeked into the game room. She could see Trent, eyes intent on the large screen, and could distinctly hear voices coming from the headset.

"Stop dawdling! Evan's already waiting to pick each of us off," Trent said and Juliet slipped in closer to watch what was happening on the screen. Juliet had never paid attention to games, but seeing Trent play was fascinating and her interest was piqued. Silently, she entered the room and made her way unobtrusively to the love seat where she could still see the screen and also be granted a clear line of sight at Trent in action. Juliet snuggled into the soft sofa cushions and viewed the game unfolding like a movie. She quickly recognized that each player had their name displayed so she was able to follow her new friends as they ran across the screen dodging bullets.

"Eddie, you shoot in my direction again and I'll stick a mortar up your…"

Juliet clearly caught Elton's warning through Trent's headset and she noticed Eddie's soldier quickly altered his position. She followed Trent's soldier keenly, holding her breath as Trent ran across an open field and not releasing it until the soldier was safely behind cover. She quickly got caught up in the game, watching the story unfold and hearing the constant chatter running through Trent's headset. She stretched her legs out a little and laid her head down on the sofa arm to watch Trent play and just to be near her. Juliet loved that Trent had something she was so passionate about. Trent's large hands deftly flew across the control pad and Juliet remembered what those fingers had done to her only hours ago when Trent had her held against the wall. She wished they could have continued what they had started downstairs without Trent's watch signaling their time was up. She thought back to her own cell phone going off just as she was preparing to make love to

Trent so many nights ago. *Damn technology, but it won't always stop us.* Her eyes drifted shut, lulled to sleep by the music, the sound of game play, and the soft burr of Trent's voice as she spoke to her friends. Amid the roar of the fighting, safe in Trent's favorite room and close to Trent herself, Juliet fell into a contented slumber.

CHAPTER TWENTY

Trent couldn't believe Juliet had slept through the sounds of war and her constant chatter. The game was drawing to a close. Everyone had played their best, but the Reapers had once again won most of the night's battles. Trent had bid her good nights to everyone and had answered Elton's sly "Say good night to Juliet for me," with a simple "I'll do that," before taking off her headset and exiting the game. Out of habit she checked their ranking and was pleased to see her clan among the top names, some of which she recognized as worthy opponents they'd be sure to go up against if they could get everyone online at the same time again. Trent switched off her console, turned off the TV, then rested her chin in her hand and just stared at the sight of Juliet fast asleep on her sofa. Trent hadn't been in the least bit put off by Juliet walking in on her game. She didn't distract her, hadn't called for her attention. Instead she'd been so quiet Trent had almost forgotten she was there. *Almost.* Trent greedily took in the tiny pair of sleep shorts Juliet wore under an oversized shirt. Slowly, so as not to wake her, Trent eased herself out of her chair to kneel in front of the sofa.

She let her eyes look everywhere, from the mane of blond hair, over the finely arched eyebrows, to the rich mouth that even in sleep quirked with a knowing smile. The sleep shirt was bunched up, revealing Juliet's soft stomach, and Trent had to restrain herself from leaning in to press her mouth against the pale flesh and just breathe her in. She longed to lick her way up Juliet's shapely legs, rest her face between her breasts, and slide her fingers deep inside Juliet, wringing out an orgasm that she could watch take hold of Juliet's body before clutching her tight and relishing the closeness. Trent sucked her lip in between her teeth as she pondered her current dilemma. *How the hell do I get you off the sofa and into my bed, seeing as where you're sleeping is supposed to be my bed for the night?* She was just wondering if she could slip her arms under the back of Juliet's knees when Juliet stirred and her eyelids flickered open.

"Hi, babe, are you still playing?" Juliet's soft voice made Trent grow hot, as did the whispered endearment that Trent had never heard from Juliet's lips before.

"I'm all done for the night. Dave's wife came and called time on him so we all decided to call it a night. You know what they say about gamers the minute they get married?" Trent paused for effect."*Game over*," she intoned darkly.

"I'd never expect you to stop playing," Juliet said. "You love it too much. It's who you are."

Trent warmed at Juliet's appraising look. "Can you get up?" She noticed Juliet's surprise at being found on the sofa.

"Did I fall asleep here?"

"God knows how. We were blowing up buildings and shouting and you just slept right through it all. Even when I cursed at someone for lobbing a grenade in my direction."

"Wow, I must have been tired." Juliet rubbed at her face and shifted to sit upright, bringing her legs between Trent's knees.

"This presentation is sucking the life out of you. The sooner it's done, the better." Trent stood and drew Juliet up with her. "You need to go sleep on a proper mattress. I just need to make sure everything is locked up for the night and then I'll get ready to turn in too." She undid her watch. "I can't believe we all ended up turning in early. It's only just past two in the morning. We're usually still up when the milkman delivers." Juliet's hand slipped into hers and Trent took pleasure in the simple gesture. She turned out the main light and left just a small one burning for her return. She gently pushed Juliet in the direction of her bedroom. "I'll just get my pj's and then I'll..." She gestured to the bathroom. Juliet's warmth was spreading a fire all along Trent's side.

"Before I woke up, were you planning on picking me up and carrying me to bed?"

Trent nodded. "I figured if I was careful enough I could slip my arms around you and lift you. I was just calculating the variables when you woke up."

"And saved you pulling your back out."

"You're not that heavy. I could have done it with little strain. It was the waking you up part I was most worried about."

"It was nice to wake up and see your face."

Trent swallowed hard at the sensual, sleepy lilt of Juliet's voice. It did nothing to calm her. She was still wide awake from her gaming, revved up and wired, and Juliet looked so damn sexy in her sleep shirt that Trent wanted to rip it off her and climb all over her. "I'd better go check all the locks," she muttered and quickly took herself away from temptation. The house duly alarmed, Trent paused in the kitchen for a long moment, taking deep breaths as she listened to Juliet move around above her. Trent went back upstairs, gathered her nightwear, and slipped into the bathroom. She washed her face briskly, brushed her teeth, in fact did everything she needed to before being unable to delay any longer. She turned the bathroom light off and headed back down the hallway to her game room.

"Trent."

She halted at the sound of Juliet's call. The bedroom door was open and Trent could see Juliet kneeling on the mattress facing her.

"Please don't let me sleep in your bed alone."

Trent stood still in the doorway. "My invitation for tonight wasn't for this, Juliet."

"I know, which just makes you all the more special." Juliet edged forward to kneel at the end of the bed. "But I want you."

Trent feared she was glued to the spot. Juliet's shy look was disarming. Seeing her waiting on the bed wearing just sheer nightwear was banishing any thoughts of chivalry Trent could conjure up.

"Go turn that light off in your game room and come back to me."

The sensual tone Juliet used spurred Trent to hustle to do as she bid. She locked the door haphazardly, a first for her, then she hurried back to her bedroom door. She leaned against it, almost weak with need for Juliet waiting for her.

"Do I need to come get you?" Juliet said, sensing Trent's hesitation.

Slowly Trent walked over to the bed and stood before her. "I can't believe you're really here."

"In your bed?"

"In my life." Her breath was suspended as Juliet edged ever closer and raised up on her knees. Chest to chest, they just breathed each other in. The flame in Juliet's eyes set her own need ablaze.

"I'm frightened I'll hurt you," Trent said. "I want you so much I might be too rough, and I don't want to frighten you off."

In answer, Juliet speared her fingers through Trent's hair and tugged her down. "You can never want me enough." The kiss was electric. Trent moaned as Juliet's tongue pushed in deep, seeking hers. Soft lips devoured her and Trent let herself be taken, thrilling to the desire that exploded between them. Too hot, too fast. Trent pulled back gulping for air, not used to someone else setting the pace.

"Fuck, you know how to kiss," she said, breathing against Juliet's lips. Then she took over the kiss, taking control and delighting to hear Juliet moan.

"So do you," she gasped, surrendering to Trent's ardor. "But I want more than kisses from you. I want what you started downstairs. I want to feel your body on mine."

Trent pushed Juliet back upon the bed and quickly followed her down to lie on top of her, covering her with her long length. Juliet wrapped her arms tightly around Trent's back and pulled her even closer. Trent could feel her breasts pressed into the softness that was Juliet's. Hardened nipples rubbed between them, and Trent shifted, enjoying the friction that sent bolts of electricity down her spine. Tugging at Juliet's shirt, Trent growled, "I need to touch you, need to taste you. You're so damn soft." She licked down Juliet's neck and eased back to allow Juliet to move. Juliet twisted and managed to remove her top, throwing it to the floor. Trent's breath whooshed out of her chest as if she'd been punched. "You are so sexy." Mouth watering, she moved to take as much of Juliet's breast into her mouth as she could. She ran her tongue over the pebbled areola and then sucked on the diamond hard nipple. Juliet bucked beneath her, nails digging into Trent's back, scratching her lightly then with more fervor as Trent flicked her tongue roughly over the rigid tip.

"That feels so good," Juliet said, pushing more of her flesh to Trent's mouth, arching off the bed and pressing into Trent's firm flesh. Juliet's leg slipped between Trent's, and Trent jerked as her heated center suddenly had pressure applied.

"I need to move before you have me come all over your leg."

Juliet's answer was to press her thigh even tighter, and Trent nearly exploded as the pleasure rushed through her clitoris. "I'm not kidding." Trent hastily shifted position and ignored Juliet's moan of disappointment. "You've got me so fucking wound up I can hardly see."

"I want you to come, babe. I need you to." Juliet tugged Trent to her as they lay side by side. Her hands were driving Trent to distraction;

they seemed to be everywhere at once. Soft kisses landed all over her face, fingers were chafing at her nipples, and the way Juliet was rubbing against her in a sensuous dance was making Trent wetter than she had ever been. She pulled back a fraction, determined to set the pace, and got a hand free to rub her fingers over Juliet's naked chest. She traced patterns all over her skin, followed them with her lips, and slowly worked her way down until she reached the barrier of Juliet's skimpy shorts. She pulled them down Juliet's legs until she lay naked before Trent's eyes. Although Trent had seen Juliet naked before, the sheer beauty of it stirred her soul, and she paused to just stare.

"What?" Juliet asked, brushing her hand over Trent's cheek.

Trent looked deeply into Juliet's eyes. "You are the most beautiful woman I have ever seen." Gently she ran her hand over every contour of Juliet's body, breathed in Juliet's unique scent, and then rested her cheek where Juliet's heart beat. "You turn me inside out." She took Juliet's lips with hers. She kissed her until Juliet was writhing beneath her again. Trent's hand drifted down to play in the soft hairs that framed the top of Juliet's legs, legs that instantly parted for Trent to explore further.

Teasing a finger through the wetness, Trent very diligently committed to memory every fold, crease, and pleasure point that she touched upon. She kissed down Juliet's body, then settled herself between Juliet's outspread legs and pressed a finger at the entrance of Juliet's sex. Juliet raised her hips to try to push Trent in farther. In her own time, teasing Juliet unmercifully with soft nips and licks along her thighs, Trent pressed her finger in more, and her breath hitched at the molten warmth that engulfed her. Juliet's back arched again, letting Trent slip in even farther. Trent added another finger, starting the rhythmic tempo that made Juliet's breathing stutter and Trent's own to catch. Trent pressed her tongue to Juliet's straining clitoris. She pressed again as Juliet squealed her name. Trent pushed her fingers harder inside and sucked the hard little knot of flesh into her mouth. Juliet's muscles tightened around her fingers.

Trent sped up her rhythm, harder, faster, pressing her fingers into the ridged flesh that held her tight. She could hear Juliet calling to her—"more," "deeper," "Oh God, just like that." Trent quickly moved her fingers and before Juliet could realize the loss quickly filled it with her tongue. She licked Juliet firmly, then speared her tongue to capture all the essence she could taste. Juliet's scent was heady. Trent found it addictive and she buried her face between Juliet's legs, desperate to take her all in. She flicked her tongue over Juliet's reddened clitoris, swiftly returned her fingers inside with a firm push, and was elated as the orgasm ripped through her. Juliet called out her name and Trent's own clitoris spasmed in a fevered response to the siren's call. A hand finally batted at Trent's arm and she stilled her fingers.

Unable to stop herself, Trent laid a kiss on Juliet's clitoris as she calmed. It made Juliet jerk again and release a soft moan. Trent felt empowered, mighty, yet safe and sheltered in the hold of Juliet's body. She was loath to move in case Juliet somehow vanished and Trent was left alone.

Juliet stirred languidly under her. "God, that was so good," Juliet purred.

Trent's chest expanded at the praise. A hand reached down to playfully ruffle through her hair.

"Monica was right."

Trent raised her head from where it was resting on Juliet's thigh. Her fingers had been lazily tracing the edges of Juliet's labia. Trent was fascinated by the ruffles and the deep rose shade now shining wet with juices.

"Monica?"

"She told me that as a gamer, you'd have amazing dexterity and would be able to push all *my* buttons."

"Did she now? And she was discussing my sexual prowess why?"

"Perhaps because she could see I was all but undressing you with my eyes at the tournament that day. I was wondering myself just what kind of lover you would be if I was lucky enough to have you."

Trent held her breath, waiting. "And?"

"You make love like you play, wholeheartedly, with great passion, and you have the amazing ability to know what needs to be pressed when. You are truly amazing, and I love it when your hands are on me." She tugged Trent up by her shirt. "Come here."

Trent reluctantly left her haven between Juliet's thighs and moved to her side. Juliet kissed her sweetly, then drew back. Trent was transfixed as her pink tongue ran over her lips and she tasted herself.

"I love how you taste," Trent said, licking her own lips before leaning down to kiss Juliet once more. She let out a startled breath when Juliet flipped her over and straddled her hips. "Hey!"

"I want to taste you too," Juliet said, brushing her hair over her shoulder and leaning down to take Trent's mouth with eager lips.

Trent's breath began to escape in sharp gasps. Her body tensed up and she struggled with her fear as it threatened to overwhelm her. Breaking the kiss, her eyes slipped past Juliet's enticing body and instead looked fearfully toward the closed door. Her hands involuntarily clenching, Trent had to physically stop herself from pushing Juliet off her. Juliet looked up and then she very gently eased herself up off Trent's body. Making sure Trent's eyes were on her, she deliberately went and opened the bedroom door wide.

"Do you have the house alarm on?" she asked.

Her head still buzzing, Trent just nodded as she sat up, unable to stay lying down.

"There's only you and me in the house, Trent." Juliet began to walk back over toward her, hips swaying, drawing Trent's eyes to her and her alone. "No one else is here. No one is going to disturb us. I'm going to make you mine like I have fantasized ever since you had me in your lap and dancing on your fingers."

The room was full of white noise, and all Trent could focus on was Juliet. Her voice was all Trent could make out. She dominated the room and filled Trent's heart. Trent couldn't take her eyes off her. Juliet beckoned Trent farther down the bed, and Trent was stupidly relieved that Juliet wasn't angry with her. She hadn't been able to control her freezing up when she was on her back. That was why she never got herself in that situation with any other woman. She couldn't allow herself to be put in such a vulnerable position again. Fear of reprisals smothered all other thoughts and feelings.

It had kept her alone for so long. But Juliet was no ordinary woman. Juliet beckoned her closer and Trent obeyed, moving to sit on the edge of the bed, feet on the floor, just staring at Juliet in wonder at the kindness that lit up her face and promised so much. Swallowing hard, Trent could only watch as Juliet came to stand between her legs. Hands brushed through Trent's short hair and snagged softly at it.

"It's just you and me, Trent." She ran her fingers down Trent's face and let a finger linger on Trent's lips. Trent caught it gently between her teeth and licked at the tip. Before she could suck it in, Juliet swiftly pulled it away and wagged it in front of her. She trailed the same finger down Trent's chest, tugging at her T-shirt until Trent took the hint and pulled it off. "Much better." Juliet sighed, looking Trent over with delighted eyes. She pressed in closer between Trent's knees and nudged them farther apart. "It's just you and me. And you're playing my game now."

Trent's eyebrows rose at Juliet's choice of words. "Your game?" she asked huskily, captured by the intent blatantly shining in Juliet's gaze.

"We're playing passion's game now." Juliet sealed Trent's mouth with a kiss.

Trent's lips parted beneath Juliet's as she kissed her softly, more than aware of the nervousness still causing Trent to tremble. Taking her time, Juliet seduced Trent with gentle kisses, her hands just skimming over her flesh. Juliet held back her desperate need to take Trent hard and fast, to devour her whole to quell some of the hunger she had for her. *Soon*, Juliet told herself and filled her palms with Trent's firm breasts. She brushed her thumbs over deep red nipples and thrilled to hear Trent's sharp intake of breath. Trent pushed herself closer as Juliet fondled her, loving the firmness of Trent's smaller breasts compared to her own larger, softer ones. Trent's eyes grew darker the harder she gripped her nipples.

"Ooh, you like it a bit rougher, eh?" Juliet tugged a little more, enough to make Trent moan and lean closer still. She grabbed for a hold on Juliet's hips and held her tightly.

"You're making me crazy doing that," Trent said, rubbing her face over Juliet's breasts. Juliet gave her one more tweak, then abruptly knelt before her and sucked a nipple into her mouth. Gasping out loud, Trent grabbed for Juliet and kept her in place, soft gasps erupting from her throat.

"How long has it been since you've been touched, Trent?" Juliet asked, looking up at her and keeping up her seduction by flicking Trent's nipple with her fingertips.

"Long enough." Trent shuddered and tried to pull Juliet to her. "It was always easier for me to just fuck and run when I did find someone."

"Well, you're not running tonight," Juliet said in Trent's ear, and a shiver ran through Trent's body. She bit Trent's earlobe, then ran her tongue over it to take away the sting.

"I'm not going anywhere," Trent managed to say before Juliet pushed her back to rest on her elbows.

Juliet slipped her fingers under the waistband of Trent's sleep shorts and pulled them down her legs and off. She explored Trent's flat stomach and the muscles that were visible beneath the flesh. She barely scratched her nails down Trent's stomach and got an instant reaction.

Trent jumped, groaned, and fell back on the bed. "Stop teasing," she growled.

Licking her lips, Juliet ignored Trent's comment and instead kissed her way down each ripple of flesh. Trent twisted beneath her, hands grasping for her, trying to pull her closer. Juliet rested her face on Trent's hard stomach and rubbed her chin over the soft patch of dark hair at the top of Trent's legs. Without preamble, Juliet pressed Trent's legs wider, moved lower, and licked her with the flat of her tongue, taking in all of Trent's sex. Trent's lower lips were spread for her, leaving her open for anything Juliet wished. She first pressed light kisses to Trent's large blood-red clitoris, which strained from under its hood. She then took it into her mouth and sucked hard.

"Christ!" Trent's legs were shaking so much Juliet had to hold them still with her arms. Trent pushed her closer between her legs. "Suck me," she said, all restraint gone. Juliet complied while slipping a finger into Trent's warmth. Her fingers met with resistance. Trent was tight, and Juliet groaned at the pressure as she pushed in. Her groan in turn made Trent's clitoris twitch in her mouth, and Trent let out a loud moan.

"You're incredibly tight," Juliet said, leaning back on her heels to watch her finger be welcomed inside Trent's wet walls. Strong muscles contracted around Juliet's finger and she moved deeper, adding another finger and pressing in harder, opening Trent up. "You okay?" Juliet asked, pressing in and out in rhythm to the lift of Trent's hips. She barely caught Trent's *yes* that hissed out of her.

"Do it," Trent gasped, all semblance of control gone.

"Do what?" Juliet stood to look down over Trent's length spread out before her, held up on her elbows. A sheen of sweat beaded her skin, her muscles tight and defined, nipples rock hard and straining. Juliet thought she had never seen anything so beautiful. She ran her hand up Trent's chest, rolling her palm over Trent's breasts roughly, catching her nipples between her fingers and pulling on them. Trent's eyes were wide, drawn to Juliet's.

"Fuck me," Trent pleaded, clutching Juliet's hand to her breast and closing her eyes to the passion. Juliet pumped into Trent quicker, her desire to bring Trent to orgasm a raging fire inside her. Trent's face revealed its pleasure. Juliet loved how Trent's mouth opened to gasp for each breath, her name escaping in whispers.

"Come for me, Trent."

"I am," Trent gritted out, writhing under Juliet's touch.

Juliet straddled Trent's leg and began to rub her own needy flesh against Trent's muscled thigh. Trent clutched at Juliet's hips to help her ride. All too soon Juliet's own orgasm threatened.

"I'm coming," Juliet cried as her hips pounded against Trent. She pushed her fingers in deep and curled her finger over the spot roughened for pleasure. Trent howled, her body spasming as she came with a loud shout. While Trent bucked beneath her, Juliet came from the pressure of Trent's leg pounding her clitoris. She fell forward and was swiftly gathered up in Trent's arms. Kisses were rained on her face and Trent nuzzled her, burrowing into her neck as if seeking shelter there.

"God, that was *amazing*." Juliet eased her fingers carefully from inside Trent and brought them up to her lips. "You taste exactly as I thought, strong and spicy."

Trent just held on to Juliet as if afraid to let her go. Juliet could feel the tremors still rolling through Trent's body. Juliet looked down at Trent's face and was shocked to see trails of tears on her cheeks. Juliet began to kiss them away, laying soft kisses all over Trent's face.

"You all right?" Juliet whispered, waiting for Trent to open her eyes.

Trent just nodded against Juliet's flesh. "I don't remember ever coming so hard," she said, finally looking at Juliet.

"You inspire me with your sexy body."

Trent moistened her lips and let out a shaky sigh. "Looks like you got me on my back after all."

Juliet realized that they were laid out on the bed, her body covering Trent, who was flat on her back holding Juliet tight. "You okay with that?" she asked softly, preparing to move, but Trent held her still.

"Yeah, at this precise moment I think I am," Trent replied, sounding surprised. She took a deep breath. "God, you fuck like a dream!" Her wide, toothy grin made Juliet's heart expand with pleasure. "It's a good thing I didn't know you were that good, otherwise I'd have blown off the game entirely and left my team high and dry."

Juliet snuggled into Trent's arms and laid her head on her chest, just in reach of Trent's nipple, which she first breathed on, then touched with the tip of her tongue. It instantly hardened. Trent pressed a hard kiss to Juliet's forehead as Juliet began to tease the firm nub of flesh.

"I take it you're not tired?" Trent slipped a hand between them to capture Juliet's breast and deliver some of the same teasing she was receiving.

"The milkman hasn't delivered yet," Juliet replied slyly and moved to close her teeth around Trent's nipple.

"Juliet!" Trent jolted under her as if touched by an electric current.

"You've got to love a butch who has sensitive nipples to play with." Juliet barely had time to make her comment before she was flipped over on her back with a wild-looking Trent rearing above her.

"And I do so love the games you play." Trent kissed her soundly.

Juliet was delighted as she witnessed the passion sparkle in Trent's dark eyes. "Game on?" she asked, light-headed and almost giddy in her love for Trent.

"Oh, the game is definitely on," Trent said, slipping down the bed purposefully. "Listen to you, using gamer speak."

"I Googled it just for you."

Trent's amused sound made Juliet's heart swell with pride that she had caused that happy look on her face. *My lover, in every sense of the word now.*

"I think we need to test out your trigger button, don't you?" Trent moved lower still. "I bet you didn't have time to Google that."

Juliet's delighted giggle turned into a squeal of pleasure when Trent's tongue wrapped around her clitoris once more.

"You ready to play?" Trent asked from between her legs.

"I'm always ready where you're concerned," Juliet said, her heart pounding and her arousal burning through her as Trent took her once more.

Game on indeed.

CHAPTER TWENTY-ONE

Juliet loved being able to watch Trent sleep, her face unguarded and peaceful. Leaning up on an elbow, she unabashedly studied all she never got a chance to see when Trent was wide awake and vibrant. Her strong face, too handsome to ever be considered feminine, drew Juliet's loving eyes. *You are so beautiful you make me want to weep*, she thought, moving her gaze down across Trent's shoulders, down her arm marked by the stark tattoo. In the growing morning light Juliet was able to study the artwork that wrapped around Trent's upper arm, the small alien shapes falling down in waves. *Only you could have that etched into your skin, my darling, and have it look so right.*

Trent's hand twitched in her sleep and Juliet was drawn to the large palm with its long blunt fingers. Hands that could race across the buttons to beat an opponent in a death match yet be so gentle and tender when they touched Juliet's skin. Carefully, Juliet pulled the sheet down to Trent's hips. The sunlight streaming through a gap in the blinds lit Trent's lean chest and firm breasts. Juliet held back from reaching out to touch. For now she was just observing because the minute Trent was awake, Juliet would probably be flat on her back with Trent roaming seductively over her. Trent turned as if hearing her thoughts, and the sheet fell away from the rest of her body, baring her completely to Juliet's eyes. Juliet bit her lip to stop from reaching out and taking what she considered hers.

"What you looking at?"

Juliet peered down at a slowly waking Trent. "I'm looking at you and thinking how lucky I am you're beside me, because you are way too sexy to go to waste."

Trent's slow smile made Juliet's insides quiver. "You sure you want to garden today?" She edged closer to Juliet, who quickly put a hand to Trent's chest to stop her from getting any nearer.

"I'm supposed to be helping Monica work on your yard. You hired us to do that, remember?"

Trent pressed against her hand. "But I have a much better place in mind for you." She moved swiftly and Juliet was pinned beneath Trent's long body.

"How's it going to look to Monica, who is my boss on this project, if I beg off today because I'd rather stay in bed with my girlfriend?"

Trent kissed her then pulled back. "It would tell her that you have a whole other kind of bed in mind for this Saturday."

Juliet tried to ease out from under Trent, but Trent trapped her, raining kisses on her face until Juliet broke into helpless laughter.

"What time is Monica, Gardening Goth, due to arrive?" Trent asked.

"In about an hour," Juliet informed her, trying to dodge Trent's lips. "So I need to get up and ready."

Trent grabbed for her hand and pressed Juliet's fingers between her legs, issuing a grunt as Juliet unerringly touched Trent's waiting hardness. "I'm already up and ready." She pulled her hand away but Juliet kept hers where it lay.

"It'll have to be quick," she said, enjoying the pleasure on Trent's face as she slipped over and around the nub of flesh, making Trent's hips rock and her breath catch.

"I'll take a quick fuck before you run off to be with another woman." Trent eye's drifted closed as she concentrated on what Juliet was doing between her legs.

Juliet nudged Trent's legs more open and lay back with Trent poised above her on all fours, pinning Juliet between her arms and legs but herself the captive to every stroke of Juliet's fingers. Trent's head fell forward and she blindly nuzzled Juliet's breast before finding her nipple and sucking on it.

"Trent," Juliet moaned. "This is supposed to be a quickie."

"It can be a quickie for both of us." Trent slipped a hand between Juliet's legs and strayed through her wetness. "You're already getting wet for me. It won't take either of us long." She bucked as Juliet rubbed a little harder. "Especially if you keep doing that."

Trent's thumb begin to move around Juliet's clitoris, rubbing around the hood, teasing her before brushing across the sensitive tip, shooting sparks down to her toes.

"Monica will know what we've been doing," Juliet said, bowing her back to try to get more of her breast to Trent's mouth.

"She'd be thinking we've done this even if we hadn't, so don't worry about it."

"I'm not worried," Juliet said as white-hot heat spread through her legs at Trent's magic touch.

"No, you're excited, aren't you? Isn't this how lovers should spend their Saturday morning?" Trent's fingers grew faster as her whole body started to tense. "I'm going to come soon. You're making me come pinching like that."

Squeezing Trent's clitoris gently, Juliet had the satisfaction of Trent falling apart above her. Hearing her name called out hoarsely by Trent was the most beautiful sound she'd ever known, and watching Trent come because of her hand was equally humbling. Juliet didn't last long after witnessing Trent's orgasm. Her whole body twitched and the explosion ripped through her body like a tidal wave. Trent collapsed beside her, drawing Juliet to her while they both rode out their pleasure. Finally Trent spoke.

"Okay, *now* you can go garden."

"I can't even feel my limbs, let alone get out of bed." She slapped at Trent's arm playfully.

"You don't want to keep Monica waiting." Trent lay back against the pillows, arms propped behind her head, lounging like a big lazy panther, satisfied and indolent.

"You're not staying in bed while I'm working," Juliet said, pushing at Trent to try to move her.

"I thought I'd rest after my morning *sex*-ercise, then get dressed and maybe play a little war with the boys, then take you girls out for lunch."

Juliet sat up beside her, unable to stop from laying her hand on Trent's chest, needing the feel of Trent's flesh, not wanting to lose the connection. "Sounds like a brilliant Saturday plan to me."

Trent hesitated and Juliet cocked an eyebrow at her. "I know you need to be in work early Monday, but I figured we could spend as much of the weekend as possible doing stuff together until you had to leave."

"I just need to do my last-minute preparations, like ironing my best blouse. Truth be told, if I stayed here all weekend, I'd never turn up at work on Monday."

Trent's grin was wry. "Would that really be so bad?"

Leaning over to kiss her, Juliet thought again how much she loved the feel of Trent's lips. "No, it would be all kinds of wonderful. But if I'm going to move on, I need to finish up there so I can walk away without any regrets."

Trent nodded, then settled back down in the bed and waved Juliet away. "Go. Your gardening buddy will be here soon. You don't want to keep her waiting. After all, she's your boss and all. You want to make a good impression if you're intending to work together."

Juliet slipped over Trent to stand beside the bed, satisfied at the soft noise from Trent's throat as she deliberately made sure her body had touched as much of Trent's as possible. "So now you're kicking me out of bed. You weren't doing that a few minutes ago when you were hot and sweaty in my hands."

Trent lunged after her, making Juliet hastily step back out of her grasp. "No no no, lover girl, you've had your quickie for this morning. Some of us have a job to go to." Her chest tightened at the wicked glint in Trent's eyes that threatened retribution of a sweet and passionate kind. Juliet was tempted beyond reason to just get back in bed and spend the day loving Trent. She lay there, still flushed and wet from their lovemaking. Juliet could hardly stand to turn away from the seductive picture Trent made. "You drive me wild, wanting you."

"Good, because I feel exactly the same way where you are concerned, sweetheart. Now go before I beg you to stay."

Juliet, her heart singing in delight at the sweet name Trent had called her, blinked deliberately knowing full well what it did to Trent when she gave her *that* look. "I like it when you beg."

A pillow hit the door behind her as she swiftly ran from the room to the sound of Trent's heartfelt groan.

❖

Monica ended up joining Trent at the kitchen table having a bowl of cereal while Trent readied tea and toast for Juliet.

"And here I was worried I was running late," Monica said, looking around the kitchen with an exacting eye. "Trent, you seriously need more color in here."

Trent spooned a mouthful of cornflakes into her mouth, preventing her from having to answer straight away. She just nodded at her and hoped that would satisfy Monica's curiosity. She'd invited her in. She'd known Monica was going to make some comment or another on the fact that Trent's kitchen looked unused.

"I mean, I applaud the minimalist look you've created here, but really, could it be any more white?" Monica got up to wash out her bowl, nudging Trent out of the way with her hip as she crowded near her. "Your kitchen quite frankly makes Elton's look like it's positively bustling with culinary knickknacks."

"I have a microwave," Trent said, pointing to one piece of equipment in the room that actually showed use.

"And you probably have the same six pizzas that Elton shoves in his."

Trent was never more grateful to see Juliet descend the stairs and take Monica's attention away.

"Your tea and toast are going cold," Monica said.

Juliet brushed past Monica, leaned up to kiss Trent, and then sat at the table. "Thank you, Trent." She began eating. Trent was grateful for the look of contentment on Juliet's face as she tasted the buttered toast. She noticed Monica staring at her with an indulgent look. Trent tried to ignore her.

"You've got a nice house, Trent," Monica said when she slipped out the back door following after Juliet. "It will make a nice home one day."

Trent stopped in her tracks and considered Monica's bald words. She realized it wasn't really a home, it was where she came back to from work, played her games, and slept. It was hers, but she'd never really treated it as such, occupied only in keeping her precious possessions safe, keeping herself safe locked inside a house alarmed to keep people out and old memories at bay. She'd hidden away, secured her borders and existed, but never truly lived. Work and playing her games had become her whole existence, and she'd remained untouched in her safe little world she'd created for herself. Until Juliet. Juliet had slipped right in past all her defenses and claimed her place beside Trent.

I know I love her. I just need to find the right time to tell her. Trent leaned against the back door while Juliet removed plants from their trays and prepared holes for them to be transplanted. *Now isn't the time. Not with the presentation looming so big in her mind. But soon, I need to tell her soon so she knows how I feel before I blurt it out when we make love. I don't want bed to be the place I tell her first. I need to say it because I don't think I can be without her now.*

Juliet looked up and caught Trent's eyes on her and smiled. Trent grinned back and settled down on the back doorstep, content to just sit there and watch Juliet and Monica work away in her yard. She lifted her face to the sky, closed her eyes against the sun and let its warmth seep through her skin. Juliet's voice rang clear and Trent opened her eyes to find her stretched out over something, reaching toward Monica, the movement separating her shirt from her shorts and exposing her belly. Trent's mouth went dry. It took all her strength not to go drag Juliet out of the yard and back into the house to explore that patch of skin further. She stood quickly.

"Where you going?" Monica asked.

"To shoot someone."

Monica blinked at her, startled. "Sorry I asked."

Trent padded around her house inexplicably and uncharacteristically at a loose end. Juliet had only been gone an hour, but already Trent was aimless and moping. She wandered past her game room but barely gave it a second thought as she slipped inside the spare room directly opposite. Trent had claimed the two larger bedrooms for her own use. This room, however, had remained empty. It overlooked the backyard, and from her vantage point Trent could look down at the progress being made. She leaned on the windowsill and peered through the open blinds. She was pleased with the transformation she could see below.

"Beautiful." Her eyes followed the pathway through the flowers that led to a small area Monica had designed for a gazebo, the focal point to the yard and a place to sit in and contemplate, she'd told Trent. Trent wasn't sure what Monica expected her to contemplate out there, but she'd seen Juliet's pleasure at the design so had agreed readily. She wandered back to her bedroom, the bed made and not revealing any of the passion and pleasure that had gone on in it the night before. Trent picked up a pillow and breathed in the scent left there by Juliet's perfume. With a decision made, Trent threw down the pillow and reached for her cell phone. She pressed on a quick-dial key.

"Elton? Does your cousin Rick still have that van of his?" She smiled at his answer. "Think he'd let us borrow it for the evening? There'd be a six-pack of beer in it for his trouble." She punched the air at hearing exactly what she wanted. "What? Oh, I knew he'd be over at yours today. He usually mooches a sandwich off you every other Sunday. He's very reliable." She checked her watch. "Can you come pick me up, then? The mall is still open and I need you to help me spend some of my savings. I have two things in mind that this house needs. I'm buying myself a future, Elton. I think I'm long overdue."

CHAPTER TWENTY-TWO

Monday morning found Juliet wishing the woman in front of her would just go back to her own office and leave her the hell alone. There was more bad news on the stock market as she'd walked in, and she'd found Carnie hovering around her desk like some damned buzzard circling, bringing with her rumors of planned layoffs. Juliet's comment about there being too many chiefs and not enough Indians in their business as it was hadn't helped Carnie calm down any. Juliet had never been more grateful for her phone ringing so she could shoo Carnie out of her office.

"I just wanted to wish you luck this morning." Trent's voice made Juliet's world stop spinning so madly in its place, and she sank into her chair with a smile on her face.

"Oh, I needed to hear your voice right this second. Thank you, babe."

"Tell me, are you wearing those high, high heels that will take no prisoners if anyone gives you guff today?"

Juliet lifted her foot and inspected her shoes. "They're the highest heel I have, real serious butt kickers."

"Excellent…sexy too." Trent's voice lowered and Juliet's skin reacted to the tone. She took a swift breath as all thoughts of her presentation left her mind. "You'll do great. What time do you plan to leave work tonight?"

"Five o'clock, as always. I don't aim on hanging around today. There's too much doom and gloom here with everyone terrified what company will fall next and if this will be the one to take us down with it."

"Just know that I'm thinking about you, okay? I'm cheering you on from here." Juliet heard an exasperated sound from her. "Sorry, I have to go. Some customers are giving me the eye. I think they want something, so I'd better go see to them. Good luck, Jule."

"I'll see you later?" Juliet asked quickly, not wanting Trent to hang up but recognizing she had to.

"Count on it."

The cool, certain answer calmed Juliet's nerves, and she disconnected the call, then set to gathering up her supplies for the presentation. As she slipped out the door her cell phone rang again. Answering it, Juliet was met with an excited stream of words that she could only decipher half of. "Monica?" She listened to her jubilant voice. "Okay, I need you to calm down and tell me again, slowly and in English this time, just what has you so excited. But first give me one second." She signaled to one of her bosses as he passed her. "Gerrard, I just need to take this urgent call, can you please tell everyone I'll be in as soon as possible?" At his nod, Juliet found herself a quiet niche in the corridor and put the cell phone back to her ear. "You have five minutes. Go!"

"Juliet, I have just been offered the deal of a lifetime. Remember I was in touch with Tweedy's Building Contractors, Mrs. Tweedy's son? Well, I got a call from the man himself not two minutes ago. He's offering me the chance to head my own landscaping company, affiliated with his construction company. I'd get all the contracted work for every building project he takes on while still being able to do my own work on the upkeep of the yards I already manage."

Juliet was awed. Monica deserved this chance. "That is fantastic news. Congratulations. Are you going to take him up on his offer?"

"Well, there's more. I get to not only run the landscaping side, I get to pick my own people to work with me. He says he isn't interested in that side of things. He just wants my expertise attached to his company. My expertise! Can you believe that?"

"Your work speaks for itself, Monica. You're amazing with how you transform yards."

"I want you with me," Monica said. "I want you to come with me and be my bookkeeper, accountant, and chief flower counter!"

"Monica…" Juliet was flabbergasted by the offer.

"You've said yourself you're not happy with what you're doing now. You have never seemed more relaxed than the times you've spent with me working on Trent's yard. You've done your bit for the banking fraternity, how about you devote that same energy to making things bloom now?" Monica paused. "I'm offering you equal partnership with me, Juliet. Our own business, like we should have had years ago before you drifted to the dark side and became a corporate suit."

Juliet sagged against the wall, a little light-headed. "Did you have to spring this on me now *right* before I go do my presentation?"

"There was no better time. I have all the facts and figures before me. Tweedy was talking salary, vehicles, equipment, estimated earnings. After he and I spoke the last time, he went away and got everything planned so we could just walk right into the job. Juliet, this is what I've always dreamed of. Share it with me."

Juliet caught sight of a head poking out of the doorway searching for her. She held up two fingers and mouthed *two minutes* at him. "I have to go."

"Think about it, please."

"Like I'm going to be able to think of anything else now," Juliet grumbled. "You did that on purpose."

"I need all the help I can get to win you away from that coveted chair in the corner office."

"I'll want to see all the paperwork. It's a big decision."

"It's here waiting for you," Monica promised. "Now go wow them with all that hard work you've put into your presentation. You might as well leave on a high note!"

Juliet snapped her phone shut and hurried into the meeting room to greet all the occupants gathered there to witness her presentation. She hoped she could remember why she was there now.

"Good morning, ladies and gentlemen. Thank you for taking the time out of your hectic schedules to come here for this meeting. Let's see if what I propose can keep us moving in today's market when so many banks are falling by the wayside." Juliet plugged her laptop into the projector and booted it up. With satisfaction she opened up her file, and the first pie chart was displayed on the big screen.

"Let me tell you what I believe this company needs to do to stay in business."

❖

Trent was grateful to Elton for letting her leave just that little bit earlier to make her bus in time. She waited at the bus depot with a large bouquet of red roses clutched nervously in her hand. Checking her watch, Trent roughly calculated how long the journey should take for her to reach Juliet's workplace situated outside the main town center. *I'll be in plenty of time to meet her outside.* She checked her cell phone again, rereading the last text Juliet had sent her. Trent wondered how, after the presentation, the impromptu meeting of all senior staff had gone down. *Like Juliet wasn't nervous enough.* Her bus pulled in and she boarded it, flashing her bus pass at the driver before snagging a seat at the front. *God, I feel like a kid going on their first date*, she thought, amused at how nervous she was. She looked out the window but didn't see anything, her mind full of all she intended to do and say when she met up with Juliet.

She'd spent some time again in the spare room that morning, looking at the yard, amazed by how much work Juliet and Monica had done to transform it. Trent had been captivated by the splashes of color woven into the design that Monica had implemented. It was like seeing a canvas painted not with oils, but with soil and flowers. A living work of art. A change had taken root in her backyard and that same change was working its way through the whole of the house, starting with Trent herself. Now, sitting on the bus heading out to the business complex where Juliet's bank had office space, Trent couldn't help but be a little terrified at what she intended to do.

Time to take a chance. She fidgeted with the fancy paper wrapped around the roses. *Time to see if Juliet will be willing to take a chance on me too. A chance on* us.

❖

At five on the dot, Juliet was out of her office and heading down the flight of stairs to get out the building. She held her key card up to the guard on the door and he buzzed her out. The warm evening air touched her skin as she headed toward the car park. She couldn't believe her eyes when she spotted Trent waiting beside her car, a large bouquet in her hands. Juliet had to bite her lip to stop herself from crying. *She is such a sight for sore eyes. Oh God, I'm so glad she's here.* Juliet hurried her pace but was halted mid-stride by a deliberately honeyed voice calling her determinedly. Juliet swore under her breath as she looked over her shoulder at who had called out.

"Stacy." Juliet looked back toward Trent and mouthed *one minute.*

Stacy hurried toward Juliet, her indecently tight skirt hampering her in her haste. "I understand congratulations are in order," she said. Juliet just waited for her to continue.

"Rumor has it you're to take the senior manager's job at Chicago's head office. All paths have been cleared to fast-track you there, the way I heard it. That must have been one hell of a presentation you performed this morning." Juliet wondered if anyone but Stacy could put such a negative spin on the word perform and make it sound salacious. "Guess our office wasn't big enough to hold your obvious talents."

Juliet was amazed that someone could be so complimentary yet so derogatory in the same breath. She was about to just dismiss Stacy, but others who had been walking past had overheard Stacy's comments and started to excitedly congratulate Juliet. She tried to speak, but she was soon surrounded by so many well-wishers that Stacy stalked off in a huff.

"Really, nothing has been settled yet." Juliet tried to back away, but more of her own team had begun to leave the building and quickly hurried toward her, inviting her out for a drink to celebrate. Juliet looked over at Trent, whose face had turned ashen. Placing the roses on the roof of Juliet's car, Trent mouthed *congratulations*, gave her a smile that almost broke Juliet's heart, and began to walk away.

"Trent!" Juliet called after her, but Trent's long legs ate up the pavement and Juliet could do nothing more than watch as Trent held up a hand to call a coming bus to halt for her to get on. Looking back at her colleagues, people she'd only known for a few months, seeing how delighted they were for her, so genuine in their excitement, unlike Stacy, made Juliet raise her hands and hush them all. "I have to go," she said, ignoring their groans of disappointment. "I promise, tomorrow I'll let you know what's happening, but for now I need to leave." She grabbed her car keys out of her bag and rushed to her car, lifting the beautiful bouquet off the car's roof and cradling it to her chest as she opened the door to get in. The scent immediately filled the interior. She fingered the soft petals, then put the key in the ignition and started the engine.

"I hope you know the true meaning behind red roses, Trent Williams," she said as she drove out of the parking lot a little faster than usual.

❖

The ride back on the bus was torture for Trent. She looked blindly out of the window, her hands knotted together, her jaw clenched tight as she willed herself not to let out the bellow of pain that clawed at her chest. She blinked away furiously at the tears that threatened to spill. *She's going back to Chicago, leaving here, moving on to bigger and better things. I lose everything again. I let down my walls finally and they crash right down on top of me.* Almost drunkenly, she lurched to her feet at her stop and exited the bus with no conscious thought. *Going through the motions, just like I have been for years.* Trent walked up her street dejectedly and had never been so grateful to see her front door. Her hands were shaking so much she dropped her keys on the step and was bending to pick them up when a car screeched to a halt. Juliet slammed out of her Honda, her arms filled with her handbag, laptop, and flowers. Trent managed to get the door open, all but falling inside, so startled to see Juliet marching up her driveway.

"Jesus Christ, Juliet. Did you break every speed limit getting here so fast?"

"Probably." Juliet walked right up to her and held up her roses. "These need to go in some water." She pushed past Trent and into the house. "You've never come to pick me up at work before."

"I wanted to surprise you." Trent took the flowers from Juliet and ran a little water into the kitchen sink and placed the stems in. She took comfort in the normal task while all the time her desolation was crippling her.

"Instead, you got the surprise," Juliet said.

Trent's chest ached so bad she unconsciously rubbed at it, hoping to ease the pain constricting her. "Congratulations. I take it your presentation went well?" Trent tried to make normal conversation as her despair ripped her soul to shreds.

Juliet laid all her bags down and hung her jacket over the back of a chair, settling in. "It went great. My proposal is going to be implemented, and it should be in place by the next quarter."

"I'm proud of you. You worked hard on it. And you're obviously brilliant at your job. Chicago will be very fortunate to have you." The break in her voice betrayed her misery and she hoped that Juliet hadn't caught it. She couldn't look away as Juliet stepped closer and rested her hands over Trent's balled fists.

"Trent, I'm not going to Chicago," she said softly.

"That bitchy redhead said you'd been offered the top spot."

Juliet nodded. "I have, probably the best position I could ever have been offered, but I'm still not taking it."

"Why not?"

"First answer me one question. What do you want, Trent?"

"Me? What I want doesn't ever matter."

Juliet shook her head. "That's where you are wrong. What you want means everything to me. So tell me, what do you want more than anything?"

Juliet's eyes bored directly into Trent's soul and she opened her heart at last. "You. I want you." Juliet's soft smile blossomed. Trent was looking so intently at her that she read the word *finally* that Juliet mouthed. That simple word emboldened Trent. "I want you to stay here, with me. I need you." Trent gathered all her courage, pushing back all the years of believing she was never worthy of love and stood tall. "I love you, Juliet."

Juliet kissed her, a long, sweet kiss that made Trent wonder why she'd waited so long to reveal what was so painfully obvious.

"I love you too, Trent. I didn't want to leave you either. You've held my heart in your hands since the start."

Trent pulled her close and held on tightly. "I think you had mine from the moment I saw you. I'd never seen anyone more beautiful. Being with you made me realize that I've been living but I've never truly been alive, not until I fell for you." Juliet's arms tightened around her, and Trent relished the comfort as it broke through her wretchedness and finally gave her warmth.

"I had another call this morning not long after I spoke to you. Monica had a meeting yesterday evening with Victor Tweedy, your neighbor's son. Seems he's been watching the transformation of your yard with a very keen eye. Are you aware he's the boss of his own construction firm?"

Trent nodded. "I know bits from what Mrs. Tweedy has mentioned. There's just her son and his daughter. I know his wife died young."

"Victor Tweedy builds and renovates houses. He has builders, electricians, plumbers, and painters he's all in charge of. He asked Monica if she would be interested in being his landscaper so he can bring the full package to his customers."

"No kidding?"

"He has quite a few properties that need gardening care too, so he asked if she'd be caretaker to those as well." Juliet beamed at Trent.

"Monica asked me to join her as her partner. After my meetings today I went through the facts and figures with her. On company time too, I might add. It all sounds too good to be true, but I think we can make it work. Now all I have to do is tell my bosses."

Trent squeezed Juliet in her excitement. "That is seriously cool! That's perfect for you both."

"I had a meeting after the presentation with my bosses offering me a new job that might not be there in a year's time or I could take a golden handshake." Juliet smiled ruefully. "I was offered a severance package that is more than I could have ever hoped for considering the current climate. I know what's happening to the banks. I've been seeing it from the inside all falling down around us. I chose to jump before the ship sank."

"You're being laid off?"

"And walking straight into another job, something I've been keen to do for some time now, as you know. My severance check will be a marvelous nest egg for you and me to build our future on."

Trent was ecstatic to hear the word *future* on Juliet's lips. She kissed her, her head swimming at the possibilities that were opening up for them both. Trent pulled at Juliet's hand gently. "I have something to show you." She led Juliet to the front of the house and paused by a closed door. "This is the front room. I've never used it. As you're aware, I pretty much stayed upstairs except to venture down for food." She pushed open the door. The room was empty except for a mass of wire curled into a coil with a modem attached. "I can have this room fitted with a wireless Internet connection in a jiffy. I thought, maybe, you might like to use this room as your study. We could get a desk in here for you, a chair, move your laptop in and you could work on your spreadsheets in your own space."

Juliet walked around the room, checking it out, her eyes shining brightly at Trent's gift.

"I have a telephone line installed in here too. I just need to know where you want it placed." Juliet touched each wall as she wandered around. "We could paint it any color you wish, make it more you." Before Juliet could say anything, Trent held out her hand again. "One more thing." She directed Juliet toward the living room. Swinging open that door, Trent revealed what was inside. "I figured if we were going to have Kayleigh over here staying with us sometimes we'd need a proper family room to entertain in." She loved how Juliet's eyes widened at the new large-screen television set back in the corner, resting on its shiny new stand. Beside it was a Nintendo Wii.

"Your console is upstairs, isn't it?" Juliet said, obviously shocked by everything Trent was showing her.

"That's my new one, to be used for gaming downstairs when we have visitors who'll play."

"I can't believe you bought a TV for in here."

"I wanted us to be able to use this room as it should be. Isn't that what couples do? Make a home together?" She reached over by the TV and picked up a bright pink Wii Remote. "I even got you your own controller so you can join in when Kayleigh and I play."

Juliet took the proffered remote. "*Pink?*"

Trent shrugged. "I figured that color of cover would be more your choice. I got blue for the kid."

"You did all this for me?"

"I did this for *us*. I want to be with you so much, and through you I get your family too. I want them to feel welcome here, because I'm hoping," Trent took a breath and finished softly, "I'm hoping this will be your home too?"

"You're asking me to move in with you?"

"The buying of a controller for a loved one is kind of like a gamer's version of an engagement ring. It reeks of commitment," Trent replied solemnly, a smile tugging at her lips at Juliet's whoop of joy. She caught Juliet in her arms as she launched herself across the room at her.

"We'll need something decent to sit on in here," Juliet said.

Trent pointed to a catalogue she had nearby. "I picked this up to help you decide what we need."

"When did you decide all this, Trent? That TV was not here when I left."

"The minute you'd gone I was at such a loss…the house only ever seems a home when you're in it with me. So I decided I had to let you know how much I love you by showing you. I'm opening up my house to you, Juliet. You've already settled in my heart. Won't you please move in with me and make me complete?"

"I'd love to. I don't want to be without you either. And we'll use my severance to get this place habitable. We can start with the living room and then we'll sort out my home office." She gazed adoringly up at Trent. "I can't believe you did that for me."

"You can do whatever you like here, any room," Trent said,

burying her face in Juliet's hair to hide the fact she was grinning like a crazy person.

"Can I paint your game room pink?"

Trent pulled back to meet Juliet's teasing look. "You can change the sofa in there to something more comfortable."

"I like that sofa just fine. I wouldn't touch a thing in that room. Except for you."

Shivering at Juliet's seductive tone, Trent said, "Welcome home."

EPILOGUE

Trent kicked the front door shut with her heel and popped her head around Juliet's office door. The room was empty, so Trent headed off to the kitchen.

"Juliet?"

"Up here, sweetheart."

Following Juliet's voice upstairs, Trent padded into their bedroom but found that was empty too. "Jule?"

"In here."

Trent wandered into the spare bedroom, which was still empty save for a few boxes of Juliet's clothes she was sorting through to throw out. Trent found Juliet standing in front of the large window, the blinds pulled aside so she could see the expanse of the yard below.

"Surveying your handiwork, love?" Trent asked, slipping her hands around Juliet's waist and hugging her close. She pressed a kiss on Juliet's neck, then rested her head on Juliet's and looked down at what held her attention.

"Hey, gorgeous." Juliet hugged Trent's arms around her. "Just look at how pretty everything looks."

The yard was a riot of flowers. The last burst of summer colors was making way for autumn's turning shades. The new growth of trees edged the lines of fencing, and the gazebo stood proudly amid the pebbles in lieu of grass. Small paved steps led the way to the gazebo, laid by Juliet and Monica as the last finishing touch. Trent had to admit her favorite piece was the darker shade of pebbles that Monica had fashioned into a very distinct Space Invader alien that could only truly be seen from above. It was a perfect finishing touch, requested by Juliet.

"You and Monica did a fantastic job," Trent said, amazed as always by how her yard had been transformed from the unruly mess it had been to the gorgeous picture-postcard perfection it now was. It had become a place even Trent liked to spend time in, usually in the evening with Juliet at her side.

"Kayleigh's coming over later tonight to sleep over ready for tomorrow's event."

Trent chuckled at Juliet's exasperated amusement. "It's our first big 'kids only' tournament. She's been preparing for it for over two months now. I'm just glad the hall let us open it up to all the kids. I think it's going to be as popular as the grown-up matches are."

"Kayleigh is so excited."

"She should be. She's very good. I hope she gets a trophy tomorrow."

"You could be considered biased, her being your sister-in-law and all." Juliet leaned forward to let the blinds drop back down, giving them back their privacy in the room.

"Your sister is an awesome gamer. She's going to do well with or without my bias."

Juliet snuggled back into Trent's arms, reaching up to tangle her fingers in Trent's hair, pulling her down to kiss her long and deeply. "I'm glad you're home."

"I missed you too," Trent said, astounded every day by how much she loved coming home to Juliet in *their* house. It made her feel safer than she could ever have imagined. It never ceased to amaze her how empty her life had been. Trent cuddled Juliet close, enjoying the feel of her in her arms.

"I have had a thought on what we could do with this room."

Trent looked around at the bare walls. "You want wardrobes in here for your clothes? Elton said he would help me read the directions."

"No, I was thinking more along the lines of using it as a nursery for when we have a baby."

Juliet's softly spoken words made Trent's heart jerk in her chest. "A baby?" she repeated dumbly.

Nodding, Juliet caressed Trent's cheek. "I'd love to have a baby with you. You'd make a remarkable mommy."

Trent knew her mouth had dropped open. "You want a baby with me?"

"I want us to be a family, our own family, yours and mine. Can you imagine bringing a child up into our love?"

Trent's throat closed over the wave of emotion rising through her. "My own family." She digested this while staring into Juliet's expectant face. "That would be so cool!"

"I'm not saying we do it right this minute, but one day soon you and I will go look into a way to get me pregnant."

Letting out a whoop of joy, Trent swung Juliet round in her arms until they were both laughing and giddy. "God, I love you so much. A baby! Yes, yes to a baby!"

Juliet laughed at Trent's exuberance. "How'd you feel about us trying right this second the old-fashioned way of making a baby, you know, just to get in some practice?" She popped the buttons of her blouse and parted it to reveal full breasts straining against her bra.

Trent quickly picked her up in her arms and carried her to the bedroom.

"What time is Kayleigh coming?" she asked, peeling her shirt off over her head in one quick movement and flinging it aside.

"Later, much later." Juliet wriggled out of her jeans and scooted her way up the bed, beckoning Trent to follow.

"Good, because I think we're going to need lots of practice to get this baby-making thing down just right." Trent stared down at Juliet, loving her so much. "You, a real home, and maybe a baby to love one day. How did I get to be so damn lucky?"

"You opened your heart to love, Trent, and I promise to never let you regret it."

"I love you." Trent nuzzled her face between Juliet's breasts and barely raised her head to ask, "You are coming with us tomorrow, aren't you?"

Juliet's fingers threaded through Trent's short hair. "Of course I am. Someone has to keep the gamer groupies away from you."

"Like I'd even look at anyone else when I have you. No one begins to compare. You're my ideal."

The hands in her hair began stroking as Trent pressed kisses across Juliet's chest to roll her tongue around a nipple straining through Juliet's bra.

"Damn, I wish I'd told Kayleigh we'd just pick her up on the way there tomorrow," Juliet said, wrenching her bra off and moaning as Trent's mouth instantly latched onto her bare flesh.

Trent just smiled against Juliet's skin. "Look on it as practice for when we have a child of our own." She paused for a moment, thoughtful. "I might want to get as much gaming in now as I can as well." She jumped as Juliet hit her playfully. "Hey, don't ever think I don't know where my priorities lay." She pressed her lips to Juliet's and kissed her tenderly. "You, my love, will always come, in every sense of the word, before my gaming."

About the Author

Lesley Davis lives with her American partner Cindy in the West Midlands of England. She is a die-hard science-fiction/fantasy fan in all its forms and an extremely passionate gamer. When her Nintendo DSi is out of her grasp, Lesley is to be found seated before the computer writing.

Visit her online at www.lesleydavis.weebly.com.

Books Available From Bold Strokes Books

Darkness Embraced by Winter Pennington. Surrounded by harsh vampire politics and secret ambitions, Epiphany learns that an old enemy is plotting treason against the woman she once loved, and to save all she holds dear, she must embrace and form an alliance with the dark. (978-1-60282-221-4)

78 Keys by Kristin Marra. When the cosmic powers choose Devorah Rosten to be their next gladiator, she must use her unique skills to try to save her lover, herself, and even humankind. (978-1-60282-222-1)

Playing Passion's Game by Lesley Davis. Trent Williams's only passion in life is gaming—until Juliet Sullivan makes her realize that love can be a whole different game to play. (978-1-60282-223-8)

Retirement Plan by Martha Miller. A modern morality tale of justice, retribution, and women who refuse to be politely invisible. (978-1-60282-224-5)

Who Dat Whodunnit by Greg Herren. Popular New Orleans detective Scotty Bradley investigates the murder of a dethroned beauty queen to clear the name of his pro football–playing cousin. (978-1-60282-225-2)

The Company He Keeps by Dale Chase. A riotously erotic collection of stories set in the sexually repressed and therefore sexually rampant Victorian era. (978-1-60282-226-9)

Cursebusters! by Julie Smith. Budding-psychic Reeno is the most accomplished teenage burglar in California, but one tiny screw-up and poof!—she's sentenced to Bad Girl School. And that isn't even her worst problem. Her sister Haley's dying of an illness no one can diagnose, and now she can't even help. (978-1-60282-559-8)

True Confessions by PJ Trebelhorn. Lynn Patrick finally has a chance with the only woman she's ever loved, her lifelong friend Jessica Greenfield, but Jessie is still tormented by an abusive past. (978-1-60282-216-0)

Jane Doe by Lisa Girolami. On a getaway trip to Las Vegas, Emily Carver gambles on a chance for true love and discovers that sometimes in order to find yourself, you have to start from scratch. (978-1-60282-217-7)

Ghosts of Winter by Rebecca S. Buck. Can Ros Wynne, who has lost everything she thought defined her, find her true life—and her true love—surrounded by the lingering history of the once-grand Winter Manor? (978-1-60282-219-1)

Who I Am by M.L. Rice. Devin Kelly's senior year is a disaster. She's in a new school in a new town, and the school bully is making her life miserable—but then she meets his sister Melanie and realizes her feelings for her are more than platonic. (978-1-60282-231-3)

Call Me Softly by D. Jackson Leigh. Polo pony trainer Swain Butler finds that neither her heart nor her secret are safe when beautiful British heiress Lillie Wetherington arrives to bury her grandmother, Swain's employer. (978-1-60282-215-3)

Split by Mel Bossa. Weeks before Derek O'Reilly's engagement party, a chance meeting with Nick Lund, his teenage first love, catapults him into the past, where he relives that powerful relationship revealing what he and Nick were, still are, and might yet be to each other. (978-1-60282-220-7)

Blood Hunt by L.L. Raand. In the second Midnight Hunters Novel, Detective Jody Gates, heir to a powerful Vampire clan, forges an uneasy alliance with Sylvan, the Wolf Were Alpha, to battle a shadow army of humans and rogue Weres, while fighting her growing hunger for human reporter Becca Land. (978-1-60282-209-2)

Loving Liz by Bobbi Marolt. When theater actor Marty Jamison turns diva and Liz Chandler walks out on her, Marty must confront a cheating lover from the past to understand why life is crumbling around her. (978-1-60282-210-8)

Kiss the Rain by Larkin Rose. How will successful fashion designer Eve Harris react when she discovers the new woman in her life, Jodi, and her secret fantasy phone date, Lexi, are one and the same? (978-1-60282-211-5)

Sarah, Son of God by Justine Saracen. In a story within a story within a story, a transgendered beauty takes us through Stonewall-rioting New York, Venice under the Inquisition, and Nero's Rome. (978-1-60282-212-2)

Sleeping Angel by Greg Herren. Eric Matthews survives a terrible car accident only to find out everyone in town thinks he's a murderer—and he has to clear his name even though he has no memories of what happened. (978-1-60282-214-6)

Dying to Live by Kim Baldwin & Xenia Alexiou. British socialite Zoe Anderson-Howe's pampered life is abruptly shattered when she's taken hostage by FARC guerrillas while on a business trip to Bogota, and Elite Operative Fetch must rescue her to complete her own harrowing mission. (978-1-60282-200-9)

Indigo Moon by Gill McKnight. Hope Glassy and Godfrey Meyers are on a mercy mission to save their friend Isabelle after she is attacked by a rogue werewolf—but does Isabelle want to be saved from the sexy wolf who claimed her as a mate? (978-1-60282-201-6)

Parties in Congress by Colette Moody. Bijal Rao, Indian-American moderate Independent, gets the break of her career when she's hired to work on the congressional campaign of Janet Denton—until she meets her remarkably attractive and charismatic opponent, Colleen O'Bannon. (978-1-60282-202-3)

The Collectors by Leslie Gowan. Laura owns what might be the world's most extensive collection of BDSM lesbian erotica, but that's as close as she's gotten to the world of her fantasies. Until, that is, her friend Adele introduces her to Adele's mistress Jeanne—art collector, heiress, and experienced dominant. With Jeanne's first command, Laura's life changes forever. (978-1-60282-208-5)

Breathless, edited by Radclyffe and Stacia Seaman. Bold Strokes Books romance authors give readers a glimpse into the lives of favorite couples celebrating special moments "after the honeymoon ends." Enjoy a new look at lesbians in love or revisit favorite characters from some of BSB's best-selling romances. (978-1-60282-207-8)